The Leah Chronicles

Book Two

Piracy

Devon C Ford

Published by Vulpine Press in the United Kingdom in 2019

Cover by Claire Wood

ISBN: 978-1-912701-62-9

www.vulpine-press.com

Dedicated to the memory of Leah Anne Johnstone.

Born 5th March 1994

Died 7th May 2011

May this Leah have been a shadow of the woman you could have become.

Set in the UK in the immediate aftermath of a mysterious illness which swept the country and left millions dead, the series follows the trials facing a reluctant hero, Dan, and the group that forms around him.

Piracy

PROLOGUE

"Three hundred metres," Dan said in a low voice, "reckon you can make that?"

I didn't answer. The air was still and flat and the sea was only rolling slightly, but that undulating movement of the waves was enough to only give me two chances to fire with each swell.

He lay beside me, his own eye up close to the scope of the rifle which had little hope of matching the killing power of my own at that distance. In these conditions on dry land I was confident that I could put the bullet in the right place, but the risk of the shot falling or drifting in the air between our boat and theirs posed too much of a risk; I couldn't be responsible for killing our own people.

"We need to be closer," I said before raising my voice, "Mateo?"

"*Si?*" came the response in Spanish from the captain of the fishing boat. He understood far more English than he spoke, and his French wasn't strong enough for us both to communicate that way.

"Take us closer. Another hundred metres."

The boat's engine chugged faster as the revs were increased and the prow I lay flat on raised slightly, removing the lower hull of the other vessel from my sight.

"Not too close," Mitch warned from his spot on the stern, "not within weapon range."

I doubted Mateo knew what he meant, or even the range of the weapons Mitch was talking about; we were already within weapons range of our own guns, but he wouldn't take us any further than he thought was safe. He was reluctant enough to get as close as we were after the distant rattle of automatic gunfire had caused him to reverse course until I had calmed him.

He was a big man, strong and with muscles that reminded me of the tough sailor he was, but he had never liked violence. Perhaps because he had a talent for it. His brother was the opposite, becoming a soldier leading the men and women of a militia in another settlement, but Mateo disliked the gunfire on a cellular level.

"I count four," I said, before correcting myself. "Mateo? Are any of our sailors on that boat black guys?"

"We have only one man with the dark skin who fish," he answered, "he no on this boat."

Four then, I thought, *at least four I can see.*

"Circle us around them," I said, indicating a swirling movement with my left hand which I took away from my rifle briefly, "but keep your distance."

He turned the boat again, chugging it slowly over the open sea before backing it off again.

"Boat," I told Dan as soon as it came into sight. "Mateo, stop."

The engine note died.

"Can't see it properly," Dan muttered from beside me.

"Small. It's got two of those engines that hang off the back."

"Outboard motors," Mitch responded pointlessly before saying something more useful but concerning, "means there's a bigger boat out there because that one won't have made it far on its own."

That gave me pause, and I asked for the others to keep a watch on the horizon with binoculars.

"I see it," a voice said from behind me in accented English, spoken for our benefit most likely, "to the right. Is very far away."

I moved the barrel of my rifle an inch at a time to the right as I scanned the faint line where clear sky met the clear water at an almost undetectable threshold. I saw it, faint but huge with only the top part of its bulk visible. I knew curvature of the earth from studying how to kill things at distance, but the term *hull down* came to me from nowhere. I swung the barrel back to our other boat, stationary and riding the small swell like it was a goat tied to a post in order to attract a predator.

Lured or not, we had to go and get our people.

"I've got a shot," I said softly.

"Describe him," Dan instructed, wanting to be able to make out my target when he only had half the magnification before his own eye.

"Stood near the back," I said as I concentrated, "holding a long."

Shorts and longs, how Mitch had taught me to quickly differentiate between the weapons people held.

"Any more detail?"

I paid closer attention to the shape of the weapon.

"No stock... curved mag... AK I think."

Dan made a noise which meant nothing; an acknowledgment that I had spoken and conveying opinion on the words.

"The foreskin of Africa," he grumbled without explaining. "Can you see the others?"

"One in the boat… three on deck… standby," I said slowly, "another one coming from below. Five in total now. Five hostiles."

Dan said nothing for a time.

"You're sure of the shot?" he asked me, not questioning my ability, merely checking.

"Yes."

"Mateo? Wait for the shot, then take us in fast," he said, turning away from his firing position and groaning as he got to his feet.

"In your own time, kid," he said.

"Relax, Granddad," I said as I slipped my finger onto the trigger without taking the pressure out of it, "you just get ready."

Breathe.

Hold.

Relax.

Breathe.

Hold.

Squeeze.

4

MATERNAL INSTINCTS

I didn't quite know how to say it, especially when I wasn't sure, but it was the first and last thing on my mind that day.

I was late. Not for the start of the supply run but, you know, *late*.

I'd been living with Lucien for just over a year, and that was after he had flitted around me like a moth around a candle for months beforehand. Dan wanted to send him off to the farm or to Andorra or The Orchards. I declined his request, relenting enough to allow him to be sent as escort on as many of the summer supply runs as possible, if only to create a little distance.

He never returned to his post in the watchtower, and that was because I came up with reasons to keep him from climbing the cliff path and not being around me anymore.

Eventually I relented, spending a lot of my downtime with him until everyone around us stopped smiling every time we were seen together. When the novelty wore off I realised it was what I wanted, and he had stayed in my room every night since then. I guessed it was *our* room after that, despite Nemesis grumbling and moving into the room beside the bedchamber at the unwelcome interruption to our girl time. It didn't stop her climbing on the bed first, on his side, and refusing to move until I pretty much had to drag her away.

He didn't have much, but his bags got unpacked and he moved in with me. I had just turned twenty years old, although my life was very different to that of anyone staring down the barrel of the big two-one. As Dan always said, *It's not the age of the car, but the mileage you need to consider.*

I was still sure to give Lucien plenty of jobs that took him away from me, because I still needed some time to myself, but I always looked forward to his return.

That morning I was going towards the nearest city, Perpignan, with Dan, Neil, Mitch, Adam and a half-dozen others, and Lucien was staying behind to take charge of Sanctuary in our absence. We were using some of our precious diesel to clear the last of the supplies from one of the huge hypermarkets found on the outskirts. These places needed a lot of hands to get done properly, because there was fuel to pump and a lot of heavy stuff to carry. I usually used young female prerogative and claimed overwatch during these things, preferring to watch the heavy lifting rather than taking more of an active part.

I couldn't face speaking to Marie about my worries, nor could I go to Kate in our medical centre because I knew she would forbid me from leaving the safety of the walls, and would probably tell Dan just to make sure I complied. I couldn't deal with that, and I couldn't deal with the hassle of people knowing.

It's not like I even know for sure, I lectured myself, *it's probably a false alarm anyway.*

I kitted up, fed and exercised my dog, ran over everything with Lucien for the fifth time to be sure he knew what to do in the tiny off-chance that something happened in the whole day that Dan and

I weren't around to stop it. He assured me that he had everything under control and tried to tell me to relax.

"Never," I told him sternly, "in the history of women, has one *ever* calmed down when they were told to. Try to remember that."

He smiled at me, one corner of his mouth just screaming amusement at my expense but not pushing his luck so far as to actually piss me off. I hated it when he did that. And I loved it.

I shot him a warning look, only half serious, and turned to the big stone pot filled with sand from the beach. I pulled the charging handle on my M4, my worn camouflage-painted weapon that I felt oddly superstitious about even though there were arguably better guns available, and pointed the barrel towards the sand trap in case any errant bullet decided to pop from the suppressed muzzle.

Safety first and all that.

I turned to leave but he called me back with a "Hey," before wrapping me up in a big hug and kissing my hair.

"I'll be back tonight," I told him, hoping that he mistook my pensive mood for the distant supply run and not for what it was truly about, "just don't bugger anything up while I'm gone, okay?"

He muttered something playfully sarcastic in French which I ignored, mostly because I didn't understand it. The language was hard enough to learn without all the little idioms he came out with; like an East-Londoner and a native of the Yorkshire Dales having a conversation in what was technically the same language but neither could understand a bloody thing the other said.

I left him, pushing down the pang of wanting to stay, and walked past Marie's room where I peeked in and saw my younger brother playing on the woollen rug. It was still chilly outside that early in spring, but Marie still encouraged the younger ones to be outside as much as possible. She wasn't one for coddling them and encouraging comfort until they had learned to endure a little hardship first to toughen them. He was nearly seven years old then and had never quite been as *robust* as the other kids. Marie was great with him, which I knew she would be, and surviving the ordeal to get here and cross thousands of miles of post-apocalyptic Europe in shitty conditions to have him safely probably meant that seeing her son, even now when he was a walking, talking person, made it all the more miraculous that he survived.

I stepped inside, unclipping my carbine and propping it against the doorway before telling Nemesis to stay outside by the gun. It wasn't that I didn't trust the dog at all, but I got annoyed when kids tried to mess with her like she was a pet. I imagined it would be like owning a specialist race car and seeing people just wanting to marvel at the colour of it.

"Hello," I said to him with a smile which he returned and jumped up to hug me as best he could with all the kit protruding from my vest. He made do by wrapping his arms around my waist and ducking his head to hug my left hip. I gently moved his hand away from the gun on my right thigh, not because he was reaching for it but because it just concerned me with him being so close to it.

"We're off," I told Marie, who smiled politely and nodded her understanding before dropping the smile and returning to the paper she was reading from.

"What's up?" I asked, feeling duty-bound to check but fearing the answer would not be a short one.

"Ask your father," she said in a tone of voice that sounded almost serrated.

"*Okaaaay*," I said, drawing out the word and backing up one exaggerated step at a time as I tried to untangle myself from my little brother.

"Actually," she snapped, "don't bother. He'll just ignore you anyway."

Here it comes, I thought, *wait for it...*

"And while you're at it," she said, slamming down the paperwork, "remind him that he doesn't have to do everything himself. Remind him that he does *actually* have the power to delegate once in a bloody while."

"I will do that," I said slowly and solemnly, fearing that it came out as a little sarcastic.

I found him near the gate. He looked tired, but then again he was old. At least old by my standards. On that thought, I guessed he would always be old to me.

"In the doghouse, are we?" I asked his broad back, which had put back on some of the timber he used to carry. He turned, frowned and pursed his lips as though not sure how to respond, before evidently deciding to tell me.

"Yes. Most of the time," he said flatly.

"What have you done now?"

"Me?" he responded, his voice full of injury and objection. "Why is it always *me* who is at fault?"

"Err, because it usually is?" I told him seriously, as though he didn't know this fact.

He huffed, turned back to his kit bag, which was on the lowered tail of the big truck bed, and I counted it down in my head...

...Seven, six, five, fou–

"Well if you *must* know," he said in a louder voice as he whipped back around, "it's not actually my fault this time. She doesn't want me to go outside the walls. Ever!" He threw his hands up in exasperation as though he didn't understand why he wasn't allowed to go and play.

For starters, although I didn't tell him this, referring to Marie as *'she'* was dangerous enough in itself. "Maybe she has a point?" I offered softly. "You could always delegate the odd mission and stay at home."

"Delegate?" he asked, a dark scowl inspecting my face for signs of conspiracy. "Sounds like she got to you too... *Brutus.*"

"Maybe," I said, slipping one arm out of my bag and swinging it around to land it next to his, "but you know women stick together. And don't call me Brutus."

"Women," Dan scoffed without malice, "I preferred it when you were a kid."

"Isn't that what everyone says about their kids?"

Dan mused on this for a while before shrugging as though to convey his sentiments of *meh*.

We were saved from any further difficult conversation by the ebullient arrival of Neil. His belly arrived just before he did; it wasn't so much that it was in a different time zone but enough to be noticeable. His glee at the success of his latest batch of yeasty home-brewed beer still shone on his face, specifically his red nose, and his gut betrayed the amount of complex scientific experiments on said home brew he had been doing over the past year. Belly or not, Neil was still Neil and there were always a gaggle of younger men and women around him eager to learn any of his ingenious tricks.

Neil's Life Hacks. That's what his own encyclopaedia had been dubbed, by him at least, and had become a separate tomb of knowledge aside from Victor's precisely penned records. No doubt the academic would want to rewrite them at some point, but Neil was insistent that something would get lost in translation and his valuable knowledge would be lost in the nuances of language.

"Shall we away then?" he asked Mitch in an appalling Scottish accent. Mitch just scowled at him, fully believing that the hour was too early to tolerate Neil being so… so *Neil*.

"Aye," he said deadpan, "let's away now."

As we drove along the bumpy roads, so degraded by the passage of time and the lack of maintenance that some sections were more like gravel tracks than the concrete and tarmac roads they had been before, I mused that we would probably have another scorching hot summer after the brisk spring. There would be a period of thunderstorms soon, sudden and vicious which would drench our world and swell the river running through Sanctuary from the mountains, and I looked forward to those big firework displays and the earth-shaking thunder that followed the bright flashes.

My head bumped against the passenger window, prompting a loud 'ow' from me.

"Sorry," Dan said without much meaning, "pothole."

"Bloody potholes," I moaned, "why hasn't someone been on to the local council to complain?"

"I wrote a letter last year," Dan answered seriously as he played along, "and they assured me that they were assessing the situation and promised to get back to me with an update. They never did, you know… I should've written to my local Member of Parliament."

"Maybe you should," I said, "but seriously, some of these sections are going to be impassable next winter."

"I know," Dan answered having dropped back to normal, "Neil is planning to take his little army of fixers on our three main routes in summer and fill in the worst bits with gravel and cement to smooth it out."

We drove in silence for a while.

"What do you think has really got into Marie?" he asked carefully.

"You, probably," I said bluntly, "it usually is anyway."

"Ouch," was all he replied before holding another period of quiet contemplation, where he no doubt went over the last bickering session they had shared.

"Why are we still doing this?" I asked. "I mean, we don't need any food or anything, so why are we still scavenging?"

Dan craned his neck to check in his mirror, satisfied that he still led the convoy of three vehicles, and took a deep breath as he considered his answer.

"It's comforts mostly," he said, "things like spices that we can't make ourselves here. The processed chemical products like bleach. The medicines. We're using up the last bits of what the world had before and why shouldn't we?"

He glanced at me to see if the rhetorical question had prompted any deep connection before continuing.

"Have you noticed how people are slowly getting out of the habit of taking a paracetamol for a headache and instead drinking more water? Most headaches are dehydration and we are adapting to it, slowly. People are using herbal remedies where before they'd go to pharmacies and expect someone else to solve their issue for them. Everyone is going back to a simpler way of life because we've lost all of our modern comforts, but it'll take a couple of generations until we've got over the easy life we had before."

I thought about that, realising that what he was saying was true. We were returning to *the old ways* for a lot of things, but I still missed luxuries like sweet-smelling shower gels and deodorants. We had started making our own soaps in the last year, when the increase in our livestock allowed for the fat to be used for other things, but it was never the same. I guessed that Dan was right though; if I'd never experienced a decent shower gel then I wouldn't notice anything wrong with our homemade chunks of soap.

"I dunno," Dan said to bring me back to the present with a change of subject, "maybe I'm just being too much of a bloke about Marie. I don't have that maternal instinct that she does."

I said nothing and just let him drive.

HYPERMARCHÉ

I'd never had the chance of a foreign holiday in my 'before' days, but Dan had visited France a few times either by car ferry or via the 'Chunnel', as he called it. He always said that the big supermarkets there were like a day out by themselves as most Brits had never seen their like back home.

He said you could literally buy everything you needed in there. You could have an empty house and kit it all out in one single trip; everything from every grocery product known to mankind to white goods like massive American fridge-freezers and garden furniture. They literally stocked the lot. Many had cafés inside as well as full pharmacies. They were their own butchers and bakers. He told me about one where they even sold new cars which you could drive away if you felt so inclined.

These places saw thousands of people every day, all cramming into the acres of available parking and smacking their car doors into each other's rides without seeming to give a shit. Dan joked that he reckoned brand-new cars in France actually came with a few dents in the sides just so that they didn't feel out of place among their peers.

This one was one of the biggest he had ever seen, and it looked like a whole town under one roof to me. We drove in slowly, looking for the easily detectable telltale signs of human life which were massively obvious to anyone with their eyes open. After seven years the world had reclaimed so much of what we had already taken that the buildings were covered in green weeds to make unnatural-looking natural structures. *Mother earth didn't make straight lines*, Mitch always said as he quoted one of the first lessons of camouflage and concealment. Break up the straight lines of you and your kit and you'll be hard to detect as long as you don't break the other rules.

As we pulled into the entrance to the massive singular complex in our rolling convoy I marvelled at the sheer scale of the place and wondered out loud why we hadn't cleared it five years ago.

"Because we wouldn't have had the manpower to empty it or the storage for the stuff we'd take," Dan said. "Plus, it was a little more important to become self-sufficient for food than it was to live off canned beans."

We drove a slow loop of the parking area, seeing that every one of the cars there sat on flat tyres and sported that post-apoc rusty grime colour that was so popular everywhere, and came to a squeaky rest outside the main doors.

No sign of life at all. No indications of human activity. But then again if I had taken over that place then I would be certain to not use the main entrance. I said as much to Dan who nodded as though I told him something he already knew. If I followed it logically it would be right as he was the one who had taught me almost everything I knew.

He killed the engine to the open-backed truck we drove as the two dogs sparked into life from the rear section. It wasn't a crew cab as such as there were no seats there, but there was as storage space which fit two German shepherds easily enough. Dan made himself visible to the other vehicles, indicating that they should stay where they were while he made a loop of the perimeter. I climbed down and let the dogs out, glancing up at the building that was so large it would take half an hour at least to do a thorough circuit.

Mitch and Adam jogged up, kitted out and ready to work. Dan pointed at them and then to the far end of the building, then pointed at he and I before doing the same with the other direction.

"Split," I said, "dog in each direction that way."

Dan thought for a second then nodded, pointing at Adam who fell in step beside him as Mitch and I set off.

"Find it, then," I said to Nemesis who bounded away to criss-cross the ground no further than twenty paces ahead of us. I wasn't worried as I was certain the place was abandoned, but having Nem range out ahead of us would provide enough warning to raise my weapon should it be required. I walked in a relaxed way, not tacti-cally in a tiring crouch, and rested my right hand on the trigger guard of my gun to stop it swinging around on the sling attached to my vest. Mitch cradled his own rifle, longer and heavier than mine, in both arms and tucked it close to his body as though we were both on a gentle stroll and only happened to be heavily armed and armoured by chance.

"How's the little one?" I asked him, seeing his usually blank face break out into a broad smile of pride and happiness.

"She's grand," he said, "and Alita's taken to it like a fish to wa-ter."

"Aww," I said, unsure of how to answer such fatherly pride es-pecially with the heavy weight I had pressing on my own mind.

"You'll have to come and see her when we get back," he said, eager to share the happiness of his own daughter who was less than a month old. "She gets bigger and stronger every day."

"I will," I lied, not wanting to have such a worrying premonition given how exhausted Alita had been the last time I had seen her. Lucien had held the tiny bundle with deft hands and made all the right noises when, in stark contrast, I looked like I was attempting to defuse a dirty bomb with less than half a minute on the clock.

The 'baby boom,' as Marie had called, it was probably a by-product of a safe environment; we hadn't seen a shot fired in any of our four allied settlements since the bloodbath in Andorra, and people drifted away from thoughts of survival and started doing what we did best: self-replicate.

I tried not to think about it, to push it away and block it out. I just couldn't imagine myself even being pregnant, let alone forcing a whole human being out of my…

Focus, I told myself as I raised my gun to peer through the scope.

"See something?" Mitch said softly.

"Thought I did," I lied again, inventing some half-seen movement ahead to change the subject and enforce some silence. Nemesis hadn't changed her behaviour at all which indicated pretty clearly that there was nothing within smelling or hearing distance, but we scanned through our optics until we reached the corner of the building where it was closest to the tall fence surrounding the non-public parts of the complex. I lowered the end of my gun and stacked up on the corner, waiting as Mitch tapped a hand on my shoulder and stepped wide to raise his own rifle and scan the next quarter-mile of straight-sided building.

"Clear," he said after a heartbeat, but that didn't stop me pretending to remain at DEFCON 3.

17

We said nothing until we reached the next corner when it was my turn to step into the open and raise my weapon, my muscles tightening as I saw two shapes in my field of view. I relaxed as I instantly recognised the shape and movement of Dan.

"Clear," I said, "friendlies in the open."

"Roger," Mitch replied automatically, relaxing as he stepped out and lowered his weapon. We walked towards them, sending Nem to bound ahead to fuss at Ash who tried to ignore her as he watered the overgrown bushes sprouting from everywhere. It made me wonder how much pee that dog actually carried and how he decided to ration it to leave a few squirts on every minor landmark he encountered.

"No sign?" Dan asked us. I shook my head, sensing Mitch doing the same beside me.

"Us neither," he said, "can't believe this place hasn't been touched in years…"

"This end should be better," I said, indicating the huge vehicle bay doors ahead of me and behind Dan and Adam.

"If we can get them open," he said as he rubbed a hand over his stubbled chin.

"I'll go back and get the others to drive round," Adam offered, waiting for Dan to hand over the truck keys for our ride. He took them and jogged away as Mitch started to inspect the control box for the shutters. He prised open the box with his knife and peered at the contents as he tapped the tip of the blade against his pursed lips like some tradesman trying to figure out the cheapest way to drag out a job and quote an extra amount.

"Needs a power supply," he said. "Neil will probably be able to work some witchcraft on it, I don't doubt."

Neil could. He cut away the thick insulation around the cables running to the box and attached jump leads to the battery on his makeshift fuel truck, stepping back smartly as he issued a slightly feminine noise at the sparks from the live wire. Mitch had removed the bit that needed a key to activate the mechanism, so Neil used a tool of his own to force the shutter into the 'on' position.

With a juddering shriek the roller shutter jerked upwards like some mechanical zombie reanimated from death, rising higher up to expose the dusty dankness of the air inside. We all stepped back in distaste at the stale, oxygen-deprived atmosphere inside as the opening shutter exposed ranks of stacked boxes covered in thick dust. With just as sudden a noise as it started, Neil killed the mechanism to return us to silence.

"Big place to clear," I offered.

"On two legs anyway," Dan answered. I smiled, telling Nem to search with the command of 'find 'em' and watched her streak away as Ash whined and danced on the spot waiting for permission to join the hunt.

"Seek," Dan said simply, rocketing the dog away like he'd just set light to his tail.

"And now," Neil intoned solemnly, "we wait."

I didn't get the film reference, like usual, but the others found his impression as amusing as always. We didn't have to wait long, despite the enormous size of the place, because both dogs returned within a few seconds of each other.

We went inside, finding the reason why they had returned so quickly was because the public part of the huge store was blocked off by closed doors from the back sections. Nothing on the stacks of boxes gave much away, and the effort of opening them would probably reveal a whole lot of nothing useful in the form of rotted food or the spoiled contents of tins and jars, so we carried on into the store properly.

Heavy bolts into the doorframes gave way easily and allowed us into the main aircraft-hangar building of the main part of the store and something immediately hit me as strange. The air had a thicker quality, like it was some kind of greenhouse. It was on the verge of being damp and felt instantly more difficult to breathe.

I turned to Dan, seeing his own nose wrinkling up as I pulled my *the fuck?* face.

He returned it with his *dunno* shrug.

Non-verbal communication. The pinnacle of inter-personal relationships.

We sent our dogs away, pacing out from our entrance into the vast building with our guns up as we waited for the sound of clattering claws on dusty polished concrete floors to echo away. The way they worked, with Nem sent to the left and Ash sent to the right, they would meet up somewhere in the centre depending on who cleared their areas the fastest. As I stalked through what used to be the fresh food counters, set out like a marketplace, I could see the long-ruined pieces of meat withered away to nothing after having been eaten by whatever small bugs had found their way inside since the closed for the last time. The fruit and vegetables left only dark traces where they had rotted.

We were in the wrong section to where we wanted to be as there was nothing useful to us there, but we waited for the dogs to return before we split and searched. They came back after a few minutes, panting from the exertion with their tongues out to shed the body heat they had generated.

"What the…" Dan said, standing up from where he had bent down to Ash, "he's wet."

"Wet?"

"Yeah," he said, perplexed, "come on."

He led the way in the direction that Ash had first gone, and I followed with Adam and Mitch behind us as I glanced back to Neil. He nodded without me saying or indicating anything, agreeing that he would stay with the others while we went to explore.

I didn't see it from the front, mainly because I'd gone around the other side, but one edge of the building was given to a glass-roofed section like an indoor garden centre. As soon as we approached the heavy plastic curtain strips separating the two parts we could feel the hot dampness seeping through. Dan used the barrel of his weapon to poke it in between a gap and step aside to raise the curtain enough for me to step through. I sent Nem ahead of me, with Ash following, and walked inside where I instantly felt my skin prickle with sweat. The dogs snuffled around, legs moving fast and noses to the ground as they tracked the myriad of scents to no particular conclusion.

The skylights were open, and the plants had grown tall as though the sunroof was left open on a car and plants had been left on the cloth seats. It was like a sweaty patch of jungle inside a supermarket and seemed totally bizarre to me.

What was most annoying was that there was nothing useful in there, so we returned to the others to tell them what we'd found. Neil shrugged it off as irrelevant, leading the way towards the aisles of chemicals and organising his team of helpers to start ferrying trolleys of everything back to the trucks. Mitch and Adam went back to keep watch on the vehicles before I could volunteer myself for the task, which left me lugging boxes of tablets until my sulky looks at Mitch resulted in his offer to swap spots.

"Come on, lad," he said loudly to Adam for my benefit, "let's speed this up. You take over for a while, Leah?"

I sat on top of the truck cab for the next hour as Nem lounged in a patch of nearby shade, watching as the train of boxes came from the shutters to fill the backs of the trucks. Dan called a stop so that people could eat and drink, and because I'd been sat on my arse for too long I climbed down and stretched my back before going back inside.

I wandered between the aisles until I found the section where they sold the things I was after, struggling with some of the words on the unfamiliar packaging. I found them next to the condoms, which I thought was either weird, sensible or else very ironic.

"Leah?"

I jumped and suppressed a yelp as Dan's voice came from the end of the aisle, and I managed to shove the two packets up under the back of my vest and distance myself from the shelves as I took three fast paces towards the sound of his voice.

"Sup?" I asked him, making out like I was just strolling through.

"Just checking where you were," he said suspiciously, eyeing me like I was hiding something, "what were you doing?"

"Looking for mouthwash," I said as I snatched the lie out of thin air.

"Next aisle," he said, "with all the toothpaste."

"Oh, cool. Thanks," I said as I smiled widely and walked past him, turning as I went to keep my back from his sight. "I'll be back out in a minute," I told him as I walked backwards past the end of the aisle before I grabbed two big bottles of mouthwash and scurried back outside. I glanced back to make sure I was out of sight before transferring the two pregnancy tests into the left leg pocket of my combats.

The trucks were filled and the fuel collection went without a hitch. I ate my food as they took turns and spun the wheel on Neil's jury-rigged pump to bring the diesel up from the reservoir underneath the fuel station. It was late in the afternoon by the time we had returned to Sanctuary, but instead of the hot shower with fruit-scented shampoo I was looking forward to, we found panic.

RECORDING FOR POSTERITY

Leah leaned back from the leather-bound ledger and eased out her aching back, remembering that day with startling clarity for a number of reasons. She recalled how simple it had been to write using a computer keyboard, especially the ability that the lost technology afforded to be able to hit delete instead of having to mess up a whole page by my scribbled crossings out. She had never been one of those girls who had developed neat, pretty handwriting but instead had followed the Dan school of literacy and scribbled words like a spider had run through ink then skittered across the page, but only after the spider had chugged down half a bottle of vodka and hoovered up three lines of the finest Colombian marching powder.

It wasn't pretty, but it was a story that she had to tell, however she could, and writing it down was a good thing. It could be immortalised that way, and not diluted as the years went by to be inflated in the retelling or else miss out the parts that were most important, and she realised not for the first time how easy it was to retell a story with the benefit of hindsight and the experiences of others to add to it.

The day they were introduced to twenty-first century piracy was a day that Leah's burgeoning faith in human nature took two to the head and one in the chest. She had never encountered people with such a low regard for human life until then. Sure, they had met some real bastards along the way, but they had just been bad men intent on hurting people or, more often, taking things that others had worked hard for.

These people though, she shuddered at calling them people, were something entirely different.

Human life just seemed so... so *disposable* to them. So worthless. Like people who mistreated animals, this lot had such little empathy, almost whatever the opposite of empathy was, when it came to the suffering of others. It wasn't like they were sick in the head, not like the people who actually enjoyed seeing the suffering of living things, it was more that they just didn't recognise it. It didn't affect them or matter to them at all.

Marie said they were 'quite literally apathetic', which she took to mean that they were unable to consider the feelings of others, but that just didn't seem to be strong enough. Leah thought they were the most disgusting and vile human beings on Earth, and she hadn't lost one single night of sleep over what they, what *she,* did to them.

It was a small war of good versus evil, and it was the only conflict she'd ever been in where she never questioned whether she was one of the good guys or had to justify taking a life, like it was a 'them or us' scenario.

It was never, *ever*, going to be them. Not after what they did.

Like everyone who never watched the news on television when they were younger, Leah was blissfully unaware of any current events occurring outside of her immediate circle of influence. Given that the news stopped being a thing when she was twelve, a whole eight years before this part of her life happened, it was little wonder that her only knowledge of pirates was from kids' shows and those big-budget movies where she would lose track of the plot and where the main character was, how Kate would put it, 'of questionable mental health'.

Mitch, being in the know about these things and having been briefed for a training operation in northern Kenya before everyone died, was able to shed an alarming amount of light on the subject. That said, even he was shocked to see that the shittiest slice of life survived to continue in their unique style after the whole world went to hell.

Leah walked off the inactivity of sitting still and writing, taking in the late summer evening by the edge of the clear water of the sea as her newest sidekick, who she had called Ares, bounced along in the shallow water like he'd never experienced such fun before in his short life. He was the biggest of the litter by far and although Nemesis' daughter Athena had bred with some lumpy mongrel from the town and turned her nose up at the attentions of the well-bred dog brought from The Orchards for the task, he had turned out okay in the end. The pups all had the dominant appearance of their ancestor and all looked like German shepherds unless a knowledgeable eye paid closer attention, but Ares was that much bigger than his litter brothers and sisters, which made Leah chose him over the loyalty she had found with her previous bitch.

Ash was gone by then, succumbed to old age and arthritis and buried high on the hill where she liked to think he could still look down on her, his head cocked to one side and the tips of his large ears meeting in the middle.

Ares had a wide head, a thick set of shoulders and haunches, and was already a fast dog, if he could concentrate long enough to recall the current length of his legs, that was. He was an ungainly puppy, constantly bumping into things and banging his head on doorways that had a cruel habit of jumping out on him.

Leah's daughter was approaching ten years old in that summer, and parts of her still couldn't believe that she had created such a beautiful little creature. Lucien was obviously responsible for her good looks, but gallantly claimed that she was a beautiful as her mother which still made her blush. She liked to think that Adalene's devilish streak of rebellious nature was all her though.

She returned to the central keep with the dog bouncing ahead of her, lacking the energy to force her will on the dog and letting him just play and enjoy himself. She was met in the shadows of the old castle by her younger brother, a quiet teenager with an analytical mind but no desire towards action. Dan had been unhappy about that, which was a constant source of bickering between him and Marie, but she was happy. They had her, and she guessed that one child soldier had been enough for them. Brother and sister greeted each other wordlessly with a gentle bump of fists.

"How's the old man?" she asked him.

"Grumpy as ever," he said as he brushed his light brown hair off his face, "what you up to?"

"Walking this chump," she said, pointing at the long-legged dog who had stopped to slurp loudly at an itch and proudly expose his boys to anyone who saw, "before that I've been writing down some stuff."

"Oh?" he asked, eyebrows up in question.

"Yeah," she said, not offering any more.

PIRATES... AS IN *AARGH*?

We got back from our big supply run to find the gates open ready for us, which in itself wasn't a big deal. What was different though, was the three armed militia members blocking the open gateway. They looked nervous, which was never a good thing, and my spidey-sense kicked off instantly. Our four trucks rolled through and the gates shut behind us. Being in the lead vehicle we had the furthest to go before we stopped so that the others could get inside, and by the time Dan had eased the truck to a stop I had the door open and was sliding to the cobblestones before breaking into a dead run back towards the gate.

"*Qu'est-ce qui se passe?*" I snapped at the nearest people. "What the hell is going on?"

"Calm down," came the smooth voice from behind me as Lucien walked out of the dark stairwell leading up to the ramparts, before quailing ever so slightly under my answering look that reminded him about using that specific phrase.

"Tell me," I said, hearing footsteps stop behind me and feeling a presence over my right shoulder. I saw Lucien's eyes flicker up to where Dan's would be boring into him from behind me.

"Not here," he said softly, "please come." He led the way straight across the courtyard towards the docks. I saw that he was dressed as we were: fully kitted and carrying his long rifle in addition to the carbine and sidearm. He was dressed for war.

We followed, Dan barking instructions at people to unpack and sort the haul, ending with a familiar sounding request for the company of specific people.

"Mitch, Neil, Adam. On me."

He sounded riled, and with Dan that came out as angry and had a habit of spilling over to make others feel as though they were the ones to have done wrong. I was on edge too, and that had the outward appearance of being ready to commit murder, but I held onto my indignant anger until I had heard the facts. Clearly somebody had threatened Sanctuary in some way, and that offended me deeply to my core. Lucian stopped finally on the sea wall, well out of earshot of anyone else, with the only people in sight being the two men and one woman in the small, covered guard post at the mouth of our small harbour. All three were pointing their weapons out to sea beside the mounted heavy machine gun which had been stripped of the heavy canvas cover it usually wore.

Three? I thought as I realised instantly where the threat must have come from. *That's a one-man post.*

"One of our fishing boats came back to the home more early than we expect," Lucien explained. "The crew was five, but only three come home and one is shot." He held up both hands and took an involuntary step back as three of us began firing questions off at him like the commencement of an ambush. "Please," he said, refraining from adding the words *calm down*.

We stopped talking and waited for the rest of the information.

"They were fishing in a pair and were attacked by a boat. They were shot at, and one boat escaped."

Dan spoke before I did.

"One boat and crew lost, one other crew member dead and one injured," he said, making sure of the facts and receiving a nod from my man. "Severity of the GSW?"

Lucien glanced at me for help.

"*Blessure grave?*" I asked, translating Dan's use of acronyms into more simplistic language.

"It is bad. The man loses a lot of blood from his leg."

"Is Kate working on him?" Dan asked.

"Yes," Lucien said, "she is stitching in the wound."

"Who attacked them?" Mitch asked almost softly, hiding the anger behind professionalism.

"That is what is the problem," Lucien answered, "come to speak with the fishermen with me."

He led us back towards the docks and into a small house that was far taller than it was wide. A gaggle of people were in there surrounding two sweat-stained men. Both held small glasses of the local liquor and both bore the appearance of men who had faced the realistic prospects of their own imminent deaths.

Lucien said something loud and clear, which roughly translated as 'give us the room'. People filed out, some placing reassuring hands on the shoulders of the two frightened men. When the small room had cleared Dan pulled up the nearest chair and leaned forward to speak to them after readjusting his carbine.

"*Parlez-vous anglais?*" Dan asked in his roughly accented French.

"I speak English," said the nearest man in an accent that made me think of Denmark or Sweden, surprising us all.

"What's your name?" Dan asked.

"William. Will."

"Tell me what happened, Will," Dan said carefully. An open question, not 'can you tell me?' but an invitation to explain and not inviting any annoyingly simple yes or no responses.

"We were trawling," he explained, "in a pair like usual. This little boat came towards us from the deep water. At first we were thinking, 'this is good, more survivors', but they went straight past us and had guns. We were scared. They came past again and started shooting at us. Antoine, he…" Will ducked his head and screwed his eyes shut for a moment before continuing. "Antoine waved his arms and tried to make them stop. He was shot and fell overboard. The other boat cut away their nets and tried to leave, but they chased them. We ran away. Antoine was not to be found in the water and Rémy started screaming." He lifted his blood-encrusted hands to stare at them. "I tied his wound."

"You did well," I reassured him, not knowing for certain whether he did or not but guessing that the application of pressure or a tourniquet to a gunshot wound most likely saved the man's life. He smiled weakly up at me.

"And the other boat?" Dan prompted.

"The last thing I saw of them was when they climbed on board."

"Who attacked you?" Mitch asked, a hint of premonition in his voice as though he already knew the answer but wanted it confirmed.

"They had black skin," Will answered, "and were very thin men. They wore things around their faces that showed only their eyes."

"What language did they speak?" he asked in a more intense

tone of voice.

"I did not understand it," Will said almost apologetically.

"When did this happen?" I asked.

"They came back less than one hour ago," Lucien answered for them.

"It's okay," Dan told him, "you two rest now and leave it up to us. Lucien?" He looked at Dan in answer, waiting for instructions. "Show them a map and ask them for their last location," Dan said. "The rest of you, on me."

We went back outside and wandered towards the sea wall where we had the privacy of isolation. Dan paused to light a cigarette, blowing the smoke upwards as he prepared to launch into the speech I knew was coming.

"So we have hostiles out on the sea," he began, then glanced towards an uncertain-looking Mitch. "Mitch? You know something?"

"I *suspect* something," he said carefully, "but I can't be sure. It sounds pretty bad, but we don't know if it's isolated or not."

"What does that mean?" I asked, slightly annoyed at his ambiguity.

"It means," Mitch said measuredly, "that we need more intelligence before we can make a thorough threat assessment." The formal tone told me in no uncertain terms that he had dropped back into professional soldier mode, and that he wouldn't waste his or anyone's time giving an opinion unless it at least tipped the balance of probability to be correct.

"So we go out there," Dan stated with the most imperceptible shadow of doubt in his own words, hinting at, but not quite implying, the question mark after his words.

"We go out there," I echoed in a more certain tone.

~

Mateo took us out with two of his crew. He didn't use the hulking fishing boat he usually captained in favour of a smaller and faster craft which covered the distance to the spot where our missing crew had last been seen in just over thirty minutes. The smudge of some shape out on the open sea grew larger and more obvious the closer we got, and when Mateo backed off the engines to allow us to look at our beleaguered fishing boat I got my first glimpse of one of them.

With the sea's movement I had little hope of scoring a clean hit at that distance which is why we went in closer. We still had five of our people on that boat, and I didn't want to be the one who accidentally killed or injured one of them. One of them had fired shots when they saw us approaching; nothing aimed or disciplined with a design to hit us, just wild firing in the air like the automatic weapon they carried was a toy. That annoyed me. I'd seen it in movies in the past where someone would rattle off an entire magazine into the air without considering for one second the potential death toll of all of those bullets finally returning to earth still in possession of more than enough velocity to kill the members of the crowd, who were usually seen baying and shouting around the idiot pulling the trigger.

Even a mounted machine gun with a high firing rate and in a heavy calibre would have struggled to hit us with any kind of accuracy from the range they had seen us, but I guessed it was just a territory marking threat. Dick measuring, Dan called it.

We went in closer and I saw the exact thing Will had described to us: a skinny guy, arms like sticks or a young child, wearing a filthy vest that appeared beige and brown in desert camouflage but had most probably begun its life as white. He had a white and red checked scarf tied around his head exposing just the flash of his face around the eyes and he brandished his gun in the air like it was some kind of holy talisman of power.

I told Dan I had a shot and he made sure everyone knew the plan.

"In your own time, kid," he said.

"Relax, Granddad," I said, internally cursing myself for using the words without considering their meaning, "you just get ready."

I took the shot.

It took a moment for me to reacquire my target in the scope in time to see him thrown backwards off the deck to flip over the railings. A rattle of undisciplined gunfire came back at us as the bow of our boat surged upwards again to hide them from view. I slid backwards a little, turning and sitting up as I did to rest the big rifle in an empty bucket lashed to the deck. Once settled, I swung my carbine around to my front ready to engage these bastards at closer quarters.

Precious long seconds went by as the sound of incoming fire whistled through the air. I saw bright white splashes in the sea around us, but nothing seemed to hit our boat; I couldn't hear any round connecting with our thin hull which gave me some solace. I reminded myself that a lucky bullet killed just the same as a carefully aimed one. The engine note backed off rapidly and disappeared almost entirely and my body was pushed to the left by the forces of inertia when Mateo swung the wheel to put our left side against the other boat.

Dan was up, squeezing off single shots in rapid pairs at a target I couldn't see because I'd lost my purchase on the slippery deck. I got up to one knee, accidently flicking my safety catch all the way up to full-auto because the boats bumped heavily against one another. I rose up, seeing and hearing Dan and Mitch engaging two others off to my left as I looked to the right towards the prow of the taller fishing boat.

Looking back on it I actually laugh, even though it was far from funny at the time. I shouted something I never thought I would have a reason to say, and it sounded just like a line from some over-the-top action movie. Another one, bareheaded and wearing similarly filthy rags with prominent yellow buck teeth, ran towards the railing of the boat carrying something so utterly preposterous, so out of place for the world I lived in, that it momentarily stunned me.

"*RPG*," I screamed, dragging out the last syllable in perfect mimicry of something worthy of Hollywood. The sound of my voice was cut off by three rapid bursts of automatic fire which, I didn't fully appreciate until afterwards, had all come from my own gun.

His momentum, arrested only in his upper body as my shots hit him at brutally short range, carried him under the railings as his legs crumpled beneath him. He slipped overboard, smashing his face off the edge of our own boat with a sickening crunch, and for one moment, one awful, bladder-emptying moment, I saw the tip of the rocket pointing straight at my face as it tumbled with him into the water. I froze, my brain for once trying to catch up with the events in real time as opposed to the other way around.

"Clear," I heard in a loud Scottish accent, before a responding "clear," came from Dan who had somehow got on board the boat in a few seconds.

An engine note screamed from the far side as the smaller craft shot away with its prow pointing up at a forty-five-degree angle with the force of the full throttle. Two of them were there, wide-eyed and staring back at us as they hung onto the boat to stop themselves from being rolled out backwards under.

My body switched back on and my eyes narrowed as I took aim and began to stitch the remainder of my magazine into their path. It ran dry and I reloaded without taking my eyes off them to resume firing in bursts as I tried to gauge how much lead to give them. I didn't know if I had scored any hits on the boat, and I'd never tried to make shots under such difficult conditions as I tried to hit a moving target from a moving target. The boat carried on hard even after the sound of their engines, like a lawnmower on crack, disappeared away into the grey-blue of the Mediterranean Sea.

"Are we good?" Dan yelled.

"Fine," Mitch replied.

"I'm good," I shouted, checking my hands for the tremors I expected at any moment from the delayed reaction of the adrenaline.

"Two down," Dan called.

"One down," I shouted back, "two escaped."

"Five tangos accounted for," Mitch said loudly from the deck of the fishing boat. "Going below. Dan?"

Dan stacked up behind him. Mitch had slung his rifle and drawn his sidearm to activate the small torch mounted underneath the barrel. He held the weapon close to his chest in two hands ready to clear the cramped interior of the boat's lower deck as Dan drew the shotgun from over his shoulder and slapped Mitch once on the back before they both disappeared out of sight.

I got to my feet, putting one foot on the railing and timing my jump to wrap both hands over the bar that RPG man had slid underneath, to land awkwardly on the higher deck. I looked around, seeing nobody but finding a lot of equipment stacked as though ready to be offloaded.

"Leah," Dan bawled from below, "medkit. Now."

I looked back at Mateo, pointing to my bag which he leaned down to grab, steadying himself quickly before tossing it up to me. I caught the strap, stepping back from the edge in fear of slipping and falling into the water between the two boats which now drifted away from each other. Moving into the dark interior as quickly as I could I found the five crew members tied and gagged, being cut free by the others. One of them was badly beaten, eyes swollen shut and blood soaking his shirt from the cuts on his face. I worked on him, calling loudly into his face to try and get a verbal response but none came. His head lolled badly as I laid him down and opened his eyes to look at his pupils. He was out cold.

"Get us back home," I said to nobody in particular.

Back on deck, as the two boats went hard back towards land, I found Mitch on the stern looking at the body of a man with a bandolier of linked bullets criss-crossing his narrow chest.

"Pirates," he said.

"What?"

"Pirates. Somalian probably. East African at any rate."

"But… *pirates?*" I asked. "As in *aargh?*"

THE BRIEFING

"Somalia's government collapsed well over twenty years ago," Mitch said to us. "Our boys have been out in East Africa since forever, and a lot of that work is classed as humanitarian, but the real reason is because a lot of the European terror attacks can be traced back to the region. The ones that didn't happen mostly, because they were intercepted, but some of the ones that did, too. When the central regime collapsed there was no navy, and other countries exploited that by fishing their waters and some even started dumping their toxic waste there. It was like there was a vacuum or something and it followed the typical flow; NGOs swooped in under UN guidance and there was an international arms embargo in place to try and stabilise the region."

He saw my eyebrows asking the question for me and explained that nobody was allowed to sell or give weapons or training to any force in the country.

"It split up into three main territories, all very tribal, and the south was a major problem. Northern Kenya and Southern Somalia had serious issues with Islamic extremism; Al-Shabaab, Boko Haram and other smaller groups all linked to ISIS and Al-Quaeda, or what was left of them. You've seen *Black Hawk Down?*"

A few nods ran around our group.

"Mogadishu, although thank God I've never been there, is one of the most dangerous places on Earth. At least it was back before. The threat rating was as high as Helmand Province at the height of operations in Afghan. Some of these bastards treated the world like it had ended even when it hadn't. It was not a place to go to on holiday, put it that way. The fuckers did things like getting kids to blow themselves up in marketplaces to fight the interference of the West, but all they did was kill innocent people."

He cleared his throat and shifted position.

"Some of the fishermen were attacked or driven off by the foreign boats in their waters, and because there was no government to stop it they started fighting back. At first, I'm told, it was just defending their own livelihoods but it progressed a little faster from there. They started hijacking foreign boats and ransoming the crew and cargo back to the owners. It was seriously big business; I'm talking millions of dollars each capture. There were combined task forces of all different navies out there, usually commanded by us or the Americans."

"The Horn of Africa cuts off the Gulf of Aden and is basically a gateway to the Red Sea and the Suez Canal," Dan chimed in. "Busiest shipping lanes in the world and we used to pay millions for our naval ships to pass through. Without protection the piracy was rife and everyone started making money off it. The biggest crooks were the insurance companies who offered the ransom sureties."

"So," I asked cautiously knowing that I would probably look stupid for asking, "what's that got to do with here? We're miles and miles away from there, aren't we?"

"Yes," Dan said, "but look how far we've travelled over the years. What's to say that they didn't survive and have found their way through the Suez and into the Mediterranean?"

I shrugged to accept his point.

"You mean like that Tom Hanks film? Seriously?" Marie asked, a mild look of horrified shock on her face.

"Exactly like that," Mitch said before frowning and amending his assessment, "probably worse, to be honest…"

"Shit," she responded as she glanced at Dan, "what do we do?"

"Well they know we're here, or here abouts," he said simply. "Two of them out of the five that tried to capture our fishing boat escaped. They operate a little like a colony of bees, sending workers out from the hive to bring stuff back. There will be a kind of mothership most likely, and the smaller boats like the one we saw would go out and capture something. That fits with what our fishing crew said because they were arguing about who got what before they took the boat back. Back to *where* is the issue."

"That big boat further out to sea?" I asked.

"Quite likely," Dan said, "although there won't be just them."

"So," I asked, "what do we do?"

Dan opened his mouth to speak but stopped as Mitch spoke.

"We do nothing," he said firmly, brokering no further argument. Dan closed his mouth and looked at him, unaccustomed to the man being so forthright.

"We do *nothing*," he said again, stabbing a finger into the table, "and we hope they don't come back." He let that hang in the room and looked at everyone in turn to make sure he was understood.

Something in his eyes made me believe him because he had lost all trace of the unflappable man I had known for years.

"Increased defences?" Neil asked.

"Absolutely," Dan said, "we've got the fifty cal covering the bay, but I want the guard doubled at least with a standby force ready. One of us will need to head that up at all times."

"What about night time?" said Neil, his forehead wrinkled in thought.

I was glad that nobody suggested searchlights or anything else similarly daft as to light a beacon signalling our base.

"I can sort something," Neil said, "leave it with me and I can fix it tomorrow in full daylight."

We melted away. Dan went with Lucien to inspect the guard post overlooking our seaward vulnerability, but I said I'd catch them up. I didn't say it was because I wanted to speak to Mitch, which I did, because I preferred to do so alone.

"You okay?" I asked him quietly.

"Aye," he said unconvincingly, "it's just that these bastards worry me."

"Worry you how?"

He sighed, allowing his mask to slip and show me a glimpse of stress and fear.

"I've fought in Afghanistan, Iraq, and a half-dozen other places all over the world. I've worked on clean-up operations after earthquakes and hurricanes and major floods, but nowhere, *nowhere*, has frightened me as much as that place."

"You've come across them before?"

"Not pirates specifically," he said, "but we got into a contact in northern Kenya back in the day. We were there as a training and outreach kind of thing. You know, mentoring the locals. Their officers had been to Sandhurst, but the men were just recruited because they were able bodies of the right age. Basic training for them was mostly feeding them enough decent food that their legs didn't break when we started pushing them physically. Half of them were probably connected by family to someone in Al-Shabaab or one of the other groups, because we were always warned not to give any intelligence to them or discuss things within their earshot. Bit hard to get them to trust you and listen to what you're trying to teach when you've had the seed planted in your head that they're the enemy.

"We'd driven them out to the arse-end of nowhere, dropped them off and marched back with them on a training exercise. I was with the lead group, only eight of us in total including my daft boy of a lieutenant, and as we walked into a settlement the trees just erupted with incoming."

He bowed his head for a moment, making me stay very still and silent so as not to break the spell of his story.

"There we were; one minute giving it all 'jambo' to the kids and handing out a few sweets and pens to make them like us. Hearts and minds and all that stuff. The next the lads were all dropping like flies and screaming. You ever seen someone hit up close by a seven-six-two? What am I saying? Of course you have; you know it's not pretty. Their boys didn't know how to react, but my lot hit their belt buckles and found cover. Loads of them went down, including some of the kids from the village who had run up to see us. Now, we were told that we were there to observe and train, not to get involved, but my personal feelings on the matter differed from that of our officer. He was yelling for us to hold our fire, and I was yelling at my lads to flat-pack every last bastard insurgent they could see. Some of the Kenyan lads returned fire and their boss was switched on enough to lead a charge into the bushes.

"The wee boss and I had a falling out about it, no matter how many times I said my 'with all due respect' line. He was still prattling on in my ear when we were called forward to find that our attackers were just bairns, just wee boys who should nae been there. Should have been in school or anywhere apart from laying an ambush with a bloody AK-47 as tall as they were. The lieutenant, well"—Mitch gave a morbid chuckle—"he left his breakfast right there in the bush and did nae say a word more about it. I thought I'd never find a place on Earth as bad as Afghanistan, but yeah, Africa scares me. I've never encountered such a friendly and welcoming people who live shoulder to shoulder with the most bloodthirsty animals I've had the misfortune to meet."

I took it in, realising why I hadn't heard that particular story before, and just looked at him. Despite all of his mirth and his uncomplaining nature, Mitch was shaken up by the thought of pirates coming to our door.

"Mitch?" I asked after a while, as something Dan had said played on my mind.

"Aye?"

"Dan said that the AK was the 'foreskin of Africa'," I said a little sheepishly despite having tried to figure out the joke, "what does he mean by that?"

Mitch laughed.

"I've heard different versions." He chuckled. "But he means that every last cock in Africa seems to be born with one."

"Oh!" I said. "What other versions have you heard?"

"I'll not say the C-word in the company of a lady," Mitch

answered as he stood tall and collected his weapon. I stood up too, rustling the packaging in my left leg pocket.

"You holding out on us?" he exclaimed gleefully. "Have you got sweets you haven't shared?"

"No," I said hurriedly, stepping out of his reach as I remembered what I had after the excitement of our return, "it's lady stuff. Nothing you need."

The embarrassment tactic worked.

"Oh, I, er," he stammered, instantly glancing around for the safest route of tactical withdrawal, "carry on then."

I went back to my room to dump my kit, knowing that Lucien wouldn't be there and that I'd have time to sort it out before I was expected at the sea wall. I took the two pregnancy tests out of my pocket, looking at the packaging and only recognising them from the pictures I had seen on TV years ago, and stuffed them in between the collection of black tops of different sleeve length and thickness in the drawers. I left my bag and set off towards the sea at a jog.

"…a series of buoys," Neil was saying as I caught up with them, "the lobster pots would do. Little solar lights on each one and a channel in the middle for our boats to get in and out. As long as someone is watching then any boat trying to slip into the bay would show up against them. They won't be visible from far out either."

"That would work," Dan said, "and a flare gun for if they do try?"

"Yep," Neil answered, "we have plenty of those from all of the dead boats we've cleared."

"Raise the alarm too," I said, thinking back to the only time the bell had ever been rung by was by me shooting it to try and get the attention of the others when we were under attack.

Dan nodded his agreement.

"I'll take tonight," he said, "someone else take over for the morning and another in the afternoon."

"I'll take the morning," Mitch and I said in unison. He turned to me and explained, "I usually put the baby down in the evening."

"I'll take over after lunch then," I said as I hurriedly tried to change the subject away from babies.

"I'll sort the militia out into three watches," Adam said. "It's an easy job, and I'll get them all to sleep down by the docks."

The others left, happy with their plans for the morning until we could fine-tune things, and I remained with Dan who was having a one-way conversation with Ash who was grumbling at him for smoking again.

"We can't stop the fishing boats going out," I told him, "we'd starve and have nothing to trade for starters."

"I know," he replied darkly, "but we can put a halt on it for a week and hope they pass us by. Maybe they're heading for America?"

"Who knows," I said, "but we need a deterrent at least."

"A deterrent?"

"Like a flamethrower," I said with evil relish, "or another mounted fifty-cal onboard."

"That would certainly deter me," he said.

I got back to my, *our*, rooms late that night after running through all the 'actions-on' for the eventuality of an attack by sea. I was exhausted even before I slid under the sheets because it had been one hell of a long day, and before I blew out the candle beside my bed, I stared at the second drawer down and tried to put the contents out of my mind.

HURRY UP AND WAIT

Bored people were annoying. When you stop fishermen from going out on the sea like they did every day, and combined their inactivity with stress and fear, then people really got on my nerves.

I had offered to take the standby force, which was in reality just four people with guns ready to run the hundred or so metres to the sea wall if anything came into sight.

Dan and I had debriefed the terrified fishermen taken captive after breakfast, mostly because Kate had done her usual trick of puffing up her chest to signify that she outranked Dan when it came to medical matters and insisted that they be left alone until they had rested. Dan protested, obviously, pointing out that the memory was a fragile thing and that getting the information from them as early as possible was crucial.

He lost, because their health and sanity was of greater importance.

We sat them down individually, being very careful and gentle about it, as Polly helped with the translation. Her laid-back attitude actually made her a good interrogator if she didn't mind me and Nemesis playing bad cop.

We learned that the pirate crew had come screaming out of the open water towards them, on a direct intercept course, and simply bumped up alongside them much as we had when taking back what was ours. They jumped aboard waving their machine guns and beat the crew into submission with rifle butts and threats of death by numerous methods. Being unaccustomed to violence, the fishing crews just folded as any normal person would do. They went into self-preservation mode, promising to comply just to stop the fear and the pain.

I had to admit that it seemed an effective tactic. Just as Dan and I practiced what he called 'psychological *kah-ra-teh*' when we would both stand in separate fields of view to someone and both took it in turns to speak or shout so that they were totally overwhelmed and didn't know where to look or point their gun.

We did learn some interesting facts, however. The leader of the raid, apparently the one who had taken my opening shot straight in the chest, went overboard holding the radio he had been speaking into. Nobody recognised the language they used, which went a long way to supporting Mitch's dark premonitions about their point of origin.

"What words did you recognise that they used?" I asked one of them gently, doing what Marie had taught me to do and never asking a question that could be shut down with a one-word answer. I didn't ask, 'did you recognise any of the words they used?' because anyone who wanted to stop reliving the ordeal would just answer 'no', but I forced them to think back over it and search for the answers.

"One said something about 'the American'," he told me, "that was all I knew that he say."

"Mercenary?" Dan opined. "Or more likely a hostage."

"Either one is likely," Mitch said, "there was always a big US presence in the Gulf with the combined task force. Usually a full carrier group: a sub, destroyers, missile boats and the like. Stands to reason that some of those would have survived the thingy. Quite a lot of private security companies operated out there too, back in the day."

The 'thingy'. The global pandemic that wiped out most of the human life on Earth. Only Mitch could play that down with such dismissive nonchalance.

"True," Dan said, "but unlikely that we'll ever find out."

Neil was out with one of his eager apprentices who rowed the wooden dingy for him as he spent the afternoon carefully depositing weighted cables connected to floats that each held a solar lamp. They were the kind that people bought on a whim from supermarkets and garden centres to spike into the grass of their lawns and provide a little night time decoration. They had been loaded up on one of our supply runs over the years on a similar whim, only this time used to light the darkest walkways of the town for safety reasons instead of an adornment to complete some green-thumbed person's masterpiece.

They were collected up and he had spent the morning fixing them firmly into the blocks of polystyrene which he had kept stored for no known reason other than that they would come in handy one day. He crowed in delight as that hoarder instinct finally paid off.

I took over the watch at the sea wall after the midday meal, and Lucien had engineered his command of the standby force so that he could still be close to me. As I stood in the sun wearing short sleeves under my heavy vest and let it bathe me with warmth despite the briskness of the breeze coming in from the sea, he stood beside me and rested his big rifle on the stone wall to scan the horizon. I had rested my own rifle against the wall as my carbine hung from my vest, opting instead to use the big binoculars that would very likely have been incredibly expensive if they had been bought instead of removed from a dusty glass display cabinet.

"Nothing," I said, surprising myself that I felt a little disappointed. Then I felt guilty as I recalled the look on Mitch's face when he spoke about Africa. If he was scared, then it was damn good sign that I should be too.

"How long do we stay inside?" Lucien asked.

"Not sure. Depends on how long Dan decides, but we need to be fishing again within a week or we'll be dipping into our winter stores and we won't have enough to make the first quota for the start of the summer trade runs."

Lucien shot me a look, hearing me speak with such authority about the economic situation when it didn't usually feature on my radar.

"Polly told me," I admitted with a shrug.

"So we send guards out on the fishing boats," he said, as though the solution was really that simple.

I thought about that, looking for holes in the suggestion and finding none.

"Maybe wait until tomorrow to suggest that one," I said before changing the subject. "Adam's got the night watch again. Dan's going to take the sleeping watch with the QRF. Marie's not happy though."

"What is this *QRF*?" he asked me as he pronounced the letters carefully.

"Sorry," I told him as I bumped my right shoulder gently into his arm, remembering how he still struggled with all the little sayings and acronyms that we used, even after all this time and how far his English had developed. "It's a Mitch thing. Quick Reaction Force. The standby team."

"Ah," he said, "why do you not just say this?"

"What?" I said with mock horror. "Say the words when a TLA would do?"

"And this? This *TLA*?"

"Three-Letter Acronym," I said, using Dan's joke on someone else who hadn't heard it before.

"I will never understand you English," he said with a resigned huff as he looked back out to sea.

"So stop trying," I told him, "just go with it."

He kept me company until the night darkened and Neil's array of bobbing solar lights twinkled in the swell. He had gauged the increase of the tide well when cutting the length of each cable, and none of the lights were submerged as the tide came in to swell the bay. Adam and Dan took over, Adam with a smile and Dan with a scowl as he carried his kit bag to throw it on a folding cot in the building that had been opened up to house the relief fighters.

Leah leaned back from the ledger again, her back aching from the inactivity. She stood, stretching and hearing a pistol shot of a crack from somewhere up near her shoulder, and let out the stretch with a relaxed breath. She thought about the next part of the tale, about how they found themselves way out of their depth, quite literally, and how the turn of events shattered the boredom into pieces.

She wondered how best to describe what had happened, but because that part of the story wasn't hers to tell she went to find the one person who could fill in the seven years' worth of gaps.

"Come on, dozy bollocks," she said to Ares who jumped up from his preposterous sleeping position in a patch of sunlight where he lay on his back with all four paws sticking up and his body bent in half as though he tried to sniff his own butt in his sleep.

He came awake instantly, thrashing and spinning as though electrified before looking up at her, sneezing loudly and shaking his head before giving her a daft look. He followed her outside, walking at her heel as he'd been taught to but needing constant reminders not to run off to inspect everything that caught his interest. She did this in the form of wordless noises and growls, like she was his alpha dog, and each time he slunk back to heel.

It seemed harsh whenever Leah had to train a new dog, at least to people who didn't understand, but being too soft or kind with an animal that you wanted to be able to rely on to save your life was a bad idea. She formed a bond with the dogs. She'd done it with Ash when Dan first taught her how to give him commands so that he didn't think he could make decisions. And with Nemesis who took to her so naturally that half of the time she just knew what Leah wanted her to do and had acted independently when she'd been in-capacitated, which was the only time she'd ever want that to happen; if Leah couldn't give her commands then the chances were that she'd been knocked out or stunned, in which case she'd want her dog to tear apart the person who had done it. She'd been like that with Athena, Nemesis' daughter, but she had never really worked properly, which was a blessing because Leah had never really been called upon to use her like she had Nem. She'd proven to be a great breeder though, and had carried two litters in near perfect health without losing any of them.

Ares, as dumb as he seemed, had really warmed Leah's heart after feeling the loss of that kind of connection since Nem had gone. She just hoped he could switch on and stop being so ungainly soon, because he was almost old enough to start learning how to track and do the 'chase and detain' drills which were really just a polite way of saying that you're teaching your dog to bite someone and drag them to the ground. That usually cost her a hefty bribe to one of the younger boys in town who was prepared to take the risk and wear the thick leather sleeve to protect their limbs.

Leah was musing about whether to offer the task to one of the few hopeful teenagers who wanted to be part of the militia, just to test their resolve, when she bumped into the man she was looking for.

"Hey there," Joshua said in his broad accent from one of the American states she had never visited, which remained unchanged despite the dilution of everyone's language. He even spoke French with the same accent.

"How's things?" Leah asked him as he stood tall from the outboard motor he was tinkering with and nursing back to life.

"I'm all good," he said, "I was just fixin' to finish up here. How you doin'?"

"I'm good," she said, smiling genuinely as she always found his genetic sense of hospitality so infectious. "I was hoping you could do me a big favour actually…"

Leah's smile worked on him, like it always did, and he picked up an oily rag to remove the residue from his hands. He was tall and heavy but had a permanent streak of happiness that reminded Leah of Neil in so many ways, but his sayings and mannerisms were a world apart and still made her laugh after a decade of hearing them.

"Man, you're as cute as a button when you're after something. It's like you've weaponised charm. How can I help you today?"

"I'm, err," she said, feeling the natural apprehension of every writer everywhere who was about to admit that they were writing a story, "I'm trying to write an account about what happened when you first came here, but I don't want to write something which isn't true."

"Happy to help," he said, beaming, "you know that."

"Awesome," she said and returned his wide grin, "after evening meal?"

"It's a date," he said wickedly, knowing that Lucien would roll his eyes at the intentional goading.

Adalene went up to the rooms with her father after the evening meal and Leah took Joshua up to her favourite spot on the ramparts. They had the same idea, because Leah produced a bottle of the local sweet fire-water and he smiled to reveal a half-bottle of his favourite tipple.

"Have you met my brother?" he asked with a grin. "Leah, this is Jack. Jack, meet Leah."

"Hi Jack," she said.

"Funny you should use that word…"

"Ah, sorry," she said sheepishly.

"It's fine," he said, "I ain't gonna have a hissy fit now. So, what do you want to know?"

"Everything," she said, "from the beginning to the end." He took a measured pull on the bottle as his eyes glazed over into uncomfortable memory.

"It ain't over yet," he said, "but I'll tell you how that part started."

ALONE ON THE WAVES

My name is Joshua "Junior" Bucknor, and I was born and raised in Lutts, Tennessee which I thought was just a dot on the map but the townsfolk believed it was the centre of the world. It was mostly farms and churches, and I had little interest in finishing high school and turning my Saturday job at the hardware store into a full-time gig. On my last day at school I walked out with a *three-point-oh* and partied like everyone else.

The next day I took a two-hour ride on a Greyhound bus to Jackson and marched my ass right up to the US Army recruiters.

An hour I waited there, all the while getting the stink eye off this master sergeant who no doubt thought my skinny body wasn't up to his own personal standards. I took exception to this; I may have been skinny back then, not that you'd believe that of me now, but I was tough.

I was so tough that I got up and asked the guy for directions to the US Navy recruiters. To his credit, he smiled and told me where it was, right down to the proper turns and he wrote it all down for me.

The son of a bitch sent me on a five mile walk for a one mile journey, so I was sweaty and pissed by the time I got there. The conversation went something like this:

"How can I help you, son?"

"Sir, I have a mind to become a Navy SEAL."

"Well, son, only the toughest make it through. You sure you're up for that?"

Well after a half-hour of him talking to me like I was a grown-up, the first man to ever have done that, I agreed to begin my new life in the dizzying world of mechanical and electrical. I took the bus home, then dealt with the bullshit from my parents and all the drama that followed. My dad went and got three sheets to the wind and my mom just cried. They told me how I'd never be home and this and that, which I kinda thought was the point. My appointed time came around and I went back on the bus, telling Momma and Daddy that I was a man then and didn't need their help to get to Jackson. What I really meant was that I didn't want to hear them going on at me to not go.

I went. I signed my life away and I don't mind telling y'all that I felt knee high to a grasshopper when I walked in. My ass did not touch the ground for the next year, but I fell into it alright. I learned how to fix engines of all kinds and before I hit twenty years old I found myself looking down on something I ain't never laid eyes on before: the open ocean.

We weren't a poor family, but like a lot of kids my age I didn't have a passport back then and I'd never been on a vacation outside of the closest states. I'd been to Panama City Beach in Florida, what they called *The Redneck Riviera*, but the Gulf ain't nothin' compared to the real ocean. The navy showed me a whole big new world, and my new gang had never been busier since nine-eleven. I went all over the world in a few short years, but that was just a backdrop to what happened.

We were part of the CTF, the Combined Task Force, as a petty officer third class onboard the *USS Jean Evelyn* Arleigh Burke-class destroyer. Best damn ship I ever laid eyes on. We were sent across the Atlantic to Europe and spent a few stressed-out days going down the Suez. We were on high alert; terrorists – *tangos* – everywhere and round the clock watches where we manned the weapons stations until we got out into the Red Sea where, guess what?

More round the clock watches.

Now this task force was made up of all kinds of different folks. There were some Brits, some Indians, the Japanese and even a tub from New Zealand. Now I don't know how much you know about the world back then, and I don't profess to know it all, but I only thought pirates were in the movies. Turns out that this bunch of African dudes who didn't have jobs or something decided to start hijacking boats from all over when they got near the coast of East Africa.

These guys were *seriously* bad news.

We basically ranged out all over and got reports of activity in the coastal towns that the sons of bitches ran to whenever we got close. We were all set to just nuke 'em, not like *real* nukes but just to let them have it. Just send the whole bunch of them down so that they weren't a problem no more, but you know how it is; orders come down, no firing unless fired upon and yadda, yadda, yadda.

So anyway, we'd been out there all of a month with nothing but exercises and everything when the scuttlebutt went insane. There was talk of some bio-attack or something, and half our boys were sent high-tailin' it back home including the bubble-heads in the sub.

What happened next happened fast, and it was bad.

I won't go into the details. I'm sure you have your own

memories of that dark time. But I was left on the *Jean Evelyn* with just one other guy and he was losing his mind. There was no chance of us putting all the bodies of the crew in the morgue; we lost two hundred and seventy-one guys and girls in a day.

I did what I could, even wearing the sweaty respirator because I thought I'd somehow survived a chemical attack. The other guy didn't do so good. He was more useless than tits on a boar hog, I mean this dude had *lost* it. I tried to use the radio, the sat phones, everything. Nobody was answering. It was just me and my buddy, and he was falling apart.

We spent a few weeks like that, but a ship of that size wasn't designed for a crew of just one guy. One and a half at best. We were anchored up in shallower water, every day trying to just keep her afloat, when my buddy started yellin'. That was the first time I actually laid eyes on the sons of bitches we were out there to fix up in the first place. They came down from up yonder in their shitty little boats, AKs in the air and whoopin' and hollerin'.

I ran to the Bushmaster, big 25 mil auto-cannon, real doomsday bit of gear, threw on the ear defenders and started lighting them up.

I let them have it, I mean these motherfuckers started throwing themselves overboard after a few hits turned some of them into red mist. I took out two of the suckers, but the other ones got in close. I couldn't stop them, and by the time I'd gotten my hands on a gun they were there. I got bashed something fierce in the head, rifle butt I reckon, and when I came to my beloved *Jean Evelyn* was gone.

My buddy, did I tell you his name? He was Bill. Billy. He didn't try to fight them off, but he did manage to set off the thing we was able to rig up in case we had to scuttle her. I was bouncing along with blood in my eyes when I sat up to look over the stern of the shitty little stinkin' boat they threw me on, and watched my girl going down.

They took me back to their ship, every one of them taking their turn to spit in my face. To hit me. To threaten me. I was this big prize to them; the infidel asshole American sailor. I got locked up, thrown in a tiny cabin. I didn't know if it was a week or a month before they made me do the video. I tried to remember what I had to say, but I was freaked out. I was dehydrated. My mouth was so dry I could'a spit cotton, and I didn't know which way was up half the time. They treated me real ugly.

"I am an American citizen," I had to tell one of the skinnys who was filming me on an iPhone. A fuckin' iPhone for God sake!

"I am Petty Officer Third Class Joshua Bucknor, I am a member of the United States Navy and an American citizen," yadda, yadda. I did the whole service number thing, and when I refused to tell them what they wanted to know they kicked the shit out of me again and threw me back in the hole. I think it dawned on them after a while that they weren't getting no ransom for me, so I tried fixing to get myself released any ways I could.

"I'm a mechanic," I told them, "I can, you know, fix shit."

Well, they let me fix shit, and after a while they even stopped beating on me. My uniform was gone, rotted off my stinking body, and my beard had come in so that I looked the part. After a few months, maybe a year, I became part of the crew. I ain't proud of that, but it was the only way I could'a survived. I figured out that they weren't all one crew, but a few of the original pirates found anyone left and just pressed them into their crews like it was nineteen hundred. I dunno, something about the place just made it easy for them to act like that. To turn pirate like it was nothing. One of the leaders survived and he kept them all together like some asshole papa bear.

And that's how I survived. That's how I met the other hostages who found themselves some way to be useful to the pirates. There was an Indian guy, he was a good navigator. Never saw any women, but that didn't surprise me and neither did I want to think about it. Never saw Bill again. Never wanted to question why.

It went on like that for years, day in and day out. I fixed stuff, I ate, I slept, and I thought about escape for the first few years. I gave up. I didn't even have the courage to take my own life, despite thinking about it damn near every day. I was numb, and I thought I was beyond saving when their leader, Ahmad Gareer, took his whole fleet through the Suez and into European waters.

It all changed then.

"I remember it well," Leah told him, "you looked like shit."

"I think you would too, if you'd just spent seven years with them assholes," he countered gently. "Seven *years*, man. Damn. I had no idea it had been that long. I guess I'd lost track of time after the first year when they kept me locked up. Went inside myself, you know? Even missed my own birthday turnin' thirty."

"I bet," she said weakly, not wanting to consider what her life would have been like being captured by them.

Short, most probably, Leah told herself glumly, *and unpleasant all the way down.*

"You didn't explain how they got the tanker," she asked, having racked her brain but unable to recall the part of the tale when the pirates had come to get their hands on their mothership.

"Luck," Joshua said, "pure luck. It was owned by somewhere in the Middle East, UAE most likely, them suckers owned pretty much everything anyway. Gareer found it just sat in the deep-water harbour in Mombasa, that's in Kenya, next country down, all parked up and loaded with fuel from the refinery. Just sittin' ripe for the pickin'. That became their little base of operations and all them other ones just hovered around it like flies on shit. These UAE-owned boats had what we called multi-national crews: some Europeans, some Indians and quite often a white guy from South Africa as the captain. Well these dumbasses killed or injured the few people left there and guess who they brought in to start the engines?"

He leaned back, taking another swig of Tennessee's finest and pulling a face as he swallowed to relish the harshness of it.

"Well after that, after I'd proved I was useful, and seein' as I hadn't tried to escape or nothin', they sent me out all over to fix their stuff. I'd tell 'em, 'I need this oil' or 'I need that tool' and they'd scurry off to fetch it for me."

He sipped his drink again and let his eyes drift unfocussed on the distant sea.

"That's what I was doin' the day I first laid eyes on you. I'd have been the age you are now, I guess. I'd been given off to the smaller crew; they had a big fishin' boat and a couple of them skiffs they liked so much, but their main engine had a real nasty habit of runnin' too hot. First I knew of the shit that went down was when I heard yellin' and shootin' from up top. Then you hit me with that flashlight beam of yours and, as they say, the rest be nothin' but history."

SEA RANGERS

I remember finding Joshua. I remember it clearly because I very nearly killed him. The ragged, bearded, deeply tanned squinting man looked every part the Islamic extremist or pirate or terrorist at the time, then I caught myself for generalising. All I had ever known about them was from movies anyway, which was probably mostly bullshit, so it was little wonder I stereotyped him when I first laid eyes on the man.

It wasn't planned, and actually it was very ill-advised in hindsight, but after how I felt on that morning my head was all over the place and I think I was reckless. Cancel that, I *knew* I was being reckless but we all react to things differently, I guess.

Dan had finally relented to allow the fishing boats back out as long as they had an armed escort and followed the strict instructions to point their noses towards home and floor it should they see any boat that wasn't one of ours. Most of the pressure came from the peaceful side of the argument; the side that pointed out that we survived because of the sea and the fish we took from it every day, and that we had quotas to fill for trade and others relying on our productivity.

People like me who argued for action just because there was a fight to be had added weight to it, appealing to his own mentality in fact, but it was the thought of going hungry that pushed him over the edge.

He didn't act without thinking, not like he used to and not like I had begun to, and he had sent pigeons to The Orchards and the farm and Andorra who formed our alliance along with half a dozen other small settlements within reach of our little fortress. The messages warned of the threat, not that it really mattered to any of them so far inland, but the request for any additional militia was answered with alacrity and without question. Two came from the farm the same day, one from The Orchards the following morning and six from Andorra the next evening led by Rafi who had originally been one of us until a couple of years before when he and I had an uncomfortably weird holiday in the strange but stunning little country hidden in the mountains.

Our last night of relative inactivity was spent in a little gathering which I joined late after Lucien had relieved me to command the night watch at the sea wall. I went to bed early, knowing that I would be out on the water at daybreak, but the subject that had been intermittently stressed over and forgotten about for the last two days finally bore down on me with too much weight.

I opened the packaging, annoyed at the fiddly bits of plastic, and tried to decipher the instructions. In the end I had to correlate the position of the lines with the sketch drawing next to what looked like a baby face emoji, and when that first test gave me the answer I dreaded I tried the other one.

That one had the same result, despite what I willed it to say.

I was pregnant, and that knowledge didn't help me sleep at all.

I was up and dressed before the sun rose, opting for long sleeves despite the warm weather because I remembered how chilly the wind out there could be, adding my vest and instantly dropping another thirty percent of my body weight onto my feet. It was wearing the vest that kept me fit and strong as much as my running and swimming and training; ammunition weighs a flipping tonne.

With a carbine in one hand and a big rifle in the other and my face like thunder I walked up to the docks to join my crew for the day. Call it the benefit of command if you like, but I put myself on Mateo's boat just because I like him. We didn't ask any of the people from the other settlements to go out to sea, but kept them safely on land to stand guard while we went out. We were only letting the two biggest boats out, but allowed a handful of others to fish in the shallower waters near to our home just so long as they knew to keep watch and to flee back to the harbour if they saw anything. Their catches would be small, but food was food.

"Morning," Lucien said, leaning in to kiss my cheek and recoiling when I held up a hand near his face. He took one look at me and asked what was wrong; not what *he* had done, but what the matter was because he knew me well enough by then how to handle me.

"Nothing," I grumbled back, "just early. Not in the mood."

He allowed that, not believing me for a second but choosing the safer path of not pushing me for an answer when there were lots of people around to see him get his butt kicked.

"I'll be back later," I told him before looking down at Nemesis and fixing her with a look. "Stay," I told her, then watched her dance a little four-legged jig in frustration and sit beside Lucien looking up at him expectantly.

"Room for a wee one?" a familiar voice asked from the dock. Mitch threw his bag up to me which I swerved by leaning my upper body back and away so that the rucksack landed with a loud clank on the deck.

"Nice," he said.

"Sorry, got my hands full," I told him lifting up the two weapons I carried.

"Expecting trouble?"

"Always," I told him seriously, leaving out the fact that I was in the mood to actively search for it instead of letting it come to me as per usual, "aren't you?"

In answer he waggled his eyebrows and comically stroked the contraption under the barrel of his rifle, which lobbed small bombs in the direction of things and people he didn't like much.

I was right to go for the long sleeves, but it wasn't enough because I was still chilly despite the warm sunshine. The wind whipping over the deck was doubled in intensity by our forward momentum, and my skin was tight with the cold before we had even lost clear sight of land.

From a mile out, our little patch of indomitable southern France appeared tiny and barely worth a second glance. I hoped that anyone looking that way with unwelcome intentions would think the same, but I was absolutely sure that after our brush with them the pirates would be unlikely to let it pass without further investigation.

Pirates, I scoffed to myself, *can't believe I'm actually using that word.*

It still seemed ludicrous, but I was gauging that against the world from before when it was just total lawlessness. Back on land, even in the boring countryside of central England, there had been roaming gangs of men and women on bikes who hunted other survivors like extras from a bad movie. It made perfect sense for the same behaviour to apply to the seas, but that was now and not before. Now they were just another roving band of people firmly in the 'not us' category, which placed them in significant danger should our paths cross.

"Who's on the other boat?" I yelled at Mitch to be heard, realising that I hadn't seen who went out after we did and not having paid close enough attention the night before.

"Dan and Adam," he shouted back, cupping one hand to his mouth and smiling like a dog with its head sticking out of a car window. I didn't answer as there was no need. I did wonder why Dan didn't put himself with me and that nagged at my confidence until I settled on the fact that he wanted to be able to support Adam – never one to miss a training opportunity – and allowed Mitch and me autonomous control of our own day.

In hindsight, he said that was a mistake. I still think it wasn't, but I had to agree that the methods weren't exactly textbook. If Dan had done what we had then it would have been fine, just so long as we didn't tell Marie that he had done it, but he still liked to be the only person allowed to take risks like a control freak.

The engine note of the boat wound down to a low rumble and the crew got up from where they rested to start rigging up nets and winches in preparation of catching and dragging aboard the big ball of writhing and flapping silver that was our lifeblood. There were plenty of fish nearer shore I had learned, big shoals of mackerel and similar stuff, but to me fish was just fish. I didn't love it, but I didn't starve to death either. Still, nothing beat a nice bit of pork for me, and the offcuts of the fish had allowed the pigs to grow strong, so it was all part of the great circle of life I guessed.

I stood and used my rifle optic to scan the horizon, cursing myself for thinking the words and making the song from the *Lion King* run through my head on short-loop repeat, just as Mitch used a set of small binos to scan the other side. And that was how our morning went; they fished and we looked. Being a Sea Ranger was much easier, if a little more boring, than it was on land, at least that was what I thought until the late afternoon.

The first haul had been brought up and Mateo helped his crew sort them out into the hold before asking our permission to travel further out.

"The catch is small here," he said, "we go deeper and get bigger, yes?"

"Up to you, my friend," Mitch answered him, "we're just your good-looking bodyguards."

Mateo smiled, probably to cover up the fact that he hadn't understood Mitch because of a combination of his accent and a poor grasp of English unless spoken very simply.

The second haul went very much the same as the first had, only this time when the winches whined and pulled up the net there was a ragged cheer from the stern which indicated that they were happier with their second attempt.

I took my eye away from the scope to see their celebrations and smiled before Mitch spoke a single word that cut through me to connect to my 'switch on' nerve.

"Boat."

"Where?" I called out, scanning the horizon wildly.

"On me," he replied, waiting until I had crossed the rolling deck to lean on the rail beside him. "My two o'clock."

I tried to bring the rifle up to the right bearing, but the movement combined with the long barrel made it impossible. I dropped to my knee and rested the gun on the guardrail before finding what he had seen.

"Single boat," I said, "looks like it's moving fast."

"Aye," Mitch said with a hint of darkness in his voice, "look up and right of them."

I tracked the movement with my gun and saw it. A smudge on the horizon. I stared at it for a long time, casting my eyes back to the smaller boat which hadn't gained much distance on us.

"Mateo? We'll be leaving as soon as you're ready," Mitch shouted, serving only to alert the captain of our boat to the direction of the threat which he found after snatching up his own binoculars. He dropped them after a second of wide-mouthed staring, yelling at his crew to fix the nets and prepare to head home.

"It doesn't look that big," I said, meaning the bigger boat.

"And how the hell do you know?" Mitch asked me incredulously. "It may be five miles away which would make it the size of a bloody cruise ship."

"Trust me," I insisted. "Mateo?"

The captain came over to me.

"How far away is the bigger boat?" I asked him, pointing out the direction that he needed to look.

He stared for a while before answering.

"Is two mile," he said, "maybe three or four times of this?" He pointed to the deck we stood on.

"It's not that big then," I told Mitch with a wicked smile starting at the corner of my mouth. "We could use their boat and just take a look at them. Intelligence gathering."

"I don't like the look in your eye, missy," he said as his own eyes narrowed. "Dan gave very strict instructions to not mix it with them. Let's go."

I must be getting old, I thought, *my sweet and innocent eyes didn't seem to work on him any more.*

In the end I got my own way, but that was because the skiff chasing us was much faster, and we had to turn before gathering speed away from them.

The crew panicked and shouted, fearing the pursuit would stop them from getting home safely, but as we both stood at the stern of the ship the realisation that we would be caught only filled us with a ruthless resolve.

"Cut the engines," Mitch shouted as he took his eye away from the scope. "Full auto," he added to me, "light the fuckers up as soon as they're in range."

I nodded, pointlessly because he wasn't looking at me, and unscrewed the suppressor from the barrel of my carbine. I planned to let them have a full magazine from the battle rifle and then switch to the smaller calibre if they were still coming.

"Ready," I told him, and I was.

No Cover

The thing about fighting boat to boat is that there was no way to take cover and outmanoeuvre the enemy. With just one boat we couldn't outflank the smaller, more agile craft chasing us, but as that was lower and flimsy by comparison I reassured myself that we held the high ground.

I let rip with twenty lightning-fast rounds from the big rifle, of which probably four or five found the boat. It was seriously difficult being accurate with fire on a moving platform. I switched weapons, found the four occupants just popping their heads up over the lip of the boat counting their lucky stars that none of them were hit, about to raise their own weapons just as a hailstorm peppered them from ours.

Rats in a barrel was what Mitch had said afterwards, and it was just like that. They had nowhere to go but they still didn't break off or jump overboard. We cycled our weapons, reloading after the first automatic barrage had snatched one of them backwards to spin off the boat into the sea, and fired again more carefully the second time. Two more dropped by the time they had overtaken us and slammed into our side where a hooked ladder was thrown over our railings, but when we ran to that side and aimed our guns downwards the sole surviving occupant of the boat realised he was alone and was trying to unhitch himself. He was torn between escape and fighting, and as he reached for a massive, long-barrelled machine gun he found himself staring up at two separate targets both pointing weapons at him.

He made the wrong call.

Snatching up the gun that seemed as long and probably heavier than he was, the simple physical mechanics of the move was his undoing. All we had to do was apply a few pounds of pressure to our right index fingers, and the two near-simultaneous bullets hit him in the chest to drop him like a rag doll having the briefest of epileptic seizures.

"We're clear," Mitch shouted to the fishermen who had fled from sight, "you're alright now."

Slowly they emerged, peeking around the scowling Mateo who made it clear and obvious that he was unimpressed at being a part of the brief sea battle.

The silence was filled with the sounds of reloading as Mateo looked down at the gun in his hand as though he hadn't realised he had picked it up. He held it delicately, as though he was scared of it, which was more worrying than if he had pointed it at me. He went back into the wheelhouse and came out empty handed.

I retrieved my big rifle, slapped in a chunky twenty-round replacement magazine and knelt once again to check the horizon for the bigger boat. No signs of any other boats heading for us cut the waves.

"Give me a hand, Leah," Mitch yelled. I turned to see that he had climbed over the railings and down the ladder. I leaned over and he held up the big weapon to me, barrel first. It weighed a tonne. Not as much as the big Browning fifty-calibre monsters we had mounted back home, but the thing didn't exactly strike me as what they called 'man-portable'.

"What the hell is this?" I grunted as I managed to get two hands on it and haul it aboard like some grotesque deep-sea fish hand been landed as a prize.

"It's a PKM," Mitch told me unhelpfully, glancing up at me to read my face that further explanation was required. "Soviet machine gun. The world is littered with them, just like the old AK-47s. This one probably came from Afghanistan in the eighties."

"How?" I asked.

"Russia was there for a long time," he said, pausing and wearing his 'thinking' face. "That or any of the hundreds of little proxy wars fought in Africa."

"Proxy wars?" I asked, confused.

"Other countries interfering," he explained, "like us pesky Brits, but mostly it was smaller groups fighting each other and supported by communist countries. That meant that either us or the Americans would support the opposition and democracy. It was like the Cold War expansion pack."

I shrugged, having understood most of what he said. "But why Afghanistan?" I asked. "Didn't we have troops there when, you know, *it* happened?"

He searched the pockets of the three bodies on the boat, turning to stack two other rifles, one without a stock and the other with a folding parachute version. "The Soviets invaded it long before that, when I was just a wee bairn, and were stuck there for nearly ten years," he explained as he handed up the two AKs and set his footing on the rickety ladder. "They claim they were supporting the rightful communist government and everyone else said they were invading.

All the same kind of Cold War proxy shite, you know?"

I didn't, but I nodded.

"Well anyway, it was their Vietnam apparently, not like us and the Americans fared a great deal better when we went in to 'support the lawful government',," he said with his tone of voice pronouncing the air quotes. "But against the Russians, or the Soviets as we called them back then, the West supplied a shit-load of weapons, China and Pakistan supplied a lot of training, and the result was, twenty years later, an international terrorist group attacking the West. Fucked up, eh?"

"Yup," I said, not understanding the politics, but knowing the stupidity well.

Mitch hauled himself back over the railings, picking up the captured weapons and eying their state of care with evident distaste.

"And that's why these things are so bloody popular," he said to himself as he dropped the magazine out of one rifle and checked the action. "Bloody filthy, but you could cock this and leave it in a muddy ditch for a few days and it'll still be able to kill someone without blowing up."

"What do you mean?"

"These things are simple," he explained, showing me an empty chamber and handing it over for inspection, "crude even, but that doesn't stop them sending a big fat bullet your way. That thing's older than you. Twice over."

I looked at it, hating the weight distribution and clunky feel of it in comparison with my own lightweight weapons.

"And that's why they're known as the clitoris of Africa," he said with a smirk, "because every cu—"

"I get it!" I snapped, cutting him off before he went full squaddie. I handed back the gun and glanced back towards the distant boat where they had come from. I stared, my eyes narrowing at something I couldn't see.

"What?" Mitch asked suspiciously, his own eyes narrowing at my mischievous look.

"Oh, nothing…" I said innocently.

"Let's just explore that *nothing*, shall we?" he said. "We don't look like them, to put it bluntly, so if we ride their little shit-tub back then they'll spray us with *seven-six-two* until we catch a serious case of death. No, Leah, it's not happening."

"Mateo? Can you get our other boat on the radio?" I asked, ignoring Mitch.

"*Si,*" he said, turning away and jabbering into a microphone on a stretchy cord.

"No, Leah," Mitch said again more forcefully, "the two of us can't do this."

"I know," I told him, "which is why we're getting backup."

"No, Leah," Dan's voice came over the radio, crackling and distorted but every bit as forceful as Mitch's had been.

"Told you," the Scotsman mumbled from behind me.

"It's not a big boat, and they're four down already. We could do this," I said, trying not to sound like I was pleading with him.

"It's too risky," he said, "two of you can't do this."

"I know," I countered, "so get over here so the four of us can…"

A pause on the other end stretched out for long enough that I almost started speaking again twice.

"Fine," he said eventually, "wait there, and *do not* fucking do anything before we get to you. Put Mateo back on."

I did, and the captains exchanged the information required for them to meet. It took thirty minutes before they were visible. Another ten and my binoculars could make out Dan stood at the prow looking right back at me with his own.

As they slowed, they pulled alongside for the crews to lash the boats together after they threw the lashed tyres over the side to cushion our coupling. Dan timed it badly and landed heavily as he stepped over to our deck, cursing his old knees with a tight-lipped face and annoyed silence.

"One boat," Mitch said, "four of them, one overboard and three dead inside. Recovered a PKM and two AKs."

"A bloody PKM?" Dan said as he wore a look of mixed horror and disgust, "Jesus... have you searched them?"

"Yeah," Mitch answered, "nothing."

"No offence…" Dan said, making Mitch shake his head to imply that he didn't mind the man double-checking.

Dan climbed over and down the ladder just as Adam got to our deck, all smiles and barely suppressed excitement.

"For fuck sake!" Dan yelled from below, his voice a little higher than his characteristic grumpy growl. "Fucking *basics*! Come on!"

"What?" Mitch asked.

"Two dead, one not!" Dan snarled back up to me. I leaned over to see him ripping open a filthy T-shirt and slapping a dressing onto a wound low on the left abdomen of the mumbling pirate who fluttered his eyelids as he came around.

Mitch and I exchanged a look, both horrified and appalled at ourselves for making the assumption without checking.

"Wound isn't bad," Dan called out, his anger gone as soon as it had appeared, "just winged the side of his belly, the lucky bastard. He's got a decent lump on the head though. Help me get him up."

Mitch and I both leaned over to try and grab any part of his body as Dan bodily hauled him up towards us. Ordinarily I'd protest and want to protect the neck after a head injury, but seeing as we'd just left him cooking in the sun for over thirty minutes assuming him dead then I doubted I was winning any care awards.

He was laid out on the deck just as his eyes opened, blinking slowly until his brain caught up with what he was seeing and the eyes went wide. He started yelling and trying to scrabble backwards. Four gun barrels were levelled at his head and had the combined effect of some invisible forcefield that froze his movement.

"Speak English?" Mitch snapped. "Do. You. Speak. English?"

"Fuck you," he said in a thick accent made even less legible due to his grogginess. "Americans."

"Not Americans, mate," Dan said conversationally, "how many on your boat?"

The captured and confused pirate grimaced as he clutched at his belly but I saw his eyes wander over the deck until they rested on the captured weapons.

"No," I said, snapping my fingers for his attention and pointing up to my face, "up here."

He narrowed his eyes at me and pulled the start of a face. It was the facial equivalent of sucking in a breath and pulling back a fist before throwing a wild punch, and I had no intention of him landing

77

any of his spit on me. My left boot, the closest part of my body to him, shot out and pushed his head down to the deck where I held it by leaning my bodyweight forwards.

"How many on your boat?" Dan asked again, louder.

"Many," he said roughly, the words distorted by the metal deck squashing his face.

"*How* many?" I snapped as I ground my boot down a fraction harder to make my point.

"Ten," he yelped, "maybe more."

"Guns?" Mitch asked.

"Yes, many guns," the pirate answered weakly as he though he fought for breath. I let his head go and stepped back, ready to move forward and clock him hard if he went to spit at me again.

There was silence for a while as he closed his eyes and panted for breath. I looked at Dan, who looked right back at me, then we both looked at Mitch.

"Oh no," he said, stepping back and drawing out the words, "you'll not put this on me. I say we go. Toss this bastard back over and be done with it."

"They're not going to leave us alone, Mitch," I said gently. "They'll stay out here and try to take every boat we send. We can't lose our access to the sea; it's how we survive."

Mitch turned to Dan for sense.

"Come *on*, man," he said, "you can't be serious about this? It's madness."

"Madness?" Dan answered in an approximation of Mitch's own accent, with a smile that said he could barely contain his own humour. "No. Not madness... This. Is. *Sanctuary!*"

I laughed, mostly because the impression was so badly delivered when he seemed so excited to use the joke. Neil would have got it, and probably finished re-enacting the entire scene.

"I don't get it," Mitch said after a pause, puzzled, "what was that supposed to be?"

"Sparta...? Sanctuary...? No?" Dan tried. "Oh forget it. I say we do it."

"Ah bollocks," Mitch said, "don't say I didn't warn you when they cut our heads off with a rusty spoon."

"We'll make it work," I said as I turned back to give the pirate a nudge with my foot. "Oi, nobber, do you want to live?"

He looked up at me with frustrated hate in his eyes, but seemed to swallow his pride and nod.

"Good," I told him, "you can drive us back. One wrong move and I'll shoot you. Again." I jabbed my forefinger on the bone above and between his eyes for emphasis.

TROJAN BOAT

The pirate drove, sitting at the back and controlling the outboard motor. I lay in between the benches in the stinking, blood-tinged water pooling at the lowest point, and held my Walther pointed at his face. Nobody asked what his name was, clearly nobody was bothered, but I was sure to make it clear to him that I meant what I had said.

Dan was sat behind me, his hands appearing bound before him and blood smeared down from one ear courtesy of one of the bodies we dumped overboard, with Mitch and Adam under a tarpaulin at the front, weapons at the ready. It appeared to anyone paying close attention that he had taken a hostage and brought back plunder from the fishing boat, but the absence of the three men he had left with would obviously raise some questions. I hoped to answer those questions with a little high-velocity lead projectile reply.

I craved a contact, needed it almost, and I couldn't put my finger on why. It could have been the inactivity or the stress of yet another enemy threatening us, but if I was honest with myself it was because I was stressed about what was happening inside my own body and the only way I knew how to cope with stress was by doing something.

In this case, it was doing something reckless and dangerous.

"Remember," I called over the sound of the screaming engine and the rushing wind, "try to warn them and you're dead."

He scowled at me.

"I am already dead, unless you kill them first," he answered as he adjusted the empty rifle we had given back to him for appearances' sake. He was no doubt wishing that it was loaded so that he could kill us as he turned his attention back to the sea ahead.

The short journey felt longer because I was unable to look around or do anything other than lie in the foul-smelling bilge water and keep my eyes glued to him for any sign of a double-cross. I had no idea what he was thinking, but if it was me I'd either look to make a move or hope that we killed all of his friends on the bigger boat; if he was the one who had brought us back and caused carnage on board then he would suffer their wrath. I guessed that anyway; I had no idea how pirates thought.

"We come to the boat now," he said without moving his mouth much and staring straight ahead, "three men there with guns. I take you to the back where it is low to the water."

"He's right," Mitch said from beneath the tarpaulin. I looked back at him, the man who had tried to kill me and then spit at me. The man I, or Mitch, had put a bullet through - luckily only a fleshy bit with nothing important behind it.

"Why are you helping us?" I asked.

"Shut up," Dan warned.

The man seemed to think about the question, indicated only by his slight change of expression as he bounced the boat towards conflict.

"These people," he said flatly, "they are *not* my friends. I was not like this before."

I had no time to consider his response before the engine note wound down suddenly and the small skiff lurched to come alongside the bigger boat. I felt the air grow slightly colder as the shadow overtook us and bathed us in grey instead of bright sunlight, and then all hell broke loose.

The shooting started before Dan had slipped his hands out of the loosely wrapped ropes faking his bound wrists. Mitch and Adam rose up, dropping the two men with guns standing on the low stern of the rusty boat with a flurry of controlled single shots. They were over the side and onto the ship before Dan had retrieved his weapon and stood to aim higher up and drill two more on the half-deck above the stern with a series of sharp coughs from his carbine. He climbed aboard as I stood, dripping dirty water from my hiding space in the bilge where only I could fit, and I kept my suppressed Walther in both hands to save on the time it would take to switch weapons.

"You stay there," Dan warned our captive, emphasising his point with the carbine levelled at his chest. "Mitch, Adam, topside. Left and right," he instructed. "Leah with me. Inside."

I said nothing but snatched the powerful compact flashlight from my vest, the same one as I had attached to my own carbine, and held it in my left hand under the pistol to support the weight. My arms made a stiff kind of triangle with my body, and everywhere the gun pointed was where my eyes were, making me able to react in a flash and squeeze off rounds should I see something hostile. Dan had flicked his own weapon-mounted torch on, just a thumb's reach from where his left hand supported the barrel at the angled foregrip. Two powerful LED beams sliced through the filthy gloom of the cabins as gunfire rattled above our heads. The clattering and heavy rhythm of the enemy was answered with the more staccato reply of the lighter ammunition we used. I ignored that, or at least pushed it to the back of my mind. My fight was down here in the dark.

"Clear," Dan hissed after stepping smartly back out of a small cabin, waiting for my mirroring actions and word as I did the same on my side. We came to a hatch in the deck leading down to where the loud sounds of an engine echoed upwards. More gunfire was exchanged overhead, just as loud as the sounds coming from below, and Dan looked to me with a choice evident on his face.

"Go," I told him, "I'll clear down."

Dan hesitated, only for a second, then nodded and pushed out through the door ahead where I knew he had thrown himself straight into the fight as he had emerged in a position to flank the men swapping bullets with Mitch and Adam. I refocused, pointed my gun and torch down the sloping ladder, and descended feet-first leaning back against the rungs to support myself as I went below.

Mitch and Adam fell upon the first three men as they spilled from the cabin on the main deck. Two went left and one right, and that single foe turned directly aft and into the barrel of Adam's rifle. His eyes went wide, and he instinctively grabbed at the end of the barrel just as it began to spit flame and supersonic projectiles into and through his chest cavity. He died on his feet, three rapid-fired bullets drilling small holes straight through him, and fell to his knees still griping the hot metal that had been the instrument of his death.

Adam wriggled and wrenched the gun free just in time to see another man, bone thin and wearing ragged clothes over bare feet, as he climbed to the top of the steps and rose into view. As he grew taller, and his torso and legs were exposed, he raised the AK-47 and levelled it at Adam's chest as he depressed the trigger on the run, spitting heavy bullets wildly in all directions as though he was trying to announce his presence more than kill the invader.

Adam wanted to freeze. He thought he had, in fact, so when he felt his body dropping to the deck and his cheek pressing into the stock of his own gun he worried for the briefest moment that he had been hit. His finger spasmed on the trigger, sending a small but tightly packed hail of bullets towards the running pirate and stitching a series of holes into his thigh and hip.

As time let go of the breath it held and the world returned to normal speed for him, he stood and checked his body for pain and any sign of gaping holes showing where he had been shot. He hadn't. The man who had run at him on a desperate or brave or stupid charge was dying, bleeding out as great spurts of bright red blood shot skywards from the wounds in his groin. Adam snapped his head left, looking past the rusted metal of the bulkhead he hugged and through the grimy Perspex of the cabin windows to two other men holding the iconic-looking weapons. They were taking it in turns to point them blindly over their hiding spots to rattle off a handful of shots on automatic without any way of knowing if they had been effective. He moved forwards, only to have to throw himself down again as more wild and un-aimed shots punctured the windows and flew past him. He heard the cracks of Mitch returning fire, knowing that the old soldier would be far more disciplined in his own methods, but before he could move again to flank the two men pinning him down to his front he heard a chorus of bare feet slapping on the metal deck down to his right. He leaned over to look and saw three men running hard for the lower aft section which would lead them directly to Mitch's unprotected rear. He ran, unthinking and simply reacting, reaching the top of the steps he had climbed just in time to fire a burst of automatic into their tightly packed group as they crossed his path.

The one at the lead went down to hit the deck hard, tripping the other two who were simultaneously assaulted by the tiny storm of lead to their right. They both went over the unprotected edge and into the water, weighted down by weapons and a bandolier of large bullets criss-crossing the chest of one. Adam rose and went back to try and help Mitch but as he did he saw Dan emerge from below and turn to spray their positions with gunfire and lift the stalemate. One stood and turned to fire on him as the other was hit in the back.

There was a lull in the battle, filled only with the small scraping and clicking sounds of weapons being reloaded, then an almighty torrent of noise erupted from the bow as bigger guns entered the fight. The sounds of ricochets and dull cracks of impacts filled the air all around as Dan dived behind the cover of something large and metal. Adam dropped flat, minimising any target he might offer to the men, who didn't appear to have seen him yet, and began firing on them.

They adopted the same tactics as their friends: hiding behind cover and firing heavy-calibre bullets wildly over the top in an ill-disciplined attempt to break this new stalemate, as though their bullets would find the enemies by pure luck.

It was wasteful, it was unprofessional, and it angered Dan.

"If you're going to do something," he snarled to himself as he tucked into a small ball and tried desperately to keep his legs and feet inside the woefully small piece of hard cover he had found, "at least do it properly!"

He glanced up, seeing where Mitch was pinned down behind an annoyingly bigger piece of cover than he had found, and the single shake of his head made it clear that there was nothing he could do from where he was. Dan couldn't see Adam from where he was, but the fact that the fire was directed at them made it seem likely that he wasn't in the fight yet.

Then he heard it. The distinctive crack of the five-five-six ammunition punctuating the automatic heavier gunfire. Then he heard something else. He heard gunfire coming from a new direction, and behind that was the worrying sound of an outboard motor.

Mukami Adumbe was not a pirate, not in his eyes anyway. What he had been was a dock worker in Mombasa until he found himself totally alone save for just one woman who ran away from him when he called out to her. He had no family in the city; he'd moved there for employment and had been staying in a huge dormitory with other workers, none of whom had survived the virus.

He had survived that way for months, living off what he found and not having the first idea when something would change. He wandered freely around the docks and the surrounding areas, not finding anyone else alive for days on end and when he did they would usually run away from each other. Twice he had been robbed for everything that he carried, but he gave up those possessions freely as there was always more to be found which didn't hold any risk of being killed over.

When the wet season hit he was fine for drinking water but was beginning to run low on food. He didn't think he was capable, or at least he had never faced the concept of his own behaviour in such a situation, but human nature took over and dictated his course when he had been without food for two days and he chanced upon two people carrying heavy bundles.

He considered just asking them for help, but he knew what he would do in that scenario and knew that he would starve if he begged for charity. He followed them through the outskirts of the industrial area until the opportunity arose to strike. He hit one of them over the back with a metal pipe and ran off with his plunder before the other had time to realise what was happening. He ate that night, hating himself for becoming the bandit, and tried to consolidate those feelings of guilt with the natural urge to survive at whatever cost.

He had become feral, prowling around the docks and forcing his way into the many shipping containers in search of anything edible. One of those shipments was labelled as aid parcels destined for one of the many refugee camps in the north of the country, but when he broke open the wooden crates he found stacks of straw-packaged weapons under the topmost layers. He dropped the gun he had lifted in his hand, terrified and in awe of it at the same time. He had never fired a weapon, never even held one until that moment, and shut the door on the container until such time as he figured out what to do with it.

The answer came three days later when he saw two small boats coming in from the sea directly towards his port. They weaved between the massive container ships, going in and out of sight as they approached, and Mukami felt fear like he had not experienced since he thought he was the last man alive on Earth. He hid from them, foolishly seeking cover at the only open dock, which is where the two boats headed, and peered out. He willed the men who had their faces covered by scarves in the Arabic fashion, all carrying guns and looking like people he needed to avoid, to leave.

He was discovered quickly, having picked poorly when it came to his chosen hiding place and had knocked down a stack of plastic barrels. He found those barrels replaced with machine guns and his natural urge to survive surfaced through his mouth before his brain knew what he was saying.

He told them that he knew where there were more weapons. That he could lead them directly to them, but not if they killed him. He cowered in silence, hands raised and trembling as the men waited around for someone to tell them what to do.

That was the first time he laid eyes on Ahmad Gareer. He later learned that he had been one of the leaders of the Somali Al-Shabaab group, and was a pirate of international renown. Or infamy, but that depended on which side of the law a person lived on. He was not one of the men who had been driven from their fishing grounds by the armed boats from other countries, not one of those misguided men turned pirate at all, but something far worse. He was one of the men who used international financiers to bankroll their missions to capture multi-million-dollar prizes and ransom the white-skinned crewmembers back to their companies after their insurance policies paid out. The white people were always worth more money to the pirates. It made for good videos on the news and made the rest of the world sit up and take notice.

Gareer squatted down in front of him and used the barrel of his machine gun to raise Mukami's chin to look directly at him. He removed the scarf from his face, exposing a mostly toothless maw which smiled cruelly.

"Tell me where these guns are," he said, "and you will live."

That was how he had been recruited; out of desperation and a fear of starvation and death at the hands of this man. He remained at the docks for months after their bigger ships were brought in. They stripped everything they could over the rest of the year, using the dock as a base where other boats came and went. They brought in a white man, a captive, and he restarted the engines of the massive fuel tanker before it was piloted back out to sea. Mukami went with them, never having the option to choose another path.

Despite the terrible things he had done in order to survive, Mukami saw his opportunity when the three men were shot in front of him and he stared in horror as two of them tumbled off the deck and into the sea below. The third man, the one shot first and who had tripped the others over the side, lay flat on top of his weapon as the man who had shot them disappeared once more. He heard a heavy gunfight raging at the prow of the big boat, and acted in self-preservation as he always did. He rolled the man over, fighting with his corpse to free the rifle, and untied the skiff from the mooring to rev the engine and steer the boat around the side of the larger vessel. He let go of the controls for the outboard motor and stood. He wobbled slightly as he did but having grown accustomed to life on the sea, he steadied himself quickly and aimed his rifle.

The barrage of shots pinged off the deck, but two of them found their mark and crumpled one of his former shipmates into a heap. The man kept his dead finger depressed on the trigger of the big machine gun he had been firing and the remainder of the box magazine rattled off skywards until it ran dry with an inaudible click. The other man turned and aimed his weapon at Mukami, who switched his aim but was unbalanced by his rapid movement. As he sensed his own impending death, more shots rang out and the man aiming the gun at him fell, spinning, just as he pulled his trigger and sent three bullets spraying outwards in an arc.

The last of those bullets found Mukami's throat, punching a small hole through his windpipe and blowing a large one out of the back of his neck in a sickening fountain of gore and red mist. He dropped back into the bilge as the boat floated away, and as he looked up at the blue sky for one last time he hoped that he had redeemed himself in some small way to repent for the life that he had led these last years.

Pure Relief

I crept silently down, ignoring the sounds of gunfire above until I reached the lower deck where the noise was so loud that I couldn't hear what was going on up top even if I tried. I crept along, the heavy machinery of the engine pounding my ears and affecting my concentration to the extent that I had to squint to try and block out some of the noise.

I breathed hard through my nose, unable to stand the cloying, stifling air going through my mouth into my lungs, until I reached the loudest section of the dark, windowless sub-deck. One of them was there, wearing filthy rags and so intent on using a wrench on some stubborn part of the engine that he had no idea what was going on above him.

Finally, something cut through his intense concentration and made him stop. The sudden addition of brighter light on his task froze him, and as he turned I raised my weapon and prepared to put him down.

But something made me hesitate. Something about the filthy, ragged man in front of me stayed my hand and stopped the final few ounces of pressure going into the trigger. He dropped the wrench, the heavy metal making no sound which reached my ears, giving testimony to the massive noise down there. He looked into my eyes, his own wet with tears, and he raised his hands. I stepped back, twitching the barrel while keeping the torch beam on his chest so as not to blind him. He squinted and cowered his face away from the harsh light but kept his hand high and complied, walking slowly towards the ladder and climbing upwards as I followed.

Going up into the lighter deck bathed in sunlight through the grime-covered windows I saw him step back with two exaggerated slow steps to demonstrate that he had no intention of making a move on me as I emerged.

I kept the gun on him, feeling less certain by the second that this man was an enemy. The sounds of firing had all ceased, so I told him to go out on deck.

"Are they…" he croaked in American-accented English which threw me. "Are they dead?"

"Probably," I answered in my English accent, and the man seemed to be more confused than I was. "You're American?"

"Tennessee born and raised, ma'am," he said, smiling weakly. "Joshua Bucknor, US Navy, at your service."

"Leah," I said, lowering my weapon from his chest and clicking off the flashlight with my thumb before considering how best to explain who I was as he had done so easily. "What are you doing with the pirates?" I asked, hearing the annoying nag of the word '*Aargh*' in my head as I spoke.

"I'm their hostage," he said with an exhausted numbness, "have been since as long as I can recollect."

With that, his face contorted, his eyes ran freely with fresh tears and he crumbled. He fell to the deck, sobbing loudly with what sounded more like hysterical laughter interspersed with tears of pain and relief. The door burst in and Dan appeared beside me to point his carbine at the sobbing man. I gently reached out and placed my right palm on the barrel to make him lower it.

"What's going on?" he asked me as he stared at the man on the floor.

"We've just done our first hostage rescue," I told him, "that's what."

Joshua Bucknor, not Josh but Josh*ua*, stayed like that for about ten minutes. When his tears ran dry he stood and tried to wipe the snot away from his puffy face before looking up with a renewed smile.

"Any chance I can clean myself up a little?" he asked, as though he needed permission to do anything. I gestured with my hand, meaning to try and convey that we were in his house and not ours, so he stood and tried to make himself more presentable. He must have seen my nose wrinkle because he stepped back and mumbled an apology from behind his long, matted beard. I reached behind myself and pulled the bottle of water from my back pocket before offering it to him, which he took with a big show of respect and thanks, almost bowing to me as he reached a tentative hand out to take it as though it was a venomous snake and could strike him if he moved too fast.

"Come outside?" I offered him. "You could do with some fresh air after being down there I should think."

"Yes, ma'am," he replied in between gulps of the tepid water. "I've been working on that manifold for days now and it still ain't right." He smiled almost manically, as though he was drunk or giddy but I suspected it was the stress coming out of him like sweat.

On deck I found Dan and Mitch leaning on boxes as Dan smoked and Mitch drank from a bright red soda can bearing the logo that was at once so familiar and yet so alien. I always preferred the silver version on taste alone, but the promise of sugary goodness struck something deep in my memory and I longed for one. My eyes must have given it away, because Mitch reached behind him into a battered old cooler and pulled out another which he held out to me as he eyed the thin and filthy man following me. I took the can, handing it to Joshua who repeated his strange subservient routine as though my offer was a trick that he could be punished for accepting. His hands shook and he fumbled with the ring pull, getting frustrated as the four of us watched until he broke before our eyes.

His fumbling fingers dropped the can to the deck where it hissed and shot a frothy stream out of a tiny hole, and the man followed it, sinking down and collapsing in an exhausted heap. He sat there and dry sobbed like a toddler at the end of their tantrum when they had no more energy to cry. His eyes were screwed tightly shut and his face contorted into the rictus of tears but none came.

"It's okay, Joshua," I said gently, opening another can and crouching to hand it to him. I forced myself to ignore the smell of him, trying not to let it show in my eyes as he had clearly been through enough. I took his hand and placed it around the can, seeing such vulnerability in his eyes as they met my own. "Want to just sit there a while?" I asked gently.

He nodded, cuffing at his swollen eyes with an oil-stained hand. I stood, looking past the others towards the sound of an engine. I walked to the prow and saw the skiff, which should have been attached to the rear of our captured boat, spinning in a lazy circle. Our driver was crumpled on his back, legs and arms lying at angles which clearly announced his dead status, and his body had forced the steering arm of the outboard motor so that it chugged in a ponderous loop destined to do so until the fuel ran dry.

"Anyone going to deal with that?" I asked, turning to see the three men exchanging looks and offering shrugs. I huffed, making my annoyance clear to them, and began to strip off my vest ready to swim and retrieve the craft.

"You sure you want to do that?" Mitch asked.

"Well, how else is it going to get back here? Or would you rather stay on this piece of crap?"

"No, I agree," he said with a mischievous smile. "I was just wondering about the sharks is all…"

Bastard, I thought, knowing that there was almost no chance of finding a shark out here capable of attacking me but still unable to bring myself to swim out there now that he had mentioned the word. I stopped what I was doing, letting my heavy vest fall back onto my sweaty shirt and glared at them.

"What do you suggest then?" I shot at him.

Wordlessly, Dan chuckled and groaned as he forced himself upright from his leaning position, picking up a coil of rope with a rusty grappling hook attached to the end. He walked past me nonchalantly, dropping the coil to his feet and swinging the hook around in a circle to build up momentum before letting it soar out through the air as the rope ran through his hands.

It missed, just as it did on his next two attempts until on the fourth go it landed inside the boat with a plastic thump. At once I saw Dan's body tense as his muscles fought against the force of the boat which still tried to turn, and threatened to drag him overboard.

"A little help?" he grunted in an annoyed tone, knowing that we would all happily watch him struggle just for the comedy factor. Mitch and Adam took up the end of the rope and with their combined strength tried to haul the boat in like some kind of tug-of-war. I sighed, watching three grown men grunting like animals and thinking like babies.

"Maybe try to steer it," I said in a tone of voice that made it clear I thought they were all being dumb, "instead of dragging it like cavemen?"

They made out like they hadn't heard me, but still communicated in low grunts as they held the boat where it was and sidestepped as one to let it swing around and crab along the left side of the other boat until reached the stern. They tied the rope to the railings and Dan leaned out to try and grab the edge of the small hull.

"Jump in!" Dan said through his exertion but undirected to any one person in particular. Adam and Mitch jostled, both deciding at the last minute to allow the other to jump the small gap, so I stepped past them and hopped lightly into the bouncing, bucking hull where I shoved the dead body off the controls and looked at them.

"How do I turn it off?" I asked in exasperation.

"Hit that little button on the long handle there," called a voice from behind them.

I pressed the button on the steering arm, killing the frantic sound of the engine immediately, and looked up to see Joshua nervously smiling at me from behind his filthy beard.

"Thanks," I said as I held my hand out to be hauled back onboard the bigger vessel, "so what now?"

"We have a look at what they've got, obviously," Dan said.

What they had was a collection of badly maintained and ancient weaponry. Mitch lectured us again, or at least *me* again, about the likely source of the guns being Russia and that they were probably from the seventies or eighties.

"East Africa by way of the Middle East is my guess," he said as he wistfully inspected the second large machine gun he had captured that day. "Now, I've never been on the receiving end of one of these until today, but I can attest that they truly do sound like the hammer of god." He turned to Dan and smiled. "Can we keep them, Dad? Can we? Please?"

Dan seemed to think about it before answering.

"The PKMs yes," he said, meaning the huge guns similar to the big GPMG we once owned and mounted in the back of a Land Rover, "dump the AKs though."

"What about *this*?" I asked, hauling up the bulbous RPG and seeing the instant reaction of the others as they began to raise their hands to take the rocket gently out of my grip. I stuck out my bottom lip and pretended to sulk at having it taken away from me.

"And what about this?" I asked, gesturing at the deck of the boat to change the subject.

"Is it worth keeping?" Adam asked. "It looks a bit shit to me."

"Ask the mechanic," Mitch opined.

I turned to see where Joshua had gone and saw him sitting a short distance away and staring out over the prow of the boat absently, just letting the sun soak into his skin. I walked over to him, mindful not to startle him as I had made the mistake of doing with Lexi too often.

"Hey," I said softly as I approached, still making him flinch as he whipped his head around to see that it was just me and that he hadn't been dreaming of a rescue which hadn't happened.

"Hey there," he answered weakly, still smiling but seeming

exhausted beyond comprehension. I'd seen this before, the sudden tiredness that came with no longer having to be on your guard and protect yourself. It got to you after a while, being permanently on guard, and it was only when you felt safer that your mind gave your body the bill.

"I've got to ask," I said in an apologetic tone, "is this boat worth keeping?"

"This hunk a junk?" he said with a smirk. "Hell no. It's trash. I've been tryin' to fix the engine for a week now, but the damn thing keeps dyin' on me." He paused, hesitating, before he asked in a soft voice, "What's goin' to happen to me now?"

"Happen?" I shot back. "What do you mean?"

"I mean, what are you going to do with me?"

"For a start," I said, "we're going to get you to a doctor, put you in a shower and feed you. It looks like you need it."

He chuckled. "I'm so skinny I can't even see my own shadow," he said enigmatically as he scratched a hand at his dirty beard. "Hell, I bet I look like I've been chewed up and spat out."

"I'm sure I would too," I told him, trying to ignore the thoughts about what they would have done to a young girl instead of a navy mechanic, "but we'll get you fixed up."

"I sure do appreciate that, ma'am," he said quietly, almost as though the tears threatened to take him over again.

"Leah," I reminded him.

"Excuse my Southern manners," he said, "it's just how I was raised."

"It's okay," I said, reaching out a hand to his shoulder and placing it gently despite the flinch, "it's all going to be okay now."

We loaded up the skiff so much that it sat low in the water with all five of us along with the recovered machine guns and ammunition. Mitch said that the bullets wouldn't fit our own weapons of that calibre, explaining that we had the NATO chambers as though that made sense to everyone, and Joshua had recovered enough to offer the simplest way to sink the pirate boat. He had made a comment about pulling the plug, and checked that we were ready to depart before going below and coming back up a minute later at double the pace.

"Clock's tickin'," he said as he stepped onto the boat with a practiced skill which we all lacked.

He said nothing more on the journey back to our own boats, electing instead to watch as the rusty tub he had been imprisoned on sank ass first. The only sign he gave that he was even conscious was to raise a one-fingered salute to the vessel, holding it high and proud as it sank.

And like that, or so I thought at the time, our pirate problem was over.

NAUGHTY CHILDREN

Marie wasn't impressed. As far as understatements went, that was a huge one. Marie was livid. She was like a miniature rooster on the opposite side of the fence to a bigger, younger bird who was eying up his chickens in a way the rooster didn't like much at all.

She paced the sea wall like a caged cat as the two fishing vessels chugged into the bay in line, and I cast a look back over my shoulder at Dan in time to see him duck inside the cabin so as not to get yelled at in public.

He was like that. He didn't want the whole town knowing his business but when Marie wanted to say something to him she gave not one single shit who was listening. As the boats throttled back to bump gently against the harbour sides I hopped down while the ropes were still being lashed to hold us firmly against the artificial shore. Being the outstanding wing-woman I knew myself to be, and not really relishing the uncomfortable time spent waiting for my adoptive parents to stop rowing, I decided to cause a small fuss to change the subject.

"I need Kate!" I yelled with far more drama in my voice than was necessary. Marie's face changed from horrible temper to horrified fear and I felt a little guilty for it. "It's okay," I said with my hands up, "nobody's critical, but we've rescued a hostage."

It worked.

"A *hostage*?" she cried. "Who? Where? *How?*" I tried to wave off her questions as I turned to help Mateo place the wooden ramp to span the gap between pier and deck. Gasps sounded behind me when Joshua appeared and he tried to stand tall to wave away any assistance he was offered to step ashore.

"I ain't no first-timer," he complained kindly to the big fisherman without any force in his words. The prideful statement was undermined by his faltering feet. Somehow, the ordeal of being saved from his ordeal had weakened him; as though he was only being held together by the stress of captivity and routine. Now that he was safe, his mind had released those bonds over his body and he seemed to weaken with every minute spent free from his tormentors. As his right foot first hit the ancient cobblestones of Sanctuary his legs gave out and he crumpled to dry land for what he later said had been the first time in many months. He was helped up by more people rushing to his aid than could easily get their hands on him, despite the smell, and he wept openly as the relief of so many years spent being a slave flowed out of him.

I watched him being helped towards the big central keep, the castle that I lived in, as word had already spread to Kate and Sera that medical attention was needed at the docks. I watched Kate lugging the heavy and battered red bag that had so long ago been liberated from an unused ambulance way back in the UK. The red was faded to a dull pink in places through overuse, more like a white bag bearing a large bloodstain than the original red it had been, which I thought was probably just as possible given what they, and the bag, had been through over the last seven years. My reverie was shattered by the pointed noise of Marie clearing her throat. I turned to see her, arms folded and mouth pursed into a tight line as she waited impatiently for an explanation.

"Hi," I said innocently and tried to walk quickly away before she realised I had blown her off.

"Err, I don't think so," she said sternly, somehow nailing my feet to the ground with her tone of voice alone. I sighed and turned back to her, just as a welcome interruption stopped my interrogation. Nemesis' claws clattered on the cobbles as she snaked her way through the gathering crowds like a furry eel to get to me. Behind her, being far more polite and apologetic about forcing his way through, came Lucian with the long barrel of his big rifle extending above his shoulder like an aerial.

I bent down, letting the desperate dog lick at my mouth which I kept tightly shut to prevent the slobbering tongue from finding its way inside, and ruffled the thick fur at her neck in greeting. Another noise, that of Marie clearing her throat so intentionally that it was like a command, forced me to stand just as Lucian, Dan and Mitch joined us. Marie opened her mouth but Dan silenced her.

"Not here," he said quietly, "please. I don't want the others hearing this, not yet."

Marie shut her mouth wordlessly, stopping herself from exploding at her husband in public - not for his sake, but for the sake of the others around them. His tone told her that what he had to say was serious and that small ruse, much like my own distraction technique, seemed to work.

We went up the long, sweeping stone ramp towards the main keep as the hubbub behind us grew. Mitch had unveiled the captured weapons and asked two of the militia to take them to the armoury, where I knew he would spend meticulous hours taking them apart piece by piece to clean every last trace of neglect from their components before rebuilding each weapon with painstaking care and attention. By the time we got inside, startlingly cool under the cover of the medieval stone in contrast to the warmth outside, I was sure that half the town would already know what had happened.

Marie couldn't wait much longer and led us into the nearest unoccupied room to whirl on Dan and demand an explanation for how a simple guard duty had resulted in us bringing back a rescued hostage. Dan gave her the bullet points, leaving out names and specifics which resulted in full responsibility resting on his shoulders.

"It was my call," I told her, "I wanted to take on the bigger boat." Marie looked at me and blinked as though she had only just noticed I was there. She turned to Dan and elevated her eyebrows accusingly.

"And poor little you was powerless to stop her from forcing you to come along, was it?" she asked dangerously.

"I'll be off then," Mitch said quietly as he backpedalled with slow, exaggerated steps and tugged at Adam's sleeve to indicate his recommendation to withdraw. Marie ignored him, simply keeping her eyes on Dan's and said nothing until he broke first. The door shut and Dan seemed to relax.

"No," he admitted, "and I don't know why you're being such a bi—"

"One more fucking word," Marie interrupted, "I *dare* you." Dan returned her look blankly and breathed in to speak again.

Less sense now than the day he was born, I thought to myself, echoing one of Neil's sayings.

"Marie," I said, feeling the cold stare turn on me slowly, "I'm sorry I dragged everyone into this, but we saved someone's life and killed more of them. They're almost a dozen fighters down," I explained, "and they've lost one of their boats. I doubt they'll come back our way now. Not after this."

"Are you even hearing yourself?" Marie asked. "You two are like a pair of naughty children who keep sneaking off and getting into fights. Answer me this: if you knew there was an enemy out there somewhere"—she pointed at the wall, meaning to indicate inland I think, but the direction she had chosen actually pointed directly along the coastline—"and had a large force allowing you to send almost a dozen of your people out in a big vehicle, and they failed to return, what would *you* do? Give up? Say, 'oh well, I'm sure they'll be alright wherever they are'?" She said his part in a mocking tone before switching back to her own piercingly angry voice. "No. You'd be exactly like you were after you found out someone had tried to kill *her* in Andorra a few years back and go storming off like an ape to find someone to punish."

I was reeling enough from her words to be openly shocked as the finger she had pointed at me still lingered like the ominous barrel of a gun wavering in my direction.

"Marie," Dan said with exasperated resignation, "just calm down…" He realised his mistake as soon as he had uttered the words and tried to pull it back by speaking fast. "They don't know who we are, they don't know *where* we are, they won't be able to trace their people or their boats, and the sea is a pretty big place. So is the coast, really."

"And," I added gently whilst trying not to sound like I was ganging up on her, "we have a defended position with fortifications both inland and seaward-facing. We're safe," I added pleadingly.

She seemed to bubble for a few seconds as she considered our words.

"And how long is everyone going to last on edge like this?" she asked in a softer voice. "The constant threat of being attacked will start to unravel people. It's unravelling me!" I bit back the comment that she was already showing higher than normal stress levels even before anyone said the word 'pirates'.

"What would you prefer?" Dan asked her. "That we ignore the threat? That we just bumble along like trusting idiots and hope that the baddies won't come?"

"Obviously not," Marie said, "we… oh, *forget it!*" she snapped as she walked away. We watched her go, only then realising that Lucien was in the room behind us having remained utterly still in case he came to bear her attention.

"What's up with her?" I asked Dan. He pulled a face and gave a rapid shrug. "Come on," I pressed him, "you've got to have at least *some* idea why she's so pissed off with you."

"With me?" Dan complained. "She seems pretty pissed off with you too, you know?"

"Fine," I told him, "I'll go and ask her myself, shall I? Do your job for you?"

"If you wouldn't mind," Dan said seriously.

I couldn't find Marie, and the only place I hadn't checked was the infirmary wing where I didn't want to go and see our rescued hostage just yet. Partly out of respect for him probably not wanting me to see him in a state, and partly because I didn't want to see more evidence of his mistreatment, I avoided the place and instead went to find some solitude to gather myself.

That solitude, oddly, was found in the same way as another

person. As I neared the armoury and saw the door open a crack I put a suspicious hand on my hip near the sidearm as I pushed the door open, only to stand tall and relax as I saw a sight I had grown accustomed to over the years.

Mitch had converted the small, round room from the empty store it had been when we first arrived, to an ordered and full workshop. At some point someone had been asked to line the walls with timber to act as gun racks, and the bench he worked at was wide with an old hand-turned vice on one end. He was stooping over a whiteish cloth laid flat with all the parts of the PKM laid out like a kid with crippling OCD preparing to make a Lego model.

"Velcome to my hhhumble abode," he croaked in an appalling Dracula impression before turning to beam at me. He was happy; the disassembly of a big machine gun to him was as relaxing as a cocktail and a book on the beach to others. I had to admit, I probably preferred to field-strip a weapon more than I did read.

My mind wandered off to television, something I hadn't watched in years by then, and Mitch brought me back to the present with a scathing report on weapon maintenance discipline by the pirates.

"The gas piston is bloody filthy," he complained as he held up the part for my inspection. "I mean, look at it! Caked in carbon. I'd have had my arse and my face rearranged for that back in the day. Soldier's gold, we called a bit of rust. Any of that shite on your weapon would cost you a pretty fine, I can tell you." I took the small component and studied it, feeling the pitted metal where the residue had baked a hard green and would need scraping off to return the part to a polished state.

"You see," Mitch went on, "no discipline. That's what makes

the difference between us and them; we have discipline and they don't."

"Maybe not," I said, "but they seemed to have done fine just like we have. Lucky bullets kill just the same as disciplined ones." He made a noise in response, halfway between a grunt and a *hmm* which just gave him the impression of having trapped wind. "I'd really like to know how many of them are out there an—" I stopped, shutting my mouth as the most sudden and unexpected jolt of nausea hit me harder than I thought natural. It was a smell which had triggered the response, and as I focussed on the dirty piece of metal in my hands I could smell it again so intensely that I actually gagged and clamped a hand over my mouth and nose.

"You alright, lassie?" Mitch asked, wearing a look of obvious concern on his face. I tossed him the part and stepped back, taking my hand slowly away as though I didn't truly trust what would happen when I did. I took a few long, deep breaths and steadied myself against the doorway.

"Yeah," I lied, "too long on a bloody boat if you know what I mean. That oil stinks!"

"Does it?" Mitch asked as he took a tentative whiff of the metal he had been attempting to clean and tried to detect any kind of strong odour from it. He laughed and recounted something relevant: "Remember how bad Ash got when we first crossed the Channel? Ach, that dog was a right mess..." He stopped talking as he grew concerned about me again. I tried to keep my breathing steady as I focused on a single spot on the rough stone floor and warned the contents of my stomach to stay where they bloody well were.

"I'll catch you later," I blurted out as I fled the room, desperate to get away from the intense smell. I didn't hear him shout after me as I was fast-pacing down the corridor in eager search of fresh air. When I reached it I rested my back against the wall and closed my eyes to suck in long pulls of air through my nose, which made a tickling whistle noise that only I could hear, and blew them out slowly through my open mouth.

Of all the people in our town, of all the people who regularly came and went through trade or through the seasonal worker exchange, who fished from the walls or the boats out to sea or tended the livestock and crops of Sanctuary, it just had to be Lucien who saw me.

"My love," he said in accented English which always sounded more melodramatic than the French translation, "are you okay?" He reached out for me, concern morphing into fear on his face as I tried to brush him away and stand up straight.

"I'm fine," I said, "just seasick from being out on a boat all day."

"Are you sure?" he fussed. "You look the colour of the seaweed..."

"I'm fine!" I snapped, the effort of not being sick making me speak more harshly than I intended so I tried to soften it with a hand on his arm. "I'm fine," I said again, "I just feel like shit."

"Come with me," he said as he put an arm around my shoulder and tried to pry me away from the wall and force me to lie down somewhere.

"I said I'm fine," I insisted, pushing him away gently but firmly. "Aren't you supposed to be on watch anyway?"

"Dan is taking a turns there," he explained. "I wanted to find you and check you were okay and I find that you are not."

"Seriously," I told him in French so that he understood me

better, "I am fine." My eyes held a small hint of warning which he seemed to detect and he relented. His interruption had worked, miraculously, as I no longer felt sick and proved that I was fine by walking away with a smile.

THE UGLY TRUTH

Joshua's story came out in parts and the chronology was all over the place. Kate said it was normal for the brain to rearrange things after trauma and Marie agreed, saying that the sailor probably blocked out long parts of memory which were only now coming back to the surface because he was safe.

"He's probably going to have a period of high mood before he crashes again into depression," she explained to us in a private discussion that evening. Her anger at Dan getting himself into conflict had abated temporarily but she was still a little frosty. Kate agreed with her, saying that Joshua needed to be watched as the risk of suicide was heightened after rescue from long-term imprisonment.

"And watch what he eats, too," she warned. "He'll get sick if he starts shovelling fresh bread and sweet stuff down his neck after living on shitty scraps for years."

"How are we going to monitor that?" Dan asked. "Keep him in medical?" He still referred to the French infirmary as 'medical' even after almost a decade since the first incarnation of the department had sprung up in an old prison thousands of miles away.

"For a few days at least," Kate said, "we can keep an eye on him, but I'll attach one of the trainees to stay with him after that." Kate and Sera, their veterinarian turned part-time surgeon, had their own rooms opposite the infirmary and had spent years training others in emergency care and basic diagnosis and treatment skills.

Like Victor in his tower, they had recorded their knowledge in large books which were added to every time a new symptom was presented to them. They had trained people who had returned to other areas inland like the now-sprawling farms and The Orchards, and had even travelled to Andorra at times and used their surviving medical facilities.

"One of the more *experienced* girls, I think?" Sera suggested, giving everyone the impression that she believed putting a young girl in charge of his recuperative care might not be as effective as someone else.

"And what about the bigger picture?" Dan asked, forcing the issue of Joshua's captors onto the table in front of more minds he thought inclined to support him.

"What of them?" Marie demanded. "Weren't you telling me that they'll never find this place and will leave us alone now?"

"That's not *exactly* what I said," Dan began awkwardly. "We need to keep the armed patrols going out on the boats for a few more weeks at least." Kate and Marie opened their mouths to protest but it was me who silenced them.

"No armed patrols means no fishing boats go out," I said flatly. "Not safely anyway. And no fishing boats going out now means no peak haul of fish. No excess fish means less winter stores, which means less trade in winter for other food from settlements inland. It means we go poor and hungry for the next year if we don't take advantage of the season, and that means we have to stay on alert." I had tried to soften my words a little so that I didn't sound like I was slapping them down, but I think it still came out a little like that. I smiled to show some humility and tried to bring it back.

"I'm not a fan of being out there," I admitted sheepishly, "and I felt sick after a day on the water but it needs to be done. We need to use our best people to keep our fishing boats safe until we can afford to dial it back. Until then?" I spread my palms open to show that we really had no choice and had to just roll with it.

"We're all agreed then?" Dan asked, seeming like he wanted the discussion brought to a close quicker than usual. Nods rippled around the table and he stood, snapping his fingers for Ash to follow as he snatched up his carbine and pushed out of the doorway.

"Where's he going in such a hurry?" I asked nobody in particular.

"You mean you don't know he's opted to take the evening shifts at the dock on a permanent basis?" Marie asked in a sweet voice that I knew disguised a wickedly sharp edge.

"No," I admitted, "I didn't."

Everyone else filed out as I stayed sat at the table opposite Marie. Lucien hovered at the doorway, one hand scratching Nemesis under the chin as he waited for me until I gave him a subtle nod to go and leave me alone with Marie. She knew I was loitering to speak to her, knew that the hostility between her and Dan was palpable, and seemed prepared to defend her position.

"You going to tell me?" I asked gently.

"No," she said, ending the conversation before it had begun so I tried a different method: talking until she told me to leave.

"I was thinking about this," I said as I leaned back and looked up at the high ceiling, "and you were pissed off with Dan even before the pirates showed up."

Argh, my brain echoed until I told it to shut up.

"I think there's something you're not telling me," I goaded her as she tried to pretend that she was reading something and ignoring me. "I think you two are arguing over something and his way of *coping*"—I emphasised the word theatrically and stitched the air with double fingers curling over in air quotes— "is to go out and try to get himself in a fight or just do stuff so he doesn't have to talk about his feelings."

Marie took a sharper intake of breath through her nose as her eyes still pretended to focus on the words on the page in front of her, but still said nothing.

"I think," I went on, having smelled blood in the water in search of an answer, "that you two are fighting over something that he refuses to listen to or accept is real, and I think tha—"

"Do you remember a little over a year ago when I got sick?" she asked quietly, turning to face me for the first time. I did, just about, because the whole thing was played down at the time. I thought more about it and wondered why Dan chose that time to go off for over a week doing the rounds of the other settlements.

"Yeah…" I answered, eyebrows meeting in the middle.

"Well I had a miscarriage then," she said, "just as I had another one a couple of weeks ago."

"Oh," I said, not knowing what to say and only just managing not to show visible relief at keeping my own secret from everyone.

"Yes," Marie said softly, "oh." She dropped the page of writing and folded her arms while staring at me. "I didn't tell him, I just asked him to stay inside the walls for a while and not run off to look for a fight. I feel like he's literally itching to get himself shot at so he doesn't have to worry about me."

"I, err…" I said.

"And instead of just hanging up his bloody guns for a couple of months," she went on in an angrier tone as though I hadn't spoken, "instead of staying home with me like I asked, he goes out spoiling for a scrap with… with… *bloody pirates*, and *you* aren't helping."

"Me?" I shot back, failing to recall that I was the one spoiling for a fight with the bloody pirates. "What am *I* doing?"

"Well you aren't helping by suggesting gunfights on boats and bringing back hostages, are you?"

"Bringing back… hang on," I said as I pointed an ill-advised finger at the older woman, "I'm not even sorry for that. Not one bit. These bastards are out there; I didn't choose for them to show up and I didn't go looking for them. They came here looking to steal and hurt people just like every other tosser has since all this"—I waved a frustrated hand over the air in general—"this *shit* started. I'm sorry the timing sucks for you but it sucks for me, too. You thi—"

"Why does it suck for you?" she asked. My face froze and for a second I didn't know what to say. My mouth flapped like a cat flap in a strong wind for a second or two which was long enough for her to know with total certainty that I was hiding something.

"Why," she asked me slowly, "does it suck for *you*?"

"Because it just does," I moaned. "Spring and summer are supposed to be fun and happy and warm and… and *busy*. Not full of twenty-four-hour guard rotations and spending all bloody day on a boat making me feel sick."

"Urgh," Marie let out involuntarily as she puffed her cheeks and put a finger to her closed lips, as though just raising the subject of sickness had a negative effect on her. I knew enough from having suffered three of my own unexpected waves of sickness already that day to be quiet and let it pass instead of forcing her to speak in response to stupid questions like, 'are you alright?' and 'can I get you anything?'

It passed and she came back to me. "So we just have to suffer?" she asked.

"Yes," I said, meaning more than she knew I did. "We're just going to have to suffer. For a little while, at least, until we're safe again."

I managed to avoid going out on a boat just once over the next three days, as Lucien had caught me having another turn at the cruel hands of nausea and insisted that I rest to allow him to go in my place. I took the offer willingly, because another second spent in the company of fish-stinking water was definitely going to bring my breakfast up for everyone to see.

I got myself to the little bit of cover on the end of the sea wall and leaned on the barrel of the fifty-cal to suck in fresh air from the refreshing breeze whipping in from the sea. By the time Lucien's face, almost pathetically worried for me, went out of focus on the fishing boat I felt better. Nemesis whined beside my leg and danced all four feet on the spot for a second, which was her signature move for showing her concern for me.

"I'm fine," I told her, reflecting that all I seemed to say to people at the moment was that I was fine.

The patrols had encountered no other boats, and despite taking an extra person on each voyage to keep a careful watch through powerful binoculars, the tense mood began to abate.

Joshua had slept for a day and a half, waking only to rush to the bathroom and void himself of the rich food he had enjoyed in spite of the warnings to avoid such things until his body had begun to adapt to a better standard of living. As anticipated, he seemed full of life and on top of the world whenever I saw him, and the knowledge that he would crash back down soon saddened me. He waved to me every time he saw me, and stopped once to thank me again for saving him. I told him I didn't do much, leaving out the fact that I was literally about half a second away from dropping him, and just said that I was happy he was with us.

A week of inactivity was all it took for almost everyone to go back to unsuspecting normality, and the few of us who were still on edge were exhausted by the constant state of alertness.

THE STORM ON THE HORIZON

Despite trying to hide how I felt the second I opened my eyes each morning, it started to become obvious to anyone paying attention that there was something up with me.

I countered some of the effects, the effects of people noticing that was, not the actual nausea, by working later into the evening and staying in bed while Lucien got up as quietly as he could to leave me asleep. I had to admit that there was something of a contrast on the rare occasions that I got up before him, as he accused me of playing a one-man band as though my intention was to wake him.

I woke every time, despite his silent creeping, but I just pretended not to so that he didn't see me hanging my head over the bowl I kept under our bed as a chamber pot. It hadn't been used for that purpose in a long time, but at that point it was a god send.

As soon as he clicked the door latch shut like a burglar making his stealthy exit I threw back the covers and slid the bowl from beneath the bed frame and tried not to groan out loud too much. Willing myself to not throw up and breathing hard in the hope that it would pass I reached for the glass of water beside my bed and took small sips. Nemesis woke to my grumbling and moaning, yawning loudly through her wide mouth and turning the noise into a whine of concern as her long muzzle nudged my face.

When the door burst back open to reveal me half out of bed and dribbling water from my mouth and eyes over a large ceramic bowl, with a startled looking dog staring back at the door beside me, Lucien took the scene in with a confused look until he shook it away.

"You must come," he hissed with more than a hint of panic in his words. "The dawn is breaking and there is a ship."

It's always amazing to me how quickly the mind can exert control over the body. I've been hurt before and not noticed it until afterwards, and I've seen plenty of people with injuries that should be debilitating, yet they were still running around shouting and fighting. On that occasion, my mind simply chucked out the crippling nausea as though it was no longer a priority and replaced it with the need for sudden physical action.

I sat up, not even thinking that such a rapid change of body position should've emptied my stomach all over the bed, and swung my legs out to throw clothes on as I found them. I was glad I had switched to a lighter pair of boots for the summer, ones I only had to lace once as the sides fastened with a zip. I stuffed my feet into them and pulled on the zips simultaneously before shrugging into my vest and nodding in the direction of the corner of the room for Lucien to pick up my carbine.

He bent and retrieved it, standing straight to pull back the charging handle a fraction and check the chamber to ensure it was safe before handing it over.

When you handled weapons enough on a daily basis, these things just happened automatically.

"What ship?" I asked pointlessly as we fast walked in synchronicity towards the sea exit to the castle.

"I do not know," he whispered back over the stereo sounds of our footfalls and the sharper clacking of Nemesis' claws, "but it must be big."

Lucien wasn't exaggerating. We jogged side by side towards the sea defences, my bladder screaming at me for having neglected it when I woke, and as the faint grey sky lightened with each passing second, a looming feeling of foreboding nagged at my senses from the direction of the dark expanse over the water. When I stopped and focussed I saw it. Not directly, but if I let my eyes wander out of focus and glanced to the side of the darker patch of dark ahead of me then I saw a glimpse, a snapshot of the outline.

It was huge. Bigger than any single mode of transport I had ever laid eyes on in real life. It was the size of a city; longer than our walled town and taller than the tops of our ramparts and it spanned a distance of the sea wider than any one thing had a right to.

I stared at it, trying over and over again to see more and focus on the shape of it just hoping that we were all wrong at it was a kind of pre-dawn mirage or just a simple trick of the light and we could all go back to bed.

The silence hung heavy like there was an electrical charge in each of us ready to arc and jump outwards should any conductor stray into reach. I became aware of three other people on the pier beside us, no doubt the three members of our town militia on night duty, and none of us said a word as the sky grew lighter with each passing second. A slight cough and a scrape of claws on cobblestones behind me snatched my mind away from the boat but my eyes stayed glued to it. The faint sounds of an artificial packet rustling preceded the click of a cigarette lighter before the pungent aroma of smoke drifted over me.

It was too much. I turned and hung my upper body over the stone wall, my equipment scraping on the rough surface, and I vomited noisily into the black water below. Twice more I heaved, expelling the remnants of the small meal I had eaten late the night before and stinging my eyes and nose with the acrid smell of bile. I spat twice to clear my mouth and stood, leaning on the wall to steady my dizziness, to see Lucien, the three militia members and Dan staring at me. A whine from beside my left boot reached me and I looked down to see Nemesis' eyes reflecting the weak light of the pre-dawn back at me.

I returned their looks of concern and shock, only for the backdrop to their silhouettes to snatch my full attention.

"Ho-ly *fuck*," I said, drawing out the words as they left my mouth of their own accord. As one, the other faces turned and looked out to sea as the first slither of light emerged far off to our left beyond the high cliffs in that direction. Curses in French echoed my own inadequate language until I pushed myself away from the wall and brought my weapon up to my shoulder. Scanning through the optic I saw the outline of the gigantic ship in slightly better detail, only to feel the very opposite of reassured when the unimaginable size of it was solidified in my view. I lowered the carbine and spoke out loud.

"Raise the alarm," I said softly, swallowing hard to keep anything else in my stomach firmly in place. One of the militia turned to obey before another voice rang out with more authority.

"No," Dan said, "*arrêtez*." The shape kept moving towards the radio set.

"*Detener. Espere*," Lucien added in Spanish telling him to stop and wait. The shape froze and retreated back to their original position.

"There's no point in causing panic," Dan said, "and waking everyone up at daybreak with this kind of news is a bad idea; panic spreads like a virus and we need to control it." He stepped away from us, closer to the sea wall, and flicked the cigarette away into the wind.

"People will see this when they wake up and be frightened, there's nothing we can do about that, but we can reassure them by not panicking ourselves."

Lucien muttered along in Spanish as Dan spoke, somehow recognising the militia members and knowing that the two French among them spoke enough English to not require a translation but that their Spaniard had to be caught up with events.

"Send someone to fetch Mitch," he asked Lucien, "and another for Neil." Two of the militia were dispatched to bring the men Dan wanted as he stepped into the covered guard post and picked up each of the three radios in turn. One led to the watchtower, another to the front gate and the last to the sky fort high above the road approach to Sanctuary. He spoke softly and slowly, alerting the other positions to the unexpected arrival. Only the people of the fort were unaware by the time he called them, as their main focus was on keeping watch inland.

"We were about to raise the alarm," the voice from the watchtower said. Dan looked up at the far cliff on the opposite side of the bay as he spoke. None of us could see the watchtower in the early morning gloom but that didn't stop him from trying to make the physical connection as he spoke.

"Don't do that," he said, "a flare would only cause panic and show whoever that is out there how long it took for us to notice them." He gave his instructions to them and signed off just as Mitch jogged up to our position.

"What's all the hullabaloo-*ohmyfuckingchristonabike!*" he said, the comedic curse rolling into one single expletive to accompany his open-mouthed stare at the big boat anchored off our shore. The sun crept higher in the far east with every second, and if I stared at something for long enough I could actually see the world growing lighter as though someone was slowly dialling up the picture with a manual control.

"Mitch," Dan greeted him solemnly, "could I trouble you to take over here for me?" Mitch nodded his assent, still staring out at the vast intruder with his mouth hanging open. He seemed to snap out of it quickly and looked round for a subordinate to command.

"Alejandro?" he said to the Spanish boy of the militia. His grasp of Spanish and his natural Scottish sound made the language seem infinitely more guttural. "*Los demás,*" he said. *The others.*

Alejandro, what seemed like all fifteen years old of him, scampered off down the pier to where the team of people kept on standby were asleep.

"What do you want us to do?" Mitch asked Dan.

"Nothing," he said as he pointed to his dog to stay on the ancient stone of the sea wall's walkway. "Keep their eyes open and their guns ready." With that he waked a short distance and hopped down into the belly of a small boat, little more than a large canoe really, and started the tiny outboard motor.

"Whoa, where the hell are you going?" I asked him.

"You mean where the hell are *we* going," he replied, gesturing to the tiny bench seat opposite him.

"Oh no," I said warningly, "for one, you're – *we're* – not going out there. For two, I need to do some stuff before you drag me out there."

"Go do your stuff then," Dan told me.

I went to the nearest building that could accommodate my needs to save climbing back up to the castle and my own rooms. I did what I needed to do, finishing with a mouth rinse of bottled water and a squeeze of precious toothpaste that didn't belong to me. As I tried to gargle it, the third wave of dizzy nausea swept over me and threatened to undo all of the repair work I'd just undertaken. I managed to keep that one down by breathing slowly and staying very still with my eyes closed until it passed. When I walked back to the boat Dan had occupied I found it empty and saw Marie storming down the slope towards the docks with a tired little boy on one hip and a look of biblical fury on her face.

I sped up, despite not wanting to at all, because I felt some sense of protection over Dan and didn't want to have him torn to shreds by Marie. I needn't have worried, because all of her anger and frustration was directed at the now clearly visible tanker ship anchored a mile or two out to our immediate front. Others began emerging with the dawn as they did most days. Fishermen prepared to go out to work, militia members woke to take their turn at the guard posts and allow those who had been up all night to get a few precious minutes of sleep ahead of their official finish times. One by one, all of them saw the overnight arrival and all of them froze in uncertainty.

The standby force had arrived in a collectively groggy group spurred into immediate action by the shrill arrival of Alejandro having woken them only minutes before, and Mitch set them to work, spreading out his forces in preparation for any eventuality.

"Change of plan," Dan said quietly from behind my shoulder like a bad ventriloquist. "We're not going out to meet them."

"You mean not now Marie's watching?" I asked. He ignored my question, electing not to give the obvious answer.

"We'll watch them for today," he told me, "see what they're up to. But make no mistake, kid," he said in a dark tone, "this isn't going to end well for somebody."

WRITER'S CRAMP

Leah stopped writing, putting down the pen to massage some life back into her right hand. She had lost track of time, having spent a few hours so deep in thought that she had neglected to break after midday and eat. By early afternoon her absence had been noticed and her daughter came looking for her.

"There you are!" Adalene beamed as she burst through the old wooden door and startled the sleeping Ares into jumping up and yapping a flurry of shrill barks at the sudden intrusion. The puppy stopped barking, sneezed for no discernible reason, and sat to scratch an oversized ear with an even more oversized paw.

"I'm here, *chérie*," Leah said as she leaned back to the sound of her clicking back and rubbed her hand.

"What are you doing?" she asked as she did that curious thing so many children did and stood far too close to her mother so that she couldn't even see her clearly. Easing back the chair and standing, Leah kissed her on the forehead on the way up, letting out a squeak of a groan.

"I'm being silly and sitting still for too long," Leah told her, "you know what happens when you sit still for too long?"

"You turn into stone," Adalene said with confidence.

"No," Leah corrected her gently, "you get cramp. Who told you

you'll turn to stone?"

"Papa," she replied, allowing a touch of uncertainty to creep into her voice.

"Ah," Leah said, trying and failing to be annoyed at Lucien for filling their daughter's head with so many untruths, "*he* turns to stone if he stays still, but normal people like you and me just get cramp."

"But why Papa and not us?" she asked seriously.

"Because he's a goblin," Leah replied with the same confidence and seriousness, then broke into a smile as the young girl stared at her to find the truth in her words. She erupted into giggles when Leah's face cracked.

"He's not a goblin," the girl said, laughing.

"No," Leah replied, "but he is a silly man for filling your head with nonsense. Come on, I'm hungry."

"But you missed the midday meal," Adalene said with concern as they walked out of the room where Leah had set up her writing studio.

"Then we'll have to sneak into the kitchens," she told her daughter conspiratorially. The girl matched her mischievous expression and giggled again. They took a route via the outside of the castle walls, still inside the town, and went the long way to the kitchens that had evolved much over the eighteen years since Leah had first walked up to the gates and begged for help. She was only a few years older than her own daughter was then, and the two girls could not have been more worlds apart if they came from different planets.

Adalene was a young girl, prone towards daydreams and make-believe, but she had been raised as a resourceful member of their society and her education had been focused on the real-life things she needed to know. She had learned the basics of reading and writing both French and English, and was adept at picking up a lot of Spanish verbally. She had learned mathematics and science, much as she would have done in school, but she had learned what she needed to learn for a reason.

She could send and receive messages in multiple languages, should the need arise. She could translate between members of their wider group who had yet to learn a second language. She could calculate distances between places on maps, and work out the equations to tell her how long it would take to walk, or ride, or even drive between them. As for the science she learned, she hadn't even known she was being educated. She was taught how to purify water using the power of the sun. She learned engineering from studying how the water wheel worked in the bubbling stream falling from the cliffs and how that in turn moved the grindstone inside the barn beside it. She learned electrical engineering by building her own wind-powered battery bank using parts of long-dead cars.

She learned domestic skills and could gut and clean a fish before she turned five years old, as well as being able to safely cook and start a fire to stay warm and dry. She understood how to work a dog as support and protection, she kept a wary eye on the horizon out of ingrained habit, and even if she hadn't realised she was being taught the skills of survival she had learned from the best.

Leah led them into the kitchens via the small side door where the scraps were taken out to travel the quickest route to the pig pens. Feeling very much like they were sneaking around where they shouldn't be, Leah told Ares to sit and stay in a patch of shade under the low-hanging branches of a fruit tree. The dog did as he was told, grumbling comically as he flopped down to rest his chin on both front paws in an obvious sulk. Slipping inside, and despite having the complete freedom to roam anywhere inside the walls, including the private rooms of the residents if she had justification, Leah looked around for a friendly face. She found every face looking back at her to be friendly, but one was even more so than the others.

Pip, then in her late thirties, was still the diminutive lovely who had ventured across half of Europe with them, even though her adventurous nature was strictly limited to having tried a different kind of hot chocolate before bed once. She was still every bit as loving and selfless as the day they had rescued her from the hell she had been cast into straight after those early days of fear and shock, and her face lit up to see the woman she had first met as a young girl. They went over to her in the busy kitchen, past the women peeling and chopping vegetables for the evening meal to where Pip was in the group tidying away the remains of lunch.

When Leah had first met her she had been terribly unwell and very weak to the point that Kate had kept a tight hold on her until she was stronger. She had suffered with a miscarriage soon after her capture and imprisonment in what the legends now called 'Slaver's bay', which made it sound far more grand than the harsh truth; she had been thrown into a dirty ring of shipping containers and had to survive for months without even the basic medical or nutritional requirements being met.

Regardless of her shaky start in the new world, she had prospered in Sanctuary and had two children of her own. Both boys, who she raised with their father – a Frenchman working on the fishing docks –doted on their mother for many reasons, one of which being her ability to sneak them treats from the big kitchens.

"Pip," Leah said warmly as she reached an arm out to swamp

the tiny woman's shoulders and hug her. "How are the boys?"

"Oh, they're wonderful," she said with a genuine smile. "Little shits sometimes, just like their father, but wonderful all the same." She turned to Adalene and crouched slightly to bring their faces level. "And how are you my little lovely?" she said, embarrassing the girl. She smiled back at the small woman saying nothing until Leah saved her by changing the subject.

"I got caught up doing something and completely missed lunch," she explained, "and the little general here came to find out why." Leah leaned closer and made a show of checking over both shoulders for sign of anyone watching or listening. "Any chance of, err, you know…" Her eyebrows asked the rest of the question making Pip laugh and cover her mouth self-consciously as she always did. She needn't have. She was still an attractive woman even after seventeen years of living in a kind of hybrid medieval state of technology mixed with the odd electrical item thrown in for good measure.

"Oh," Pip said as she played along in character and shot furtive glances around the big kitchen, "I think I can sneak you a sandwich… Adalene? Keep watch for me?" The girl grinned at what she thought was a charade but was beginning to suspect was real-life danger. It didn't occur to her that the highest power in the entire region other than her grandparents was her mother, so any consequences were likely to be irrelevant. Adalene kept watch as Leah and Pip went to work putting slices of cold meat and broad leaves of salad between two slices of bread large enough to be used as cover should the world erupt into a gun battle without warning. Thick wedges of homemade butter, churned in the town for over fifteen years, adorned the bread before the contents were squashed together and wrapped in a linen cloth. Leah thanked Pip and retrieved her lookout as she made a big show of holding the wrapped sandwich down low and walking fast to make it obvious she had something to hide. Adalene ran along beside her, unable to contain her giggles as they burst from the side door and broke into a panicked run.

"Ares, heel," Leah yelled as they ran laughing towards the direction of the sea. The ungainly dog, sparked into consciousness so rudely after his sulk had become a genuine afternoon nap in the warm shade, followed and yapped excitedly as he tried to keep up and not fall over in a tangle of oversized paws and long legs.

They stopped running, their laughter taking their breath away more than the sudden exercise, and dropped onto the rocks at the very beginning of the long sea wall to stare out over the waves. Little things like that, not that Leah did them intentionally, made her a very fun mother to have. Adalene adored her, and that adoration was returned tenfold. In that specific case, it was returned by half of a huge sandwich which Leah pulled the thick crusts from as her daughter was at that awkward age when her molars began to fall out to be replaced by her adult teeth.

The crusts sailed through the air one after another, thrown expertly to the dog, who needed only to open his mouth and accept the tasty treats as reward for keeping up. Instead of casually snatching them from the air, Ares allowed his excitement to rule him and leapt frantically to overextend himself and flip in mid-air. Landing with an ugly thud, the dog regained his feet and desperately searched the ground for the crusts until he located them and swallowed them whole.

The two women, one very young and one feeling much older than she truly was, looked out over the sea and lapsed into silence as they ate.

"Tell me what you are writing down, Mama?" Adalene asked

sweetly. Leah said nothing for a moment, just sucked air in through her nose noisily before letting it out after a while. She didn't have the heart to tell her. Couldn't bring herself to describe the fear and the doubt she experienced when she first found out she was pregnant with the girl sitting beside her. She thought about telling her parts of the rest of that particular tale, but the atrocities the pirates visited on innocent people was a story not for the ears of a ten year old.

"Just something that happened before you were born, *chérie*," Leah told her. "Something not very nice, and that meant I had to do things that weren't nice either, you know, to keep everyone here safe like I always try to." Adalene didn't press her for more, just sat and enjoyed the time in the sun when she had managed to steal her mother away from the town and everyone else for a few minutes all of her own.

ATROCITIES

I'd heard the word enough times, but I'd never experienced it. Not truly. Not until that point in my life. On the rare occasions I'd managed to get Dan and Mitch to open up about the experiences of their past I had learned how seeing what other humans could do to one another, for whatever reason, left a permanent mark on the souls of those bearing witness to it.

Mitch had told me about his experiences in East Africa, about how he had to reconcile fighting child soldiers and had actually been okay with being put in the position of returning fire and killing them. He had reconciled that as a simple matter of survival, and while he hated the situation he reserved his real anger for the manipulative bastards who indoctrinated young boys and girls and put the weapons in their hands.

He had told me about a time in Afghanistan, when a man occupying one of the machine gun positions on the lonely, dusty hilltop they had been ordered to defend took a bullet high in the thigh. He looked at his empty hands as he told me the tale, his mind conjuring the blood he described as it ran into the endless dust and turned into a dark brown paste that stuck to every part of him until the young man stopped screaming and went still. His ghostly pale face told Mitch what had happened, and the bullet which had splintered his thigh bone had sent sharp fragments up into his groin to transform the blood vessels into a ruined mess. He told me how looking into the eyes of the soldier, not much more than a boy, had brought home all of the cruel brutality of humankind.

He shook off the spell of memory and smiled as he said how they had returned that violence on their enemy with all the discipline and force of the British Army, but I knew his smile was as false as his bravado.

Dan was much the same, only his dusty memories were of different places and different people. The only common theme was that people were capable of such unending cruelty to one another, and the end of the world went a long way to making it worse, as the only thing keeping those people in check was the threat of retribution.

~

I was taking my turn on the pier where I spent every day watching the distant hulk lying motionless out in deep water. I was grateful for their arrival in one way, as it saved me from having to give excuses why I could no longer step foot on a boat without feeling instantly sick.

Not one boat had been seen leaving it for the first few days, and when the shout went up from one of the eagle-eyed in the high tower, every man and woman capable grabbed a weapon and lined the sea wall ready to pour fire at anyone heading to our little slice of paradise with evil intent.

The boat bobbed towards us for a few minutes, growing larger in such slow-motion as to betray the distance the massive ship was from land. I had claimed seniority; Dan accused me of playing but I ignored him. I stretched out the headband of the ear defenders as I flicked down the bolt latch to select fully automatic fire on the Browning fifty and braced my boots wide on the stone walkway in anticipation of the thunderous vibrations the huge gun would send through my body. I glanced left and saw Mitch flipping out the bi-pod legs attached to the underside of the barrel on the captured and refurbished PKM as he handed a spare belt of linked ammunition to a bewildered young man beside him, giving instructions through the medium of sign language and shouting. He must have sensed my interest because he rested the stock into his shoulder and dropped his body weight slightly to line up the gun before looking in my direction and offering a wink.

I took a breath, let it out slowly, and waited for the little boat to come into effective range. In theory the bullets could kill at over a mile away, but the chances of me sending a bullet over that distance and taking into account the various changes on wind and temperature over the water, as well as the curvature of the Earth and a few other factors I couldn't counter, were so slim they were non-existent. I could fire the entire belt of ammunition, something which we couldn't replace, at them and still miss with every single round.

Before they came anywhere near close enough to shred with our amassed firepower, they turned abruptly to our right and headed east. We watched in annoyed silence as they went out of sight even before we heard the whine of their engines.

"Well," Dan said quietly to break the awkward silence, "that was disappointing."

It was. I flicked the bolt latch back up and released the twin handles of the machine gun, feeling like I would never get the chance to fire it, which strangely bothered me.

"Stand down," I declared loudly, feeling faint as I said it and staggered slightly. I thought I'd got away without anyone noticing but one of the militia members, a young woman who flatteringly seemed to model her look on mine, stepped close and spoke in rapid, concerned French.

"I'm fine, really," I insisted. "*Je vais bien.*"

"*Tu n'es pas,*" Lucien said as he appeared through the small crowd to emerge shouldering his way to the front. I tried to push him away, tried to tell him I was fine, but a wave of heat surged through my head and I fainted.

I came around in the infirmary with Kate scowling down at me. I scowled back, mostly out of anger at myself for appearing weak in front of people, and moved to prop myself up on my elbows.

"Slowly," the medic admonished me as I sat up and waited for the wooziness to fade. A tug at my left elbow revealed a thick needle piercing my skin, my eyes following the clear tubing running from my flesh to the bag of liquid hanging from a chromed frame.

"Is that all you do?" I asked with no real venom in my words. "Just stick a bag of fluids in anyone you find?"

"Pretty much," Kate shot back without even looking at me. "Now, what have you had to eat today?"

I thought about it and answered honestly. "Some juice," I admitted.

"No carbohydrates?" she enquired with a raised eyebrow. I shook my head. "Well, no wonder you fainted in this heat on an empty stomach."

Fainted? I thought. *I've never fainted in my life...*

"Oh," I said out loud, "I err..."

"You need to rest, and you need to eat properly. I swear you're as stubborn as Marie for taking my advice…"

"I'm okay, I ju—"

"Eat something, rest, don't overdo it," I was told firmly. "And you aren't going anywhere until I've finished topping up your oil."

I sighed and slumped backwards to flop into the pillow, not expecting a Neil joke from anyone except Neil, taking the enforced inactivity as a chance for some quiet time. That was ruined by another wave of sickness that I just knew wouldn't go away on its own. I sat up, my voice sounding strangled as I asked for help.

"Unhook me," I said, "I'm going to throw up." Kate looked at me uncomprehendingly for a moment too long, making a retching noise erupt from the back of my throat which I cut off by clamping my free right hand over my mouth.

Now, normal people would have let me off the bed. Would have disconnected the drip or else carried the frame holding it for me to puke with at least some dignity. Not Kate. Not the paramedic who'd been vomited on so many times in her life that she was almost immune to the sights and smells and sounds of it. No, she just brought a bowl over to me and held my ponytail clear while I coughed up the acidic contents of my stomach.

"*Pheeeww*," she whistled in mild distaste as she looked away and tried not to breathe in, "you were telling the truth about the juice." Her nose wrinkled and her eyes blinked rapidly as the smell of acidic orange filled the room. I finished, wiping my mouth and leaning back with an exhausted groan. I opened my eyes to see her looking at me curiously.

"What?" I asked, still out of breath.

"How long have you been feeling like this?" she quizzed.

"Just this morning," I lied, "didn't feel like eating much and didn't sleep well…"

"Right," Kate said, drawing the word out with a clearly pronounced subtitle of, 'I don't believe you'. She picked up a blood pressure cuff and a stethoscope and advanced on me like the world's kindest torturer. I lacked the energy to make her stop and stayed still as she messed around with me, poking and prodding and telling me to keep still as the pressure around my upper arm increased and a thermometer was shoved under my tongue.

"Mmff a 'ectul ffmumutah?" I mumbled through the obstruction. She just glared at me for a moment, ignoring my weak attempt at humour and probably contemplating telling me that it was indeed a rectal thermometer and that she hadn't cleaned it since she saw the last patient. She took it out of my mouth and frowned at it, muttering something about a high temperature. I glanced up at the drip and saw that it had almost finished so I carefully withdrew the needle when she wasn't looking, snatching up a small square of boiled cloth and pressed it hard into the tiny wound as I slipped down from the tall bed.

"I'm fine," I said as I headed for the door, "I promise I'll eat something whe—"

I stopped, seeing the exit to the infirmary blocked by Dan and Mitch. Both were still dressed for war and both wore faces of undisguised anger. My heart dropped, thinking that somehow they had found out about my *situation*, I think that was what people said about it, and were coming to force me to stay inside until I turned fifty.

"What's going on?" Kate asked with evident concern. "Do you

need me to leave?"

"No," Dan said, "stay. You'll need to hear what we have to say too." Kate sat down. "Looks like that boat we saw today wasn't the first one they'd sent out," Dan intoned ominously. He seemed to want to say more but was struggling to phrase it the way he thought it should come out. I wanted to tell him to get on with it but the rainbow of emotions coming off them kept my mouth closed.

"The settlements to the east," he said, "the homestead people?" I knew them. They were like a large family, only none of them were related before it all happened. They came up with their own idea of living together in what Dan called an 'off-grid' lifestyle. They reminded me of the old TV shows where people lived off the land out in newly populated areas of countryside. I liked the idea, until I realised that the ten of them had to get all of their own food and water as well as every other chore necessary to stay alive. Their way of life made me know I had it easy in many ways, as I never had to worry about what I was eating and whether there would be enough fuel to have a fire. Much the same way that the people who made food or harvested firewood never had to face the prospect of fighting with any invaders because that was what I did for them.

"What about them?" I asked suspiciously, not wanting the answer to be what I thought it might be.

"One of them is here. He…" Dan wavered and cleared his throat. "He was hurt."

Kate leapt up to grab her bag loaded with everything she might need to administer emergency medicine. "Where is he? What are his injuries?"

Dan held up both hands and took a pace towards the paramedic. He placed those hands on her shoulders to stop her frantic movements and fix her gaze on him.

"It's too late," he told her as softly as his anger would allow, "he's gone."

"Gone?" she shot back. "Gone bloody where?"

"He's bloody well *dead*, Kate," he said harshly. "And a lot more people will be if we don't do something about it." He glanced at me as his glowering eyes told me to fall in and get ready for a fight. I followed them out of the room as Kate began to interrupt and say that I couldn't go anywhere. A single warning glance from me stopped her protest, and she nodded for me to go.

That day was the first time I ever truly understood the word atrocity. I found myself walking away from the gatehouse automatically as my feet propelled me onwards in a daze. Nemesis walked beside me, looking up intermittently and whimpering as she picked up on the mood.

How that man had walked to Sanctuary was beyond belief. That he had survived the injuries they had inflicted upon him was an impossibility, but to have covered over eight miles on rough ground after having both of his hands removed at mid forearm before suffering what looked like a crude cauterisation was the stuff of nightmares.

He had survived long enough to tell one of our militia that they had attacked their home, had dragged away the woman and murdered the men. How they had given him the option of which parts of his body they should remove with a machete as the rest of them jeered and laughed at the entertainment, forcing him to pick two things. He had chosen his hands, because he knew he couldn't walk to raise the alarm on stumps and the other option they gave him would mean bleeding out or simply dying of shock.

He must have been one of the strongest, bravest, most resolved men I think I could ever have met to have survived the ordeal long enough to make it there and tell us, and his death rocked me so far over the edge that I needed to be alone. I walked out to the small bay where I still ran when I wasn't feeling sick and splashed into the shallow water as it lapped lazily towards me. Tears broke from my eyes and began their escape downwards as I tried to corral them with the backs of my hands.

I had seen death before. I had visited it on more people than I actually knew and some of that death was dealt at close range and with real malice. I had seen the results of tortured minds and bodies. What I had never seen was the results, the leftover dead meat, of pure and unadulterated sadism. These people, no, these *pirates*, had committed atrocities on our doorstep.

And they had to pay.

IMMEDIATE ACTION

Dan paced like a caged animal, barely able to contain his rage. I, like Neil and like Marie, had seen him like this once before. Mitch, despite seeing Dan angry on plenty of occasions, including more than one instance of murderous intent, had never seen him like that.

The last time I'd seen him that mad was when we'd learned about Joe's body being hung from a streetlight about a million years ago.

The only reason he hadn't left yet, hadn't taken his rage and his guns and his dog and waged personal war on anyone he could find was because Marie blocked the main gate with her arms folded.

No weapon he possessed would break that defence.

"You're not going anywhere," she ordered, "not like this."

"How am I supposed to be?" he snarled at her, totally blind to how he was speaking to his wife. "Should I be *calm* about it?"

"No," Marie said, fighting hard to keep the reaction out of her words, "but you should be *rational* about it."

"*Rational?*" Dan exploded, flinging his arms up. His outburst affected everyone in earshot, but the one frightened flinch I saw pushed me to intervene.

"Oi," I snapped as I stepped forward to force myself into his eyeline. I pointed my finger at the end of my ramrod-straight arm. He peeled his eyes away from Marie's and followed the line I gave him and saw something that brought him back down to Earth. Ash cowered, fearful of his anger instead of being riled up and ready to go into action alongside him as he should be. Dan recognised it in an instant as his emotions connected the dots far faster than he could have explained. When that realisation hit him he deflated instantly.

Marie, hiding the fact well that her husband calmed down for his dog and not her, stepped forwards and dropped her folded arms to grab his hands and get his eyes focussed on hers and make sure he heard her.

"You need to react properly, not just run out there and start a fight with the first people you don't recognise," she told him in a firm but softer voice. She had tears in her eyes, which at the time I thought was because of the fear and the anger of the situation but I later realised she had been suffering physically since her last miscarriage.

"She's right," Mitch said, "this is a come-on."

"A what?" I asked, having not heard him use that term before that I could remember.

"It's a lure to get people out in the open. To bring fighters out of cover into a killing ground. Chopping this poor wee bastard's hands off and seeing where he runs to for help is a sure way to get a response, do you not think?"

As brutal as that was, it was definitely a tactic that would work against a moral enemy. Dan seemed to deflate, reaching out to wrap Marie up into a hug that oozed wordless apology. She knew him well enough to know not to take his emotional stupidity as intentionally hurtful. He was angry, and he needed to punish the bastards who hurt and killed innocent people. He pulled away, cuffing unashamedly at the tears in his eyes.

"Who spoke to him?" he asked, his voice cracking as he spoke.

"I did," a young man answered. I recognised him, not surprisingly as I knew all of our militia members to some degree. I didn't know him well, but I appreciated his resolve as he kept his face free from emotion and recounted the last words of the mutilated man who I then realised lay covered with a once-white sheet found from god only knew where.

"How many?" Dan muttered as his brain whirred into overdrive. The answer was given and the questions came one after another. He asked about their weapons, their language, their accents, how they were dressed, how they carried themselves.

"How is this?" the young Frenchman asked, unsure of the translation he had given the question in his own mind.

"*Et leur comportement? Dîtes moi, comment se sont-ils comportés? Ont-ils eu de l'allure martiale, par exemple?*" Marie offered in French far better than my own, asking about their behaviour and whether they appeared like they were military. I think that was what she meant anyway.

"Ah... *non*. They were... *sloppy?*" he offered questioningly.

Undisciplined, I thought, unsure if that made them less or more dangerous. It made them unpredictable in many ways, and unpredictable always increased the threat level in my mind.

Dan continued interrogating the man for every scrap of information he could glean before a gentle hand from Marie rested on his arm and reminded him that he wasn't trying to drag the answers from an enemy. That unspoken communication, the soft reassurance of physical contact with a loved one, brought him back down again.

"Okay," Dan said in a growl that was more upset and disillusioned than angry. He paused as he thought, and I could see his mind weighing up the same factors mine was, as to go outside of the walls with enough fighters to remain safe meant stretching the town's defences even thinner than they already were. "Lucien?"

"I'm here," he said from behind me, taking a step forwards and reaching out to place a hand on me automatically as he always did whenever he got in easy reach. I felt the warmth of his fingers on the back of my right hip and my body responded all by itself to lean into him.

"You have command of the gate," Dan told him. "Take ten militia and hold it. Tell our people in the fort what's happened and get them to double up on their watches."

"*D'accord*," Lucien replied, waiting for the rest of Dan's instructions to be given out so that he had an overview of what everyone else was doing.

"Neil, can you man the fifty in the bay and take charge of that side please?"

"Got it," Neil answered without an accent or any humour as his eyes lingered on the covered body beside him.

"Mitch, Leah, Adam – with me," Dan finished.

"Hold on a minute," I heard myself saying, "what's the plan?" Dan looked around, seeing concern and fear radiating back at him from the assembled faces.

"The plan is to head for their settlement, see what's there and re-evaluate," he said simply.

"And if you find them there?" Marie asked. "What then?"

"You need to ask?" I questioned her gently, my eyebrows up as I purposely switched my gaze from her face to the body of the peaceful homesteader whose only want in life was to exist peacefully.

"Twenty minutes," Dan announced, causing the group to break away softly as though he had cut the bonds keeping them there and allowed them to float away. I caught his eye, my own expression one of grim determination which mirrored his. Both of our faces reflected a great sadness behind the anger; sadness that people still behaved like this to one another when there were precious few of us enough left already. We were both saddened and upset by what we had seen, and although that upset caused us to experience pain it wasn't a weakness that showed through, but instead a hardened resolve to rectify the imbalance that had come to our little slice of the continent.

Like everyone who had done so before, these bastards would pay the price for their inhumanity too. I gave him a nod and turned away, wheeling around to find my eyes directly in front of Lucien's chin.

"You," he said sternly, or at least as sternly as he could manage when talking to me, "be careful and come back to me." My eyes flickered to the covered body nearby before returning to his face. I managed to leave off the words, *in one piece*.

It was only a little after midday by the time we had headed far enough inland so as to be totally alone in the world. Everywhere I looked the subtle signs of nature reclaiming the earth peeked back at me; a reflected glint of metal covered by creeping ivy or the unnatural straight edge of a distant building yet to have been pulled down to the ground by the elements.

I always enjoyed being so far away from everything, so far

removed from the world entirely, but that day my mind was so pre-occupied with the gruesome results of barbaric human behaviour that any enjoyment I could have taken from the journey was whipped away by the warm wind rushing around us.

It was late spring, or I guessed the start of summer, technically – not that the days and months meant anything in a life dictated by the seasons that had a habit of keeping their own schedule – and we were all sweating and breathing hard as we fought to gain elevation from sea level where we began. Rapid gains in height, especially when walking and jogging under pressure and stress, was so exhausting it sapped the will from my legs before I reached the top.

"This…" I panted as I put my head down to force my legs to dig in deeper and propel me upwards towards the ridge line ahead, "is why… we run up… and down the bloody steps… at home…"

Mitch said nothing, as his recent lack of sleep through baby-related activity had taken the edge off his usual billy goat-like fitness. Dan grunted in answer, all he could manage as he screwed his eyes up and opened his mouth wider to suck in the much-needed oxygen.

When we reached the plateau, via the most direct route to save half an hour of meandering round the long way by road, I dropped to one knee and brought up my weapon to scan the ground ahead. Beside me, Dan did the same as Mitch remained stood tall and brought his heavier, longer gun up to his shoulder to view the land ahead through his scope.

"Nothing," Dan said first. I agreed but saved the unnecessary waste of breath in saying so. I just stood, lowered my gun into a low ready carry, and gave a short whistle to bring Nemesis to heel. The two dogs, unperturbed by the steep incline save for their tongues lolling from their mouths to lose the excess heat they had generated during the climb, stopped sniffing around in random tracks on the rocky ground and returned to us. Ash went to Dan and, being the seasoned professional he was, dropped into position by his left leg and waited to go to work. His age, and I guessed he must be almost nine years old given that we didn't really know his age when Dan first found him, didn't seem to slow him down. I knew it would, eventually, just as it would my Nem, but his only concession to his advancing years had been a little more bulk and a lightening of the grey around his big muzzle.

Much like Dan, actually.

I kept my own dog at heel, proud that even though she was a little under half of Ash's age she was already an experienced sidekick and had performed well the only time I had ever had cause to deploy her as a weapon against real enemies. My mind shot back to her first bite, when I had been knocked stupid by a car crash and came under attack by someone wanting to finish the job of rendering me unconscious with a rifle butt, and she had flown through the air like a furry missile to savage the bastard to pieces.

"Another hour," Dan said. I looked up to see him pointing ahead and slightly left with a flat hand to indicate the direction we needed to take. Like me, he had these routes memorised and never took the same way to or from somewhere unless it was necessary, as you never knew when you might have to go around something. Knowing the ground was an advantage I enjoyed.

Nobody spoke as we moved. Occasionally one of us would point out something: an animal or a position we should check before walking casually by. One of those was a thick copse of trees which were packed together so tightly that they created a dark void in their centre and grew so straight as though they were racing one another to get their leaves up to the sunlight.

The method was simple, just as though we were hunting game birds back in the world where such sport was a pastime for the wealthy instead of being a necessity of survival. Dan and I sent our dogs into the trees with commands to search for enemies as we tracked their progress from the sides on open ground. A rustling of undergrowth and the pistol shot of snapping branches preceded a flurry of movement as three young deer, short-legged and bounding randomly, fled the trees with Nemesis running with extreme effort after them. I knew she couldn't maintain that kind of flat-out sprint for more than a matter of seconds as she seemed to hinge in the middle of her back to get the maximum reach of front and back paws like a cheetah. I contemplated calling her back, but before I could draw in the breath to do it she realised the futility of her pursuit and broke off to loop a wide circle back to me. Ash emerged beside me, gave me an almost bored look, and sneezed once before trotting off to find Dan.

Experience over youth, I thought, watching the older dog who knew better than to try to take down such agile moving food when it had a head start. I smiled at him, prompting Dan to ask what I was thinking.

"Oh," I said, unaware that I had been the subject of his scrutiny, "I was just thinking that he's clever enough to know when not to bother chasing deer, but he'll still pick a fight with any cow he sees."

Dan chuckled. "He *does* hate cows…"

"Got something," Mitch growled, bringing us back to the moment in an instant. Both of us brought weapons up as we sidestepped to the shade of the trees as Nemesis looped in to my left side.

"Where?" I murmured.

"Twelve o'clock," Mitch told us, talking our eyes onto the target as we knew he would. As he had taught me to do. "Peak in the ridge line. Pan right to the patch of bushes…"

"Got it," Dan said.

"…come down to the patch of dead ground… see it?"

"I see it," I told him as I picked up the reply. "Where now?"

"Hold there," Mitch told us. We held there until our patience was rewarded by a small billow of smoke rising from the dead ground ahead.

LONG SLEEVES

Ten of them were sent ashore on the first dawn after their huge mothership had dropped anchor opposite the small bay where people watched from the walls of an old castle. None of them had ever seen a place like it, and almost all of them aboard the small skiff heading up the coast stared in awe at the high walls and ancient defences of the seaward side of the enclosed town.

They were more accustomed to walled towns of rusted metal sheets and mud walls topped with broken glass and barbed wire, but the most important part of their lives were spent at sea. Unlike their previous incarnation, these post-civilisation pirates spent more time on one vessel than they did previously. Instead of hiding in the small coastal fortresses in Kenya, Eritrea or Somalia and only going to sea when a hijacking mission had been financed and planned to spend weeks, often months aboard the captured ship until the ransoms were paid, they now lived almost exclusively at sea.

The small group, a single crew of raiders, was sent ashore as a reward for hard work and good fortune when they had found a further cache of weapons in Tunisia and then a supply of alcohol in a port that they didn't know was at the southern tip of Sardinia. Their leader, Gareer, who the crew simply referred to as *Boqor*, had told them to go inland away from the town so as not to test their defences yet. Their orders were as simplistic as they were ominous.

They were told to go and have some fun.

The first place they found to beach their boat safely, away from the sharp rocks, was a small bay of yellow sand, with a massed rampart of junk and plastic washed up over the years since people had stopped using the beach for leisure. They ran the small skiff aground and shut off the engine before they leapt from it to raise their weapons cautiously, if with little tactical ability.

One of them, the smallest and likely the youngest, lugged a large plastic container of water awkwardly, the long AK rifle he carried slipping from his shoulder in his haste to try and keep up with the older men as they filed up the sandy slope towards the higher ground.

It took them less than an hour to locate the homesteaders, as they were burning some wood from the previous summer which had yet to season enough not to emit a skein of dark smoke to rise up over their farm. They weren't subtle about it. They didn't conduct any reconnaissance or watch their targets with any degree of professionalism, but merely wandered up to their property wearing smiles of anticipated cruelty.

There were eleven people there that day, and of those eleven just one was chosen at random to be the messenger. He was kept until last intentionally so that he had lots to report and would be debilitated and motivated by the fear in equal measures. He had been tied to an apple tree, the sickly sweet smell of the fallen fruit rich in his nostrils above his gagged mouth, and he had watched as the men in his group had been forced to the large chopping block they used to split their firewood. The one who appeared to be their leader, a tall and gangly man with prominent, yellow teeth and stick-thin limbs, brandished a dull-looking machete with rust pitted on the wide blade.

The man watched – he had no choice as he was bound so tightly that he couldn't look away – and every time he tried to close his eyes he was struck and threatened so that he saw the full horror of the display.

"Just kill me," he begged through the gag. He didn't want to watch his friends die, but his pleas for mercy and humanity fell on deaf ears; the men who had come to their home possessed neither.

He screamed and raged into the thick cloth stuffed in his mouth as tears and mucus ran freely down his face. He bellowed in fear and pain and guilt as he watched the men lined up in turn and given a choice; the choice of which parts they were going to cut off with the machete. If they didn't choose quickly enough, if they hesitated or tried to resist in any way, the men would choose for them.

The first man, forcibly restrained and held over the block, lost his head. The thin man with the machete seemed capable of an incredible strength when his thin arms swung the ugly blade, and despite its rough appearance the edge must have been carefully maintained as just three powerful downwards strokes severed the head, removing it from the body with a sickening eruption of fountaining blood.

The next man dragged towards the block screamed and begged for them to take his hand instead. He threw himself down, sobs forcing the tears to run from his eyes and down his cheeks as he held his own hand out on the block to be taken. The man who dragged him there looked at his leader and shrugged. He shrugged in return and whirled the dirty blade through the air like he was splitting logs to bring it down and remove the hand just above the wrist with a crunch.

The amputee howled in agony and shock. It wasn't a sound the bound man had ever heard another human being make before, not even an animal, but that sound echoed in his mind until the moment he too died. With blood spurting from the severed limb the man tried to walk away on his knees as his right hand gripped the left forearm with as much strength as he could muster. It wasn't enough to stop the bleeding, not by any stretch of the imagination, but that didn't matter.

"Where are you going?" the leader asked through laughter. "You have another prize to collect!" He gestured with the machete and the bleeding man was hauled back to the block where his right foot was amputated at mid shin. This second procedure took much longer, as the bones had to first be broken and manipulated to allow the blade to bite home. It took six or seven blows for the lower leg and foot to fall away, but by that time the man had blessedly lost consciousness either through the terrible, unimaginable pain or else through the severe blood loss. His body was rolled aside like discarded meat and the gang jeered the next man as he was ordered forwards. He stood, retaining as much dignity as he could, and when one of them moved to pull him towards his execution he drew his head back and delivered a brutal sucker-blow with his forehead.

He timed and aimed his defiant blow perfectly, connecting the hardest part of his forehead with the widest part of his tormentor's nose, and crunching it into ruined oblivion. He dropped, shattered nose rendering him unconscious long before his thin frame slumped to the ground, and the defiant man reeled from the blow to his own head.

Savage strikes from rifle butts rained down on him, dropping him to the ground and continuing until another stomach-churning crunch signified that his skull had been fractured. An angry exchange took place between the leader and one of the men who had beaten their prisoner to death which none of the captured French people understood as it was in a language none of them had ever heard. Their leader seemed annoyed that he had been denied the sport and exercise of dismembering a terrified, innocent person. As their argument raged and grew louder, one of the other men took his opportunity to make a run for it in a bid for freedom. His sudden flight was noticed, thanks largely to the heads of the captives all moving in unison to watch his escape, and three loud rifles opened up with bursts of automatic fire to shred his body with the heavy bullets and throw his ruined corpse to the ground.

More arguments erupted among the invaders and the sport of chopping up their captives was put on hold as the women were dragged inside the farmhouse only for their screams to rip the air for over an hour. The remaining captives, bound and gagged and forced to listen to their friends and loved ones suffering more torture than they could endure, suffered more casual beatings until they couldn't offer any more resistance.

One man, unable to contain his rage at seeing his woman dragged away, died slowly from a deep knife wound to his belly which had been delivered by the smallest member of the invaders. He seemed to be no more than a child, but any sympathy for his age and assumed innocence was obliterated by his sick and cruel actions. He had threatened the man with the blade, kicking him back down to the ground repeatedly and shouting at him to stay there, and when he hadn't complied the boy had stood on the man's chest and pressed the tip of the knife into his flesh just enough to pierce the skin. He snarled in his face, saying something that none of them understood, and slowly, inch by heart-wrenching inch, he pushed the blade inside as blood welled up and his victim began to make chocking noises of agony and convulsed like a landed fish. The boy withdrew the blade and held it up for the others of his group to see the bright, wet blood on his hands. They made a show of seeming unimpressed, either that or they were just anxious to take their turns inside the house, and just casually watched as the stabbed man died slowly.

By the time they had finished with the women, none of whom came back outside again, the fight seemed to have escaped the men and their deaths happened with less excitement than the first few.

The man bound to the tree stared without emotion as the man he had lived alongside as a brother for over six years twitched and bled out to soak the soft, green ground in front of him with red blood from where both arms had been severed just below the elbow.

They left him there, still tied to the tree in a catatonic state, as they pillaged everything they wanted from the house and outbuildings. They took as much as they could carry, seeming to prepare to leave as all of them drank from the large glass bottles containing home-brewed cider. The bound man knew that the drink wasn't ready, hadn't fully fermented yet, and took a tiny shred of satisfaction that all of them drinking it would suffer terribly over the next few days as their guts tried to reconcile with the active yeasts still working in the sediment they ingested.

His eyes widened as a fresh hell was promised from one of them carrying a red-hot blade which had evidently been placed into the fire that always burned inside the house for cooking. He felt his bonds slacken as he was cut free and the pain of his numb hands burned fiercely as he fell forwards. Almost in a dream state, he found himself hauled forwards to the block where the smiling leader bowed to him in mock greeting.

"Do you wear long sleeve, or a short sleeve?" he asked in heavily accented English. The Frenchman knew very little English, so he frowned in response as he tried to speak but found himself unable to. "I choose long sleeve for you, my friend." The leader grinned evilly at him. He stood, nodded for others to hold his target practice still, and severed both of his hands with viciously hard blows of the machete before dropping the weapon and reaching out to carefully take the glowing orange blade. He pressed the flat of the blade to both wounds, sizzling the fresh blood and burning the flesh to produce the worst smell the now-handless man had ever experienced. His consciousness wavered as the pain somehow went away. He lay flat on his back, his ruined arms held out and above him as the world around him still moved to send muffled noises his way. After a while, which could have been minutes or hours, he became aware that he was now alone.

One of his friends, his brothers, had been dumped on top of a fire which had been set in the small pit outside they sometimes used, and his dead form smouldered and smoked to emit another noxious smell that he couldn't bear.

He stood, staggering as he gained his feet awkwardly, and set off west without being able to look back at his home even once.

WHO COULD DO THIS?

"Go," Dan whispered, having sunk low into a firing position behind a tiny patch of raised ground. Advancing through open fields with little cover was fraught with danger when you expected an attack at any moment, and even the flimsiest of cover felt like a fortified trench.

I stood from the small depression where I'd been lying flat, Nemesis following at my heel automatically, and bounded forwards in the low body position with bent legs and rifle up ready. I dropped to my left knee behind a low wall and smelled the source of the smoke instantly.

My nose turned up at the odour. I was unable to place it, but my brain conjured the idea of overcooked meat left to burn on an open fire. Wood smoke mingled with the smell of burnt flesh but there was an element I couldn't place.

When we crested the low ground into the small valley where the homesteaders had settled, the smell grew stronger until I rounded the side of an old brick-built barn to see the farm's courtyard.

I hadn't been affected by any waves of sickness since I had action to concentrate on, but when my eyes took in the source of the burning smell and connected it with my senses my stomach boiled and flipped. I wheeled away back out of the yard and vomited onto the ground, only just missing Nemesis by an inch. The dog tucked her back end underneath her body as she danced aside in confusion. Both Mitch and Dan heard me expelling the contents of my stomach but as what had caused it was just as abhorrent to them, neither passed comment or judgement.

It wasn't the sight that had caused my reaction, not that they would know that, but the smell had flipped a switch inside me.

A man, at least I assumed it was a man as his hair had burned away and only his legs and shoulders retained any kind of shape, lay on what had been his belly over a firepit. He hadn't caught fire, not from what I saw, but had burned away nonetheless, like leaving a piece of meat over a hot plate on direct heat.

A low whistle from Dan caught my hearing and I glanced around. I saw Mitch look over in the direction of the sound and nod before moving off to encircle the farm buildings and search the perimeter. Dan had ordered the move without me, thinking me incapacitated by the sight of the burned body. I wiped my mouth, sniffed in to dislodge something stuck at the back of my nose and nearly threw up again before I spat it out to startle Nemesis again - she had never seen me be that disgusting before.

Gun up, legs bent and upper body scanning over my weapon sights I went back into the courtyard and allowed my mind to block out the sensory feed from the fire. Seeing the littered body parts and broken bodies surrounding a chopping block soaked a dark red was little better, and soon the buzzing of flies filled my hearing to add another confusing element to my input.

"My heel," I muttered to Nem as I started to clear the outbuildings, beginning with the one on my immediate right and working around the courtyard until I emerged into the daylight near the main house. Ash rounded the building and loped towards us, seeming angry and subdued at the same time. It struck me that not everyone soaked up emotions from their animals, but then most people didn't live and fight alongside their own like they were an extension of themselves. Nem and I were linked somehow, just as Dan and Ash were. I glanced down at Nemesis to see her reflect the same angry nervous tension I felt.

Death was everywhere, littering the ground and clogging up what should have been the warm, fresh air of southern France in the early summer. My eyes played a vile form of jigsaw puzzles as I tried to mentally connect the severed hands and feet with the limbless bodies. I stepped closer, reaching out with the toe of one boot to flip something over in the centre of a puddle of dried blood.

"Oh my fucking god!" I erupted, turning away and trying not to puke again. This time had nothing to do with my 'condition' and everything to do with what I hadn't recognised in the twisted, shrivelled piece of human flesh. Dan emerged, looking at me with questioning, wide eyes until I pointed at what had caused my outburst. He turned, taking it in until the realisation hit him too.

"Oh," he said simply, the word catching in his throat.

"What?" Mitch called out softly from across the yard.

"They cut off..." Dan started, "they cut off one guy's..." He shook his head, unable to say the words out loud and make it real. "House," he said to the stunned Scotsman. "Leah, cover outside."

I knew the real reason he told me not to go into the house. I knew that he was protecting me from the horrors inside as his mind had already connected the dots. Quite literally dismembered men outside and no women. Either they were taken, or they were inside, and either option would stop anyone experiencing the discovery from sleeping for a very long time.

I kept my back to the door of the farmhouse and heard the faint noises of doors opening and furniture being shoved aside as the two men and Ash searched. Before they emerged, I heard Mitch's muffled voice growling "bastards," over and over again. Sounds of coughing reached me and I realised that one of them was losing their lunch too. That meant that whatever was inside was something that my hyper-sensitive nose didn't want to experience if it had made either of those hardened people throw up.

"What is it?" I called out. "What's in there?"

"Stay out there!" Dan barked back at me using his 'alpha' voice. There seemed to be an echo, a kind of resonance when he did that, and beside me Nemesis seemed to shrink a little as she took a series of nervous steps backwards. I stayed outside as my inherent need to know everything was pushed aside by fear and sickness. Unable to stay in the courtyard and hear the undulating waves of buzzing flies swell and ebb in intensity, I climbed the side of a log store and perched on top of a low roof to keep watch. Whoever had done this was long gone, but the sight of the scattered bodies was too much to take in if I didn't have to as my mind kept trying to trace the dismembered body parts back to their original place.

I looked outwards, cutting up the horizon into sections and scanning each in turn to give a structure to my watching. Every few minutes I let my gaze fall out of focus and simply let the world ahead haze out of clarity. It was easier to spot movement that way, at least that's what I had found during the countless hours of guard duty I had conducted since I had turned thirteen. The downside of doing that for too long was that it put me into a very relaxed state, and dulled my other senses which was why I jumped a mile out of my skin and yelped a little when Dan spoke from behind and below me.

"All clear?" he asked, the words thick in his throat. I turned and looked down at him, seeing his eyes red and puffy.

"Yeah," I told him, my own voice subdued also.

"Hold the fort for ten minutes?" he asked me as he pulled at the rubber mouthpiece of the drinking tube snaking over the right shoulder strap of his old tactical vest. I waited as he took four long pulls on the tube, his stubbled cheeks sinking inwards as he gulped down the tepid water.

"We're going to put the others inside," he said with his eyes on his task as he pulled on a pair of thin, black gloves without looking up at mine. I didn't know what to say to make it better, to soothe his damaged soul for what he had to do, so I just told him I'd keep watch.

Mitch was already dragging a man from the crumpled position he was in to stretch him out flat on his back. He gripped the dead man's clothing at the shoulders as he had no hands to give him any purchase on the arms. Dan slung his weapon, picking up the legs as they lifted him as reverently as they could. I watched until they had manoeuvred him inside and scanned back to where he had fallen. His hands were still there, discarded like unwanted crusts at a meal. I turned back to watch, not wanting to see Dan and Mitch forced to stoop and recover the severed body parts.

I blinked, my eyes lingering closed but instead of the darkness inside my eyelids my brain saw the gruesome scene I had just tried to escape.

Hands.

A bare foot. Another still in a boot with the shoelace untied.

The back of a man's head with his shaggy brown hair matted thick with blood above the ruin of his severed neck and exposed spine.

I opened my eyes to rid myself of the imagery, knowing that the scene would be one of those things that stayed with me forever just a vividly as when I first saw and smelt them. Most of those feelings, those extreme experiences that existed inside the vault I kept locked deep inside myself, revolved around death:

The death of my mother and younger brother before everything changed.

The death of the first man I had killed.

The death of the feral dogs who had attacked and so nearly killed us.

The death of Penny. Of Joe. Of Jack.

The feeling of fear when I was stranded and alone after being ambushed a few years before.

This butcher shop scene I presided over was added to the vault as I forced it inside to start the process of locking it away.

"Still okay?" Dan called up to me from behind again. I said nothing. I didn't turn around, just raised my right hand away from the grip of my weapon to hold a raised thumb aloft. Nemesis whined quietly below me, not liking the separation of the height difference between us.

"Grab that," I heard Mitch say. Curious, I turned then to see Dan lifting a log from the fire that still burned. He carried it carefully towards the house and saw me looking back at him.

"Be ready to go," he told me, and leaned into the house to drop the flaming wood inside. The fire didn't catch straight away which I naively expected it to, and I just watched the empty doorway for a full minute until reality reasserted itself. I climbed down and soothed Nem as she spun a circle around me to check I hadn't changed in the few minutes I had been away from her. Dan came back into view carrying something and Ash following intently with great interest and a raised snout as he tiptoed on his front paws to try and put his head into the crate in his master's hands. I saw what it was, and knew that Ash would be interested as he thought it was either a play thing or a snack.

"Gedd*awuff!*" Dan grumbled at the dog, nudging him away with his right hip with as much success as he'd have trying to stack tennis balls. "Bloody dog."

Dan pushed him away again, prompting an undulating grumble as the big dog backpedalled.

"No," Dan said conversationally, "you can't have it."

Another grumble from Ash as he sat back on his haunches and licked his chops as though he answered the man.

"We need it," Dan said as he pointed at the pigeon in the small crate made from nailed together wooden slats. "That's how we send messages home. It's not for you."

Ash issued a muted barking sound through his nose and cocked his head to one side.

"No," Dan insisted. "Piss off." He pulled the small notebook from the pouch on his vest and smoothed it out on the wooden table he had perched at. He left it there while he fished in his vest again and produced a small leather pouch which he rested down to take out a pinch of the dried, shredded tobacco and spread it evenly on the small paper he produced. He rolled it between his thumbs and his forefingers until it formed an even, thin tube and licked the edge of the paper to complete the ritual.

He pinched the errant strands of precious tobacco from one end and placed it in his mouth to produce a bright yellow disposable lighter adorned like it was a packet of chewing gum. Flicking his thumb down on the top of the thing made to look like a packet of juicy fruit he introduced flame to cigarette and closed his eyes as he inhaled deeply but slowly to lean back and close his eyes. He lifted his trigger finger up and curled it around the thin smoke, taking it out of his mouth as he held the toxic cloud in his lungs to get the full effect.

Like all addicts Dan knew just how far to push his high and blew the smoke out in a long stream of relaxed satisfaction as he picked up the stub of pencil he kept with the book. He scribbled out a short note, tore the sheet out of the book and rolled it tight before folding it back on itself and reaching inside the cage to grab the flapping pigeon. He tucked the message into the leather tube tied to the bird's leg and lifted it out of the cage to stand and toss it high into the air. He watched the bird fly out of sight, just as Ash did as he wheeled on the spot in the vain hope that it would fall from the sky into his loving embrace. He sat, took another pull on the rolled cigarette and bent to write the message again on another piece of paper before repeating the process and releasing a second bird to flap noisily upwards and turn towards the sea where whatever magic gave it the genetically formed sense of direction sent it after its partner towards Sanctuary.

"What did you tell them?" I asked him, wanting to know the content of the message.

"That we've found the settlers," Dan said as he watched his dog staring intently after the shrinking speck of the flying messenger. He took another pull on the cigarette and made a noise as he spat a loose strand of tobacco from his lips. "And that they've been killed."

"Nothing else?"

"Nothing else," Dan intoned with finality. He knew that I knew those in receipt of those messages, sent in duplicate as a standardised failsafe, would read between the lines and factor in the brutal treatment of the man who would be carried to our clifftop burial site and shown more respect in death than he had been shown at the end of his life.

"Who…" I said, stopping as I didn't know where my train of thought was heading.

"Who would do this?" Dan asked gently, taking the last pull on the small smoke and dropping it onto the ground. "Bad people, Leah. Very bad people. People like Bronson. Like Le Bloody Chasseur. Like that fat fucker in Wales. Just more bad people."

I took his point, meaning that the *who* wasn't important, only the *what*. Whoever it was, they had stirred the hornet's nest. They had woken the beast.

A cracking sound came from the house and interrupted our taught conversation making me spin to react to the noise. I lowered my half raised weapon and stood back to my full height as the reaction had raised the gun and lowered my body to meet the threat somewhere in the middle. I relaxed, seeing that it was just the fire taking hold in the house when my brain finally understood what had happened.

"We're… we're *burning* them?" I asked, turning back to Dan.

"It's a cremation, of sorts," he said softly. "We… we couldn't be sure to put the right bits of the right people together if we buried them, so we decided to cremate them all together."

"Together in life, together in death," I said solemnly. I felt more than saw Dan's eyebrows raise in answer to my uncharacteristic words. "Piss off," I told him, "just let that one ride, okay?"

Dan said nothing, just raised two palms in mock surrender and took a few paces backwards as I watched the flames lick up the wooden frame of the front door.

He was on his third smoke by the time the heat from the burning house grew too hot to remain there. We retreated outside the walls of the homestead to watch as the first lick of orange flame burst from the break in the tiled roof of the house. Black smoke billowed upwards to be whipped west and dissipate over the plateau.

"Tracks," Mitch said. Dan and I turned to face in his direction to see him bent down examining the ground.

"Six men," he said in a voice that made me think he was trying to do a Neil and quote a film, "wearing boots. They walked…" He stood and stared at the ground ahead theatrically.

"They went south east," I said, "following the obvious path to the coast." Mitch glared at me, seeing how unresponsive I was to his distracting humour at that point, and dropped the act. I led on, Nemesis at my side with Dan and Ash behind me. I glanced back to see Mitch crossing himself as his lips moved silently to say a prayer over the burning house.

I remember now that I felt like I was the only one to be affected by what I'd seen there, like the other two were hardened to it and somehow coped better. I suppose that betrayed my age and inexperience at the time, because I wasn't the only one with a locked vault deep inside my soul where all the really bad things went.

The only difference between mine and theirs was that mine wasn't full to the brim.

Contact

We followed the tracks for less than ten minutes before Dan, who had taken over from me on point as we always did at regular intervals to keep the person at the lead fresh, stopped and sank to one knee as he held out a flat hand to make Ash lie flat with the 'down' signal.

I froze when he did out of learned habit and made the same gesture to Nemesis. She lowered herself like a machine in total silence and pricked her ears up to stare intently forward. I couldn't see or hear anything, but when pitted against the ears of the dogs our own hearing was pitiful by comparison. Dan went flat, stretching himself slowly out to crawl forwards with tiny movements so as not to betray our position to whoever or whatever had caused him the concern. Being further back neither Mitch nor I went prone, but simply waited as patiently as we could to find out what had sparked his sudden caution.

The far younger version of me had learned not to ask questions at these tense moments, as I had figured out that I would always find out soon enough and distracting someone in Dan's position would only ever get a best-case scenario of being ignored. Just because I wouldn't ask what was going on didn't mean I wasn't going to try and find out though, and I slowly leaned forwards from my kneeling position to stretch out onto my elbows with my carbine held in the crooks of both elbows. I began to move forwards like a bulky caterpillar as I walked my elbows forward in turn before slowly contracting my stomach muscles and sliding my knees forward. The thought hit me that I wouldn't be able to do that in a couple of months' time and I mentally kicked myself for losing focus; if there weren't literally pirates anchored off our coast then I might have time to deal with the situation I was in. Crawling forwards with as much control as I could muster, I inched my way towards Dan's side as a rustle of dry grass made a sound beside my left foot. I glanced back, careful even then to move my head slowly to not catch the attention of any unseen watchers with the amateur mistake of fast body movements, to see Nemesis maintaining her loyal heel position even as she belly crawled just as I did. It was both adorable and ultimately cool in equal measures as I caught eyes with my dog who was more tactically aware than most soldiers we had ever trained.

Bringing myself very slowly level with Dan I carefully moved my barrel around to point forwards and allow me to use the scope if I had to.

"Ahead," Dan murmured in a voice barely above a whisper but with a soft tone that didn't carry like whispers had an ironic habit of doing; something about the range of hearing of an average human being made whispering a counter-productive activity sometimes. "Dead ground to your right as it drops away," Dan told me as he read the signs of nature who would happily announce such things if you knew how and where to look for the clues. "I heard voices."

I looked in that direction, seeing how the green grass landscape of the foreground appeared to be one and the same with the more distant ground but the subtle hints like the movements of the grass in the light breeze and the colouration betrayed the hidden dip ahead. Waves lapped and softly crashed somewhere ahead and to our right, and I knew that we would be able to see the wide expanse of the sea if we just stood and walked forwards ten paces. I looked at the barely visible line snaking through the grass where the blades had been bent in many places, giving off a different degree of shine as the sunlight reflected to highlight where people had walked recently, and followed it with my eyes to where it disappeared into the hidden ground.

"Fiver says there's a bay down there where they landed," Dan said, pointlessly betting the irrelevance of cash with me. Now, before the world had ended I had a monthly pocket money of fifteen pounds, so bizarrely that irrelevant sum of irrelevant money seemed like a lot to me. To Dan, who earned close to forty thousand pounds a year before everything went wrong, it was nothing, but to me it gave a different sense of how certain he was about his guess.

"Let's find out then," I said, turning to catch his eye. He met my look, showing me an expression I had seen plenty of times before. It was one that promised a good deal of retribution delivered in his own savage style of speed, accuracy and total violence until the job was done. I mirrored that look, my own cruel sense of redressing the balance in the eternal struggle of good versus evil expressing itself with a ghost of a smile.

I turned slowly to Nemesis and made her stay where she was. The dog lay flat on the ground, chin resting on the stiff grass as her eyes never left me. I turned back to my front again and slowly moved myself forwards to cover the last few paces to the lip of the high ground where I could see down into the natural bowl containing the trash-strewn beach below.

I saw the last of them in line climbing up and out of the bay, AK slung over one shoulder casually like it was a handbag, and shuffled myself backwards far quicker than I had reached the position before it was safe to stand and run at a crouch back to Dan and Mitch.

"Another lot of them," I muttered, screwing up my eyebrows as I thought about it, "or maybe the same lot come back again. Either way." I shrugged. "Hostiles."

Hostiles. The simple way of labelling people who weren't us and that we didn't like. Life had become slightly less of an 'us and them' affair since we rescued the Andorrans and established a kind of regional co-operative, but it usually boiled down to that principle.

This lot weren't 'us', not by any stretch of the imagination, so they were 'them'.

"Stay here?" Mitch offered. "Ambush them when they get back?" He seemed to realise the implication as soon as he had said it, but Dan answered anyway.

"And let them do the same to someone else?" he asked, his hushed words filled with force. He stood, throwing caution to the wind to walk forwards and peer over the edge to be sure there were no sentries left behind with the boats. There weren't, and I saw his eyes flick over the landscape like an expert mechanic would do glancing into an engine bay.

"Bugger it," he snarled, seeing what I had seen and knowing that the topography didn't leave any positions to conduct an ambush from. "We follow them until we find an ambush site and lure them back."

"How?" I asked before my brain caught up with my mouth. Dan said nothing, simply lifting one hand up and miming pulling the trigger. Faking a gunfight by their boat should bring them back quick enough, just like rats running for an escape when the lights came on.

We followed, moving faster than we usually did and definitely faster than I liked, but speed was more important than stealth to catch up with them before they found more innocent lives to ruin. Following their movements wasn't difficult, as anything manmade left over from before showed little sign of maintenance or care, and even the remains of the roads not often travelled betrayed the passage of feet unless care was taken. The pirates had traipsed through the dried remains of fallen leaves and trampled grass down with no care for stealth, and to experienced trackers like us they may as well have left glowing markers to show their route, until the wind had swept one patch completely clear to end our trail. None of that mattered, as even if they had tiptoed through the landscape they wouldn't have been able to hide their scent from the noses of our two dogs.

"Where are they, girl?" I hissed quickly to Nemesis to wind up her excitement levels. Behind me Dan did the same with Ash, as though he verbally turned a winding handle in the dog's back to increase the power output. He muttered his own commands, and both dogs set off with their muzzles to the ground to move in random directions until they both caught something at almost the same time. As one, they looked ahead and tracked in a straighter line. We followed, both Dan and I intermittently calling out softly to our dogs so that they didn't stray too far ahead. After half a mile the route we tracked swung a half right and we stopped to look at the remains of a cluster of buildings ahead.

We watched and waited in silence for a few minutes. None of us asked questions as none of us were inexperienced enough to not understand the benefits in watching. Guards got bored and moved around. Ill-disciplined sentries sometimes smoked. Inexperienced snipers shifted position for comfort, or else failed to anticipate where the moving sun would shoot glare into their chosen spot to blind them.

None of these things alerted us to the presence of other people, and I glanced at Dan to see the cogs turning inside his head. His eyes darted to the low roof lines of the single-level buildings. They took in the narrowest point of the tiny settlement where the road contracted to pass between two buildings, offering us an unnaturally natural choke point to exploit. He turned and raised an eyebrow to Mitch, by far the most experienced of us at that form of urban combat, and waited as the soldier considered the ground ahead.

He pointed to himself, then his larger weapon with the underslung grenade launcher which Dan still called a bomb-lobber. He pointed to the low roof of the building near the choke point before detailing me and Dan to cut off positions either side of the killing ground he would create. Dan nodded, then looked at me to enquire about my approval of the plan. I nodded back and rose to tuck the butt of my carbine into my shoulder and begin moving forwards tactically. The dogs seemed to sense when it was time to go to work, as both of them slunk low at our sides in silence, only the occasional scratch of claws on concrete reaching my ears. It must have taken an enormous amount of physical exertion for them to move like that, to keep their tongues inside their heads and stay silent just as it exhausted us moving on bent legs in a state of semi-permanent crouch as we peered intently through our weapon sights.

We moved slowly, cautiously, and at all times at least one of us was in cover providing an overwatch for the others as they moved. Mitch reached his destination and slung his rifle to begin the quiet climb up the metal frame of the fire escape to the low roof. Dan signalled for me to move ahead, leaving the pressure of being the rearmost cut off to himself - not that being the one responsible for stopping any of them escaping inland where there were people to protect was any easier, but anyone escaping on that end would endanger our route home.

As I looked for a place to set up, the world behind me erupted into the brutal sound of an automatic weapon firing.

AMBUSHED

The first thought to bounce around my brain as I involuntarily ducked my head so far into my shoulders that I must have looked like a cartoon character, was that they hadn't even waited for me to get into position before they triggered the lure to bring the pirates back through the tiny village to be killed.

My second thought, arriving hot on the heels of the first and both of them moving quicker than my physical reactions, was that the gunfire didn't come from any weapon we carried with us.

That meant one of many things, but my priority at that point was to get my precious self off the street and into cover quickly. As I threw myself behind the corner of a solid stone building my mind reflected that I probably had it easier than both of the men with me, as I had grown up without doing this kind of thing with the trappings of modern military or police infrastructure; they were used to instant communication with one another whereas I had grown up fighting as we were – in the blind.

I backtracked behind the building line, back towards the heavy clattering of gunfire which, even as I ran, stopped only to be answered by the weak-sounding response of Dan's suppressed weapon drilling rounds in the direction of our unexpected enemy. I knew it was Dan because Mitch carried an unsuppressed weapon as always, and I knew that Dan must have a good idea where the shots had come from because his answering bullets were triggered off in disciplined pairs and weren't blind suppression fire.

As the heavy clatter of more automatic fire filled the air, I could feel the concussive waves of the gunfight I was approaching. Mitch's gun joined the fight, his lighter cracks sounding smaller than the heavy bangs of the other gun. I reached the corner of another building and fast-checked around the edge, whipping my head out and back to take a mental snapshot for analysis.

One shooter, leaning over the roof parapet. Black skin. Thin arms. AK spitting flame a full hand's length away from the end of the barrel as he bared his teeth.

I also saw Dan tucked hard against the building almost directly underneath where the shooter was, trying to flatten himself into the bricks so that no part of him appeared as a target. His left hand clung desperately to Ash's scruff to stop the dog from breaking free into the open.

I took a breath, opened my eyes and readied my gun. Stepping back and around I told Nem to stay and cleared the edge of the building to point my fat barrel at the point where he had been, only to have to twitch it a couple of inches to the right because he had moved. I had a clear view of him from mid-chest upwards, and I fired on instinct with short bursts to explode dust and stone fragments from the lip of the parapet he leaned over. I missed him, but missing him had the bonus effect of forcing him to duck below the ledge for cover.

In a display of utter indiscipline, and to my extreme horror, he pointed the gun over the top of the ledge with one hand and depressed the trigger to send fat bullets flying everywhere uncontrollably.

When I look back at that point it makes me wonder why that was so horrific to me, I mean it wasn't as though the guy wasn't trying to kill us before but somehow the lack of respect he showed the weapon angered me more than when he was aiming it at us.

"Fuck this shit," Dan growled, grabbing my attention back to him for a second. "Ash, *HUP!*"

I'd seen him do this before, mostly to show off and entertain people, but I never thought I would see the trick used in real-life combat. Ash, now released, shot low away from Dan and swung around to take three long strides of hard acceleration towards him. Dan crouched allowing the dog, who moved like a motorcycle off the mark, to leap onto his back as he stood to launch Ash higher into the air. I watched in awe, my finger off the trigger instinctively so as not to shoot the suddenly airborne division of our canine unit, and saw him run vertically up the remainder of the wall with two more bounds to launch himself over the lip and disappear out of sight.

The last I saw of Ash was his tail whipping in circles like a helicopter to balance him as he dropped to the ground on the roof of the low building.

The blind firing stopped, the heavy percussive noise replaced in an instant by the screams cutting over the sounds of snarling and crunching. Beside me Nemesis let out an uncharacteristic bark of frustration. I imagined how she felt, knowing that when Dan was fighting a battle on his own, I would want to be right there beside him to tip the balance in our favour.

The sound of splintering wood made me glance back to Dan in time to see his back disappearing inside the doorway he had just opened with his boot. Silence reigned, other than the weak whimpering and the savage growl emanating from the rooftop we couldn't see, until Dan's voice rang out with a strong command for Ash to leave the man. Half expecting Dan to want to question him I was surprised to hear the double-chug of his weapon cycling two rounds into the man, the sound of the bullets puncturing his chest cavity to tear through bone and tissue echoing louder than the gunshots.

I took cover and pointed my weapon up the road just as I knew Mitch would be doing the same back where we had come from. Dan had whatever was in that building under control, and I couldn't imagine the terror that AK-man would have felt when he thought himself secure on the high ground until a flying wolf landed inside his position to tear him up.

Movement ahead of me caught my eye, making me snatch the barrel to that position and snap the other half of the sight over to add some magnification. It took me a second to locate it, but ahead I could definitely make out another AK in the hands of a similar-looking enemy. He was joined by two others and the three walked back in our direction without even trying to move tactically or use cover.

I lined up a shot and fired three single bullets in rapid succession at the one in the lead, dropping him as he let go of his rifle and clutched at his perforated stomach. I had no time to call a warning as I switched my aim to try and lead the other two with him who had cut and run the second they came under fire. They zigzagged, fleeing my carefully aimed attack and frustrating me enough to flick the switch down to fully automatic. I stitched long bursts at them, hoping to saturate the air around them with what Mitch called righteous freedom pills, and that forced them into cover. My gun clicked dry and my left hand moved automatically to drop the spent magazine and drop it into the pouch I kept empty. My hand came back up holding a charged one which I knew without looking would be orientated the right way around and slid it into the housing to click it home. I kept my eyes on the enemy as I pulled back the charging handle and settled in the fire again.

Just as horrifically as the one dead in the building beside me, these two also flailed their rifles one-handed, spraying bullets in a wide arc covering our general direction.

I ducked back, turning to make sure that Nemesis was still out of sight of the guns and waving Mitch back to the opposite side of the street.

"One down," I shouted as I lifted a single finger to aid his understanding. "Two," another finger lifted, "in cover, firing blind."

Mitch nodded, glancing to his right as Dan poked his head out of the ruined doorway to glance at both of us. Ash's big chops protruded beside Dan's padded knee, his muzzle pink with fresh blood, and Mitch communicated with hand signals for both of us.

He pointed at me, telling me to stay where I was. Looking at Dan he pointed at him and Ash, then to his own chest, before snaking a flat hand in an exaggerated loop around the back of the building they took cover beside. Dan nodded, looking to me to check my understanding. I nodded back, knowing it was my job to pin these bastards in place and exchange fire while they flanked them. To help with that, Dan raised a bloody AK-47 in his hands to show me before sliding it hard across the rough ground and following it up with a fully charged spare magazine. I nodded, watching as they slipped around the back of the building, then flinched as a heavy bullet tore a chunk of stone off the corner of the building above my head and sing out as the round whined off into the distance behind me.

I let my M4 fall on its sling and hefted the AK to yank back the cocking handle as my hands explored the weight and feel of the un-familiar weapon. I brought it up to my shoulder, focused down the iron sights, and squeezed off a short burst.

The recoil and sound of the weapon jarred me, startling me with how aggressive and loud it felt in comparison to my own gun. Rough or not, there was no denying the power of the bullets it fired. I sent burst after ear-splitting burst towards them, stitching the ground around them into plumes of concrete dust to keep their heads down. The magazine was expended in five bursts, and the unfamiliarity of it forced me back into cover as I had to look for the release catch and pull out the spent curved magazine to click the next one in pace. Popping back out of cover I immediately had to duck back as a hand-ful of bullets connected with the building I was hiding behind. One bullet punched through the brick part that offered less resistance than the stone lower section. I looked up, my mind trying to figure out what I was seeing until it clicked: the bullets were coming from behind me.

Rolling back away from the building I choked desperately through the brick dust I'd inhaled to tell Nemesis to come with me. I staggered to my feet just in time to be thrown back down by the solid impact of a body running into mine. The AK flew from my hands like I'd been tackled, and both of us hit the ground to roll with the momentum of the hit. I saw a flash of dark skin. My nose caught the acrid smell of an unwashed body until it was obliterated by fresh dirt getting in my mouth as we rolled together.

I landed on my back, the dead weight of a bigger person pinning me under my carbine which had fallen across my chest and what I guessed was his knee thumping hard in between my legs to shoot agony up my entire body. I opened my eyes, seeing the short hair of the top of a man's head move until yellowed, bloodshot eyes met mine. The stench of his breath would have made me gag if my other senses weren't screaming at me to do something, to move and protect myself with all the savagery and violence I could employ.

My arms were still pinned by the weight of my attacker and by my own weapon. I wriggled and writhed, bucked my hips upwards to create space enough to move, to do *something*, to change the situation, but it didn't work. He recovered, punching down into my chest and stomach hard to drive the air from my lungs before reaching down to wrap his filthy hands around my neck and squeeze. I dropped my chin onto his hands, trying to maintain any airway I could as I knew my body would betray me and start to give up if I was choking. I turned my head from side to side as a desperate whine escaped my mouth, only for that sound to be drowned out by a growl and snarl as Nemesis launched herself at the man.

She bit down hard on the nearest part of his body she could reach, sinking her long teeth into the back of his right leg. He reared up, screaming a guttural noise of pain and fear that only came from being attacked by an animal, and that movement was enough.

I bucked my hips again, pushing myself free enough to pull my right hand out from underneath myself. I snatched for the grip of the Glock on my chest and wrenched it free to hold it in two hands and fast-pull the trigger to punch a dozen rounds into the chest of the bastard on top of me before he even began to fall back down. The sound of the bullets, fired so fast that it could have been automatic, hung in the air as my ears rang painfully.

He slumped over me, hot, sticky blood pouring out of him and onto me in gushing waves. I pushed him off, wriggling away to get to one knee and recover the grip of my carbine, and wipe the blood off my face to see better. Nem still tore at his body, snarling as she wrenched her head from side to side and ripped clothing away complete with chunks of flesh.

More bullets hit the ground around me, and I turned in the direction of the new noise to lay flat and open up on them. I saw two, running in the open and firing wildly from the hip as they advanced with all the enthusiasm of believing themselves invincible but none of the caution that even the most basic of training would have given them.

They fell. Not to my fire but to rounds coming from their right as Mitch and Dan cut them down. I got to my feet, falling back down to one knee as the disorientation of the hit and the close-range gunfire had robbed me of my balance. I raised my gun and Nemesis left the man who was being boring by not fighting back or screaming. She nuzzled at me as my breath came in rapid gasps, the pain of the brief and violent struggle finally hitting me. I doubled over, a small cry of pain escaping my lips making my dog whine and bump me again with her bloody nose.

Dan and Mitch ran to me, both fearing that I had been hurt, and my repeated mumbles about being alright fell on deaf ears as they forced me to lie down to check me over.

Dan told me later that the sight of me covered in blood, literally sheeted from head to toe, terrified him. It took a lot for him to admit feelings, and I only wished he would do it more often to Marie so that she wouldn't take out her fears and frustrations elsewhere. Like at me.

"I'm fine," I said, back in control of my senses and my body as I pushed them away to climb to my feet, "I just got a bit… *wobbly* for a second."

"Where are you cut?" Dan asked again intensely.

"I'm not," I told him, "it's not mine." Their eyes cast to the crumpled body of the man who had fallen on me, revealing for the first time that he was a thin young man who seemed so much smaller in death than he had moments before. A sound far behind us made us spin, weapons raised, to see another one throwing down his weapon as he ran desperately away.

"He's just a kid," Dan said as we all squinted at him through our scopes. A single loud crack of a rifle's report made me jump and flinch again. I slowly straightened to look at Mitch who was lowering his gun, a wisp of gasses escaping the end of the barrel.

"You don't spare the life of a dangerous animal just because it's a young one," he intoned gravely, his face a mask of hatred. "It'll just grow up to be another dangerous bastard."

"Let's get out of here," Dan said, not so much changing the subject as simply dropping it. "I want to be back before the sun starts to go down.

A strange sensation hit me then, one that all women recognise and dread at the wrong moment.

"I, err, I need a minute first," I said, walking off towards the nearest building and slipping inside. I tried to check, even used my bright torch in the dark and dusty interior, but with so much blood covering me and soaking my clothes I couldn't tell whether any of the blood came from me as I feared.

.

REFLECTION

I look back to that point now and I can still recall the fear. I'd never experienced dread like it before then, and never since, but that fear that my desperate fight with a filthy, ragged pirate had caused me to lose my baby lanced through my chest like an ice-cold spear. I said nothing on the journey back, understandably so after having seen the things I had seen and coming too close to getting myself killed.

They didn't know what I was really afraid of, but how could they?

My first stop back at Sanctuary was a shower. I stepped inside without taking anything off and let the cool water fall over me and my kit to run off my boots with a pink tinge. I called Nem to me, forcing her under the water with difficulty to wash away the blood from her face as though seeing her proudly wearing the results of her training would paint her in a different light to people. I stripped my kit off piece by piece and laid it out, transfixed by the diluted blood running from the barrel of my battered carbine. The man's blood had covered me, getting in every nook of my kit and soaking through to my skin where it had dried to a tacky film during the hot walk home. I peeled off my clothes, scrubbing at my skin and hair as I used an entire bottle of the precious shower gel I had so recently liberated. Nemesis had escaped to shake the water from her coat and lie in the corner of the room where she shot hurt looks at me.

My stomach had stopped hurting, but the knowledge that at least some of the blood had come from me made my heart beat faster than I was comfortable with. Dressing in clean clothes without drying myself thoroughly I left my weapons still wet and untended as I walked fast with my head focused on my feet towards medical.

Luckily, I saw nobody on the way, nobody who stopped me to ask me anything anyway, and I knew that Lucien would be on the sea wall looking outwards at the threat and not inwards with a concern he didn't even know he had.

The infirmary was empty, making me go back across the corridor and knock at the heavy wood separating Kate's rooms from the outside world. She called out from inside for whoever it was to come in, and I entered to see her looking up from the chair she sprawled on as her eyes lifted up from the dog-eared paperback she was reading. She took one look at me, at my normal clothes and my subdued bearing, at my wet hair and my face which was already beginning to contort and threatened tears at any moment.

Kate dropped the book without marking the page, some image of a silhouetted man and a dog on the battered cover and rushed to me.

"What's wrong?" she asked as she grabbed my shoulders and tried to look at my face. "Are you hurt? What happened?"

I lowered my face, not wanting anyone to see me cry as I was powerless to stop the tears from flowing. I didn't answer her, just cried and hugged her to bury my face in her shoulder. She stopped asking questions and steered me back to the comfortable seat where she sat me down and held my hands to let me get it out. She didn't push me, didn't force me to speak, just waited until I told her.

"I think…" I sniffed and cuffed at my eyes. "I think I lost my baby today..."

Kate hugged me tightly, letting me cry until it all came out. She didn't admonish me for going out into danger despite being pregnant, wasn't cross with me for lying to her about feeling sick that morning, simply held me and let me pour out my fear and pain because nothing she could do could prevent the worst from happening, if it was actually happening. When I stopped and sat up, panicking slightly as my nose was full of snot and threatening to drip, she handed me a handkerchief without even checking if it was clean or not.

She stood, holding out her hand to me and pulled me to my feet to lead the way across the corridor and into the rooms that were our hospital. She sat me down, turning away and coming back with a small plastic pot and gesturing for me to go to a small room to do what she needed me to do. I came back, pot in hand in a daze and sat as she dipped a stick into it and rested it on the top of the plastic. She passed the time by checking my pulse and blood pressure again, probably just so that the wait wasn't filled with painful silence.

"How far gone do you think you are?" she asked.

"I've missed this month and last month," I explained. She nodded her understanding.

"Have you eaten anything today?"

"Yes," I said, thinking back to when I last ate something and figuring out it had been hours. As though my body had been reminded, my stomach growled audibly. "Actually, not for a while now..."

Kate smiled, turning away again and coming back with a wrapped chocolate bar which she handed to me. I smiled. She knew I had a sweet tooth and these things were rare nowadays. They were so full of chemicals and preservatives that we had evolved away from that when the sugar hit my senses it set me alight like a drug. Sugar was a drug, at least it had been before, and I had listened to Kate moaning that it was a killer that had enslaved the human race, being responsible for more health issues than smoking and drinking put together.

The distraction of the chocolate worked, and the test had given her the results before I realised it.

"Good news," she said smiling at me, "but let's be sure because hormones are funny things." With that she dug around in a drawer, rummaging as though she looked for something she didn't need to use often. Turning back to me her hands held an off-white box with a springy cable hanging from it. She fumbled with the cable, running her hand down it to raise up what looked like a tiny microphone at the end. "Lean back for me?"

I did, reclining stiffly on the old patient couch and feeling every part of the fight I'd had that day. I lifted my top, suddenly feeling self-conscious for some reason, and Kate asked me to unfasten my belt. I did, and she squirted a small sachet of something directly on my skin.

"Ahh, cold!" I gasped, as though that mild discomfort was anything in comparison to what I'd been through that day.

"Sorry chick," Kate said, pressing the small microphone onto my skin and moving it around as she twirled the dial on the box in her other hand. Tense seconds passed by as I held my breath, convincing myself that nothing would be there and the positive test had been a trick.

"There," Kate breathed, turning the volume up and meeting my eyes with a smile.

The sound I heard next was both terrifying and amazing. The rapid, echoing, swooshing sound of a tiny heartbeat fluttering inside me put the world in sudden perspective.

My tears started again as relief and stress poured out of me. She hugged me once more, letting me cry onto her and purge the emotion until it dried up and I re-emerged from the state I had fallen into. I sat up, dried my eyes and blew my nose again. I folded the handkerchief carefully, concentrating on the small actions as a reason to keep my eyes down and say nothing.

"Want to talk about it?" Kate asked me. I took a breath, looking up at the ceiling and holding it for a long time before I blew it out through my pursed lips.

"I didn't know how I felt until today," I said in a voice that didn't sound like my own. "When I thought…" I screwed my eyes shut to stop from crying again and took a few moments to gather myself. "When I thought I'd lost it, I nearly fell apart. If I was here and not out there with Dan and Mitch, I don't know what I would've done. The stupid thing is that I'm scared to tell him, and even more scared to tell Marie because…" I faltered, realising that Kate would obviously know about her miscarriage and shaking my head to clear my own stupidity, "because of her issues. She really *wants* another baby, and I don't even know if I can cope with this…"

"You can," Kate said, "if you want to. You'll have help, you'll have support, and you'll never have to do any of this on your own."

I looked at her, seeing her eyes reflecting her genuine words, and cuffed at my eyes again as I nodded. I did want this baby, and the terror of nearly dying along with the fear of thinking I had lost it just served to solidify that in my mind. I slid down from the bed I was sat on, mumbling my thanks for her time as I headed for the door for the second time that day.

"You need to stop going outside of the walls though," she told me, "that includes going out to sea." I stopped, turning to look at her.

"No, I need to stay active," I told her, "we've literally got wolves at the door and you want to take one of our best pieces off the table?"

"It's for the best, for you and the ba—"

"No," I said, "don't do that. If I don't stop these fucking *animals*, then there won't be anywhere to raise a baby. There won't be anything here left at all. You saw what they did to the guy who made it here?" She swallowed and nodded, making me guess that she'd already heard a version of what we had found at the settlement. "Well they did worse to the others," I said. "I watched Dan pick up a man's head by the hair today. We had to burn the bodies together because we couldn't see which bit went with which body. You hear what I'm saying? You see why I can't take a back seat now?"

Kate nodded, clearly biting her lip to stop her from saying something else. She let me go without saying another word, so I walked back to my room to spend a couple of hours cleaning the blood from every part of my kit and my weapons.

Because I was damned sure going to be ready when we saw them again.

THE WAITING GAME

I had sworn Kate to secrecy which was a promise I was certain she would keep right up until the point when she thought I was putting myself in danger, then she would blurt it out just to get others to keep me in line. She would wholly believe that she was doing what was best for my health, for my baby's health, but I knew I'd do all I had to do to keep everyone else safe from the threat.

I hated being under siege. The massive ship just sat there, anchored out to sea to block our access to the deeper waters holding the fish we needed to create our excess food stores for the coming winter. We never had to think of these things before, not when food came from shops or was just delivered to your door, but I knew all too well that if we didn't overproduce and store or trade it then we would be in for a hard winter.

We'd had hard winters before, when the population of our town had increased rapidly, but back then we could fall back on stores of canned food and the foil packets of the military ration packs. We had even cleared out almost all of the stores of dried pasta, rice and flour, and I mentally planned another trip inland to the hypermarché. I abandoned the thought, knowing that sparing the personnel for it would mean hardship or gaps in the defences for those left behind.

It wasn't just the physical hardships of living under constant threat of attack; the mental pressure started to show some cracks in people that would likely never have come out otherwise. Dan ran patrols up the coastline to discourage any further forays to land, and after returning to gather the bodies of the pirates we had killed he had piled them into their boat and piloted it back to anchor it off our bay.

He hoped it would serve as a warning, as a sign that anyone sent ashore would not come back.

"Why do we have a boat full of dead bodies just sat there?" Marie asked me one morning as she walked with my little brother down to the shoreline for a closer look. I guessed she was looking for Dan as he had a habit of hiding when it came to difficult conversations about his feelings. She pulled a knitted shawl tighter around her shoulders as she stood to talk to me, feeling the speed of the breeze pick up closer to the open water. The air was warm even early in the morning but somehow the sea always provided a chill to those not expecting it.

"They might come in handy," I told her, sounding just like Neil every time someone asked why there was half an outboard motor sitting untouched in a corner.

"*Handy...*" Marie started, trailing off as I guess she realised she really didn't want to know. She shook her head and turned away, wandering over to Dan who stared out to sea as though the hulking ship would do something at any moment. She looped her hand inside his arm and rested her head against his shoulder as he seemed to come back into the real world to lean his body into hers. He reached down to bring their son into the embrace and I just watched as the three of them stood there, frozen in time for a moment.

"Hello? Earth to Leah?" Lucien's voice cut into my thoughts and burst my bubble. He opened his mouth to speak again but stopped, his eyes focussing further down on my body to where I had unconsciously placed a hand just under my belt buckle. I took it away quickly, pulling a face that I hoped would signify I had some discomfort in my stomach and not what it really was.

"What?" I asked. "Sorry, I was miles away."

"Oh," he said, "okay." He seemed flustered and confused but recovered enough to tell me what he wanted to say. "The farm, they have send someone to tell us that they"—he pointed a hand out to sea—"have been seen near their walls."

I didn't have to ask how they knew it was 'them'. Appearances were fairly obvious, and even though a good portion of our population weren't white skinned, the arrival of strangers with AK-47s made it pretty obvious that they weren't locals. I whirled away, calling Dan to me in a tone of voice that achieved instant compliance.

"What is it?" he asked as I took long strides up the sloping stone walkway towards the castle and the gates of our town.

"They're ashore," I said, knowing that Dan wouldn't have to ask who 'they' were either, "near the farm." I turned to Lucien. "Where's the messenger?"

"Gatehouse," he replied, his face resolute as he flanked me beside Dan.

"*Je m'appelle Leah*," I told him, "can you tell me what you saw?" He nodded like a demented dog watching a juicy bit of fried chicken waving through the air before him, and started to babble in rapid French so heavily accented that I struggled to make out most of what he said. I turned to Lucien who translated to fill the gaps.

"He says they came two days before. He says they just stand

192

near the farm and watch, they do not come near the walls." The 'walls' were a joke in human terms, merely a wooden palisade designed to prevent predators from stealing livestock and pets. The wolf population had thrived in the absence of more humans and every couple of years we had to lead a cull on their numbers in case they threatened our dubious spot at the top of the local food chain.

"Ask him why they didn't use the pigeons," I said, turning back to the man and speaking in frustration.

"*Les pigeons?*" Lucian added the rest of the question like it was an interrogation. The man babbled again, the occasional word reconciling itself in my mind before stopping and glancing between us nervously.

"He said they have…" He dropped back into French again to clarify and spoke to me in English. "He said they have—"

"Falcons," I said understanding the word he used well enough to get a vague translation.

"Birds of prey," Lucien added for clarity, glancing between me and Dan. "How did they know to…" He trailed off, figuring out that the torture of the homesteaders must have included some questioning. It also answered the question as to why one man arrived at their gate having pretty much run all the way to get help.

"How many?" Dan asked. "*Combien?*" The man shrugged, throwing out random numbers which told me had literally no idea. Dan turned to Lucien. "Anything else? Any information on them?" As Lucien quizzed the man in more depth, I took a step back to stand beside Dan.

"We going?" I asked.

"Mmmhmm."

"Today?"

"Mmmhmm."

"Good," I said, "how many?"

"Maximum of ten," Dan told me, "all fit. All experienced fighters. Leave enough good people to cover the walls and the bay." I nodded and turned away, all feelings of generalised nausea and tiredness forgotten in an instant when there was work to do.

My first stop was Mitch, apologising to Alita as my knock at their door sparked a sudden and high-pitched crying from their baby girl. Mitch, a light sleeper at the best of times thanks to his years of cat-napping at any and every opportunity in the infantry, emerged wearing just his boxer shorts and a confused look. I had forgotten he had taken the night shift and would have had only a few hours' sleep.

"Sorry," I said, ignoring his appearance which told him that the visit wasn't a social one. I turned to Alita and smiled another apology. "I need to steal him…"

Alita turned to Mitch and smiled a frustrated smile as she tried to rock their little girl back into a relaxed state. "Away with you both, then," she said in her strange accented English, having learned most of her sayings from Mitch. He gave me a nod which I took as my cue to wait outside and he disappeared back up the stairwell to re-emerge a couple of minutes later in fatigue trousers and a T-shirt. He wore a gun on his right thigh, more out of habit than anything else, but didn't appear in full combat gear.

"Job?" he asked as he fell in step beside me on the walk back up from the seaward part of town.

"Job," I confirmed. "They've got inland somehow, and have used hawks to bring down the farm's carrier pigeons. They haven't attacked yet, at least they hadn't by this morning, and Dan wants to go and have a look at them.

Mitch knew as well as I did what he meant by 'having a look at them'.

"When?" he asked.

"Today."

"How many?"

"Me, you, him," I said, "and up to seven more. Capable but not all of our best. Don't want to leave this place short."

"That means one of us should stay back here," he said. I shot a knowing glance in his direction. I knew he wouldn't be volunteering to stay behind, and he knew that I wouldn't either. The thought that Dan would agree and decide to stay behind the walls would have been funny under other circumstances.

~

It took close to two hours to gather the six people who met the criteria to come, and who had volunteered because to my knowledge nobody had ever been ordered on a mission. We paired them off as they drew weapons from the armoury and each took a pair under our respective commands. Trained operators they weren't, but they were fit and dedicated and they knew how to work their weapons properly.

We'd trained like this, using militia as fire support and coached them accordingly. The upside of this was that they saw how to operate, so had a visual training package to follow. The training was something that I and others had conducted weekly, but with the arrival of the bloody pirates all of that had fallen away.

I travelled light as we all did, checking over my backup and stripping them of the unnecessary things they tried to take as I got them to turn out their emergency bags. We took enough to survive if we had to spend the night outside the walls, as Dan had warned us to prepare for, and I added the thigh pouch on my right leg to hold two spare magazines for the heavy rifle I planned to take.

A hand on my shoulder stopped me and I fought back the impulse to react as though it was a threat. I knew that touch, somehow instinctively, and I reached up to place my own hand on top of Lucien's as I turned.

"It should be me going instead of you," he said softly as he snaked his hands around my waist to smoothly bring himself closer.

"Why?" I shot back half seriously, as I reacted to the sudden change in temperature I felt because of the rush of blood his hands on me caused. "Because you are *ze man*?" I mocked playfully. "Because a girl can't go out and fight while her boyfriend stays at home and cooks?"

He frowned at the metaphorical bait. "I'm hardly cooking and cleaning when you are out fighting a war," he said sternly. "You leave me in command of the defences here and say that I cannot come with you?"

"No," I told him, "you can't come."

"Why?" he asked in the same tome I had used.

"Because I want to protect you as much as you want to protect me, but"—I raised myself up on my tiptoes to kiss him softly—"I'm better at this than you are," I told him with a smirk as I pulled away. He smiled back, reaching past me without taking his eyes off mine to pick up the leg pouch with the spare ammo for the big rifle, and handed it to me.

"Come back safely to me," he said with another playful smile as he turned to leave, "or else."

WHITE FLAG

Leah leaned back from her chair again, pushing the heavy ledger away and resting the pen gently down, looking out of the window to see the sun was setting and the light in the room had faded to the point where she couldn't see well enough to continue.

She had gone back to her work after spending an hour with Adalene beside the sea, talking and laughing with her daughter before she forced herself back into the uncomfortable memories of the time when she was first pregnant.

Some memories were fun to recount. They took her back to happy times, times when people she loved were still with them, still young and full of life. It hurt her to think of the people she missed; it actually ached in her chest but with that loss came the flush of happiness that she ever knew them in the first place.

She stood, stretching out her back until the rewarding cracks of things realigning along her vertebrae sounded loudly in the small room. She reached into her leg pocket and pulled out the metal lighter she had carried for years. She turned it around in her fingers to regard it and all the memories it carried before gripping it tightly and flicking off the lid with her thumb to bring the digit back own and strike the wheel to produce a rippling flame. She watched the dancing orange flicker for a moment before she picked up a candle and tipped the wick to the flame. She lit another and placed them on the desk near her work but realised that even with the light from the candles she couldn't see well enough to continue.

"That's enough for today, I think," she said as she snapped her fingers to get the attention of the sleeping dog. Ares, twisted on his back with his front and rear paws resting in opposite directions, flailed as he fought to right himself in one movement. Leah chuckled at the dog, thinking of how daft Ash was when she had first seen him. She really hoped that Ares would grow into his legs along with his ears, and that he would locate another level, another gear in his maturity because she was sad to think that he didn't have the required streak of savagery to be what she needed him to be.

She blew out the candles and patted her leg for the dog to follow her, stooping inside the door to retrieve the battered gun she had been using in the story she was writing down. Knowing it would be too early for another meal, not that she was overly hungry having eaten a late lunch, she took a walk along the ramparts as she had done so many times in her life.

The sun wasn't fully setting yet, but it was starting to sink over the cliffs on the western side of the bay, dropping down behind the watchtower where Lucien had admitted to watching her when he was stationed there for his sharp eyes and his skills of long-distance shooting. She chuckled at that memory too, only a few years before the time she had spent all day recounting, but still fresh in her memory. His admission about watching her had been turned around when she asked if he had been pointing a rifle at her, and he responded that he had the safety catch on.

"Peaceful, ain't it?" Joshua said from behind her as he walked quietly along the ramparts. Part of her suspected that he had spoken so as not to startle her by appearing close by, but she smiled and responded.

"I like it up here," she said, "always have."

"Top o' the world, sure enough," Joshua said wistfully as he gazed out to sea. Leah looked in the same direction, happy that the massive eyesore of the tanker she had been remembering was no longer there, no longer a part of their world. Joshua seemed to know what was on her mind. Their conversation the previous evening and her admission of why she wanted to drag painful memories from the past back to the front of their minds had bonded them a little more. He already felt an affinity, a platonic but affectionate sense of closeness to the young woman who had saved his life by not taking it with a bullet. Though in the months that followed his health declined and he felt confusion and resented her for not taking the shot and scrubbing out his misery right there and then. He had forgiven her for not killing him, as bizarre as that sounded, as much as he had been grateful for her saving his life, and whichever way those feelings affected him his sense of debt to her was strong.

He repaid it then with a few minutes of companionable silence spent gazing out over the darkening skies of Sanctuary before she spoke to him.

"Guess which bit I've got to in the story," she asked.

"Well, given your contemplative state," Joshua said carefully, "I'd say you had to take a break at that part when y'all went off spoilin' for another fight."

Stripped to bare arms covered only by gloves and elbow pads, an addition I'd dug out before leaving, I regretted wearing a vest top instead of a short-sleeved T-shirt. The small bag on my back, despite being strapped down as tight as it could be, rubbed the bare skin of my shoulders and chafed annoyingly. The big rifle didn't help, and after I had to resort to carrying that with my carbine strapped to my backpack Mitch had seen me struggling and offered to carry it for a while.

I accepted, because there was no time to stop and get more comfortable; we had a lot of ground to cover and we didn't want to be trying to make an approach as the sun was setting because that happened fast this far south.

The trading post, the abandoned building we had cleared and repaired so many years ago to act as a central point for our scattered settlements of friends and allies, stood proudly in the open ground far ahead of us. Dan called a halt and raised his gun to look ahead so I took back my 417 from Mitch and used the far more powerful optic to bring the building into closer view.

"I don't see anything," I said after a good half minute of watching.

"Doesn't mean there isn't anything," Mitch grumbled back like it was an automated response.

"We go," Dan said, "two down the flanks and one straight down the road." I knew who he would choose to go straight down the road, to be in the most danger of all of us, and I knew that me trying to tell him not to go himself would just be ignored. I looked at Mitch, pointing that I would go right, and he nodded to head off left. We all went with our respective pairs of militia in support, heading for the building like a three-pronged spear. Mitch's group and mine moved as tactically as we could, skirting the dips beside the repaired road as Dan walked tall and proud towards the trading post as though nothing was amiss in the world. His body might be sending out those signals, but I knew his eyes would be darting to every part of the landscape like he was being electrocuted.

I reached the position I had chosen to be able to fire on the building and cover the only other door in and out other than the front entrance. Pointing to where I wanted them, my team spread out to wait in professional silence as we watched Dan walk up to the building. I couldn't see them, but I knew Mitch and his two would be opposite our position somewhere with their guns up and ready too.

Dan stopped, Ash stopping beside him, and I imagined the low, throaty growl coming from him. I don't know why or how, maybe something about his body language, but I knew the dog was sounding his patented alarm. Dan raised his weapon as he dropped into a crouch and said something to send his two fighters ahead to the wall of the building. I saw this clearly, saw his lips moving through the powerful magnification of the big scope, and at once my heart began to bang in my chest and my breathing sped up. I forced both to slow down, at least I tried to, as I knew what uncontrolled adrenaline did to my accuracy at distance.

Dan went inside, Ash beside him as Nemesis grumbled at my side somehow sensing that there was action happening and she was being forced to watch. Tense seconds passed by as the three of them stayed out of sight inside the trading post until one of the militia ran outside and dropped to his knees, his rifle clattering to the roadway as he arched his back and vomited.

"Oh, this does not look good," I said as much to myself as anyone else, standing and slinging the rifle diagonally over my shoulder only for it to rest awkwardly against my bag and half choke me as I ran forwards. Dan came out before I got there, heading me off and dropping his gun on its sling to block me from going inside.

"What is it?" I demanded, trying to push past him. "Is it Roland?"

"Don't go in there," Dan said, holding me firmly.

Roland had been at the trading post almost every time I had passed through since it had been reclaimed and made a part of our world. He was starting to get old but not so much that it slowed him down, and I marvelled at how someone who spent a lot of their time alone knew the comings and goings of every settlement in the entire area. He was a hub of gossip, a lover of dogs, and I was incensed that someone could have hurt him.

I pushed Dan's hands off me and sidestepped him. He let me go, not wanting to escalate and actually take me down if I was intent on going inside, and afterwards a big part of me wished I hadn't seen what they had done.

The supplies, the neatly stacked food and water and other tradeable items were scattered all over the place. Whole shelves had been pulled to the floor just to wreck the contents for no reason other than sheer destructiveness. My eyes kept panning, taking in the carnage as it unfolded, until they rested on a congealing, oily puddle of dark brown on the ground. I stepped forwards, not seeing anything in the puddle and naively hoping that whoever had lost that much blood was still alive.

My gaze stopped on an abnormal item for the post: a rope tied against a fixed metal railing leading upwards to the cavernous pitched roof. Dreading what I was about to see, I followed the line of the rope upwards until I saw the butchered body of a man hung by his feet. He was stripped naked, sliced and stabbed in a thousand places and left to drip blood onto the floor like so much meat.

Scratch that, I told myself, *nobody I know would even treat their food like this.*

"We're losing the light," Dan said outside, "three miles to the farm. Let's move."

I stormed outside, walking right up to him and speaking in a low growl as Nemesis whined at the threshold of the building still not wanting to step a paw inside. It was as though she could sense what had happened and feared it.

"We can't leave him like this."

"And we won't," Dan answered equably, "but the time for that isn't now." The look he gave me made it clear that this wasn't negotiable, but leaving Roland hung there like that was too much to bear.

"Can't we at least cut him down?" I pleaded quietly.

"For the wolves and rats and god knows what else to chew at him?" he shot back. "Leave him where he is. We'll deal with him properly later, okay?"

It wasn't, but I had little choice in the matter.

We moved towards the farm, faster but more alert than before. Twice I thought I saw movement on the higher ground as though watchers pulled away from the skyline when we approached, and I didn't know if it was my imagination or instinct that slowed me before the road swung sharply to the left in the direction of the farms.

"Stop," I called, waiting as the noises of boots on the rough roadway slowed and stopped to be replaced by heavy breathing as we all fought to regain our breath. I caught eyes with Dan and pointed upwards at the higher bluff of ground which would lead back down to the road we would have to take on the other side of the bend. He nodded, telling the others to take a break.

I made Nemesis wait by Mitch and carried on, my pace slowing involuntarily as the ground angled sharply upwards. I was forced to stop running quickly, instead taking long strides until the ground became so steep I had to all but crawl up it. Slowing as I reached the crest I turned to survey the lush valley below and picked out some of the others in their obvious positions of cover. Nobody showed themselves, but I knew that didn't mean they weren't there.

Crawling slowly, I reached the summit and peered over to see that my suspicions had been right and my caution rewarded. I peered through the small binoculars from a pouch in my vest for long enough to know what was going on and slithered back down to pull my carbine up and rapidly hit the button of the flashlight attached to the barrel. I waited, seeing the answering blink of the same torch attached to Dan's weapon.

He was watching.

I held up both hands, every digit extended deliberately to signify the number five on one hand and a single finger on the other. The torch flashed once. I pulled my weapon up to locate Dan in the optic and flashed once in return. He pointed to himself, snaking his hand around the bluff of land, then pointed at me before making a gun shape with his raised thumb and extended forefinger to point it at me and drop the hammer of his thumb.

I'll go around in the open, he said, *you stay on overwatch and shoot if I say to.*

As far as plans went it was simple, if pretty risky. I shuffled along the ridgeline about a dozen paces until I nestled into a position and brought the rifle up. It was all I could do to not start taking shots, to start taking *heads*, until Dan had spoken to them. I saw AKs. PKMs. Machetes. I saw pirates relaxing around a crude roadblock made of a few branches dragged into the road and a small fire burning beside their position.

It took Dan a few minutes to come into sight of them, the first I knew of it being their panicked movements as they scrambled to pick up their weapons and point them at him.

He emerged alone, having left Ash out of sight because he never liked taking the dog into a kill zone, and walked towards them holding his carbine up with the butt on his right shoulder.

And a white rag stuffed in the barrel.

THE ART OF NEGOTIATION

Dan sat Ash down and gave him a stroke on his big head in case this was the last time he ever saw his best friend. Telling him to stay, he pulled a cleaning rag that had once been white, or at least white enough, from a pouch and stuffed it into the end of his barrel before taking a deep breath to steady himself.

He walked slowly, taking his time and trying to stay calm because he didn't trust himself not to open up on the bastards out of anger or fear - both emotions were running neck and neck for the lead - the second he saw them. He saw them before they saw him, lounging around without any discipline, angering him further because of their unprofessionalism.

They aren't soldiers, he reminded himself, *they're scum. They're animals.*

They fell over themselves to snatch up weapons and run to line the road ahead of him, not fanning out to flank his approach or taking cover at all. His face contorted as he fought to control his disgust at them. He walked, not speeding up or slowing down in response to their reaction until he stood his ground ten paces from them.

"What do you want?" he asked them. Their faces scanned among themselves as no clear leader emerged. He asked the question again, raising his voice and frightening them. He didn't want to make them react, mostly because he didn't want to test the ballistic properties of his old vest against a hail of up-close 7.62. He was pretty sure how that would turn out. Instead he wanted them flustered, scared and confused.

"Who's in charge?" he barked, taking a step forwards and repelling them like they were afraid he was contagious. "Is it you?" he asked the one nearest to him. He just shouted back in a language Dan didn't understand so he turned to another and took a pace forwards, his gun still held in a way so as not to offer any threat. "Are you in charge?" he snapped at the terrified man.

"What do *you* want?" an accented voice demanded. Dan looked in the direction of the voice as the only man not to have jumped up to grab a weapon stood. He stooped to pick up a gun with a folded stock and an elongated, curved magazine. He held a small stick, a tree root if Dan had to guess, in one hand and pointed it at him as he spoke.

"You come to here," he said as he put the root back in his mouth to his molars and chewed on it, "and you shout at my men like you are the king of these hills." He waved a hand around grandly, secure in the false knowledge that he had the upper hand.

"So *you're* in charge then?" Dan asked with a smile. He lifted his left hand up, making the symbol for a gun once more with his empty hand. He didn't glance up at the high ground to his left because he knew precisely where his daughter would be.

I saw the interaction between Dan and the man. It was clear to me before I even got the signal what was about to happen, and I gently nudged the safety catch forward on the 417 as Dan lifted his finger and gave the signal.

My mind wandered back to a story Lexi once told me. It had taken her close to three years to laugh again after her ordeal at the hands of the psychotic Frenchman who had tortured her for information about us. She told me of the time they went to a place which was now legend, even among the children born at Sanctuary after the battle of Slaver's Bay had taken place. She told me how she and Steve had climbed to the rooftops before the sun broke the horizon to be in place for the plan to work. She told me how she had shivered as she waited, freezing half to death as she lay as still as possible, waiting for the time to go to work and worrying that she would be shivering too much to shoot straight or else her frozen fingers wouldn't move. The way she described it seemed more like the effects of adrenaline to me than it did actual cold, but she was a delicate woman after her suffering and I didn't like to interrupt her.

She laughed as she told me how Dan was wearing colourful clothes that somehow made him look far less intimidating, not 'Dan' like at all, and how he went through some strange and ridiculous warmup routine before pointing his empty hand at the monster who called himself Bronson. I knew that part of the story wasn't overly embellished, as Dan himself had told me that the man must have been six-six or six-seven at least; a head taller than him and twice as wide.

Her eyes seemed to glaze out of focus and her voice grew quiet as she spoke about the killing: the moment when Dan levelled his empty hand at the huge man and pulled his imaginary trigger for Steve to end the man's life in a heartbeat, before she took her toll on the slavers to rack up a body count that she used to be proud of.

I watched and waited for the signal, only taking the shot in the instant Dan's cocked thumb dropped to his hand. I wasn't watching my target, I knew where that was and it was firmly in the middle of my crosshairs; I was watching Dan's hand.

The report of my first shot sounded impossibly loud over the open landscape and echoed far off into the distance as my second and third rounds drilled into the confused group below who were so close I couldn't miss.

Dan had dropped to the deck as soon as he had fired his make-believe gun. I was vaguely aware of how fast he moved as I made sure to keep his body out of my sights. I remember thinking that, all things considered, he moved pretty well for a man who must be what? Forty-three? Forty-four?

I continued to line up my shots and time them perfectly to take down targets one after another until none remained a threat.

Only one of them moved. He was dragging himself across the dusty ground with one limp leg trailing blood, his hands fighting desperately for purchase to claw his way closer to the fallen weapon fixed firmly in his sight. Dan stood, walking towards the crawling man to place a dusty boot on the back of his wounded leg making him cry out in pain and fear. He stepped to his side, rolling him over with a boot to expose the damage my shot had done to him: the front of one knee was all but gone.

His hands fluttered as the barrel of Dan's gun, now devoid of the white flag of truce, pointed directly at his face. I saw lips moving but heard no words as I watched intently. My tactical awareness came back to me, overriding my need to know what was happening down there, and I scanned the rest of the terrain for signs of more enemies. There were none; no silhouettes on ridgelines and no reflections of binoculars or similar. I panned back to Dan who startled me as I hadn't heard a shot from his weapon, but the man he had been questioning had evidently been dispatched. I fumbled for my carbine, seeing the same image of his below me only zoomed out, and flashed the light at him to say I was watching. His hand signals given clearly, I turned to point the weapon down towards Mitch and hit the light again, seeing his answering flash. Relaying the instructions for them to join Dan, I slung my weapons and began the awkward scramble down the steep slope.

Much like the steps, those hundreds of stone steps leading from Sanctuary to the fort high above that somehow never seemed to be the same height or shape, going *down* a steep incline was harder on the body than going *up* it.

The constant pressure on my ankles as my body fought to arrest the momentum aided by gravity was painful, and by the time I could stand tall and go with the laws of physics to run the last section and allow my movement to slow naturally the others had arrived. Nemesis ran to my side before I'd reached flat ground to check I was still the same as when I had forced her to part from me.

The militia fighters, either under instruction or by themselves, had begun to gather up the weapons and spare ammunition belonging to the pirates to take it back and bolster our defensive capabilities for a few minutes or months or years longer.

"What did he say?" I asked Dan, my voice strained with the effort to get my breath back.

"Not much," he replied, walking past me to start pulling at the woeful barricade and open the road up again. He kicked at the fire to snuff it out and snapped his fingers for Ash to join him and sent him ahead with the command to search. Guessing what he was doing

I added Nem to the task and stood as we watched them work.

Both of them picked up a trail going back along the road and began to follow it until a short, sharp whistle from me caught my dog's attention. Holding up a hand for her to wait for me, the signal for her to sit, I waited for the others to be ready before we set off to follow.

At the lead beside Dan I asked him a question in a low voice.

"Isn't there supposed to be something about respecting a flag of truce?" I enquired as delicately as I could.

"Yes," he replied flatly, "only not for these bastards, and it's not like any of them are going to tell their little pirate mates about it."

Valid point, I thought.

Urgent hand signals were given, splitting our group up into three parts again as we silently established a firing group and two flanking moves. They had set up their camp, either intentionally or by dumb luck, in a perfect spot where the natural depression of the ground offered a reprieve from the elements. Even at that time of year the wind speed had the same chilling effect there as it did by the sea, and the green bowl they occupied kept them safe from it.

I say occupied; I meant the bowl they *had* occupied, because it was clear when we arrived that they were gone. We organised a search of the surrounding area but no other trace of them remained. They were gone.

"Rest here, head back, or go to the farm?" Mitch asked, laying out our only real options.

"Farm," Dan said, "make sure the bastards haven't gone there. We'll head home in the morning."

The farm took us another ten minutes to reach as the sun was beginning to set, and despite being frightened and on edge at being circled by the sharks, the people living there were unharmed. We walked inside the low wooden palisade wall past the farmers defending their home with a mixture of military weaponry and what amounted to sharp sticks, and we were welcomed with relief to be given food and warm greetings.

"Tell me, Leah," a familiar voice asked me in French to take my breath away with shock, "did you pass through my trading post?"

"Roland?" I said as I spun around to face the old man who smiled at me through his random assortment of teeth. Despite not knowing him that well I threw my arms around him in pure relief that he was still alive, only to stop and worry that he would know who the butchered man strung up to the ceiling had been.

"Roland," I said gravely, needing him to know that the news was bad but not willing to tell him the details, "who was left at the post?" The old man frowned, the frown melting and merging into a look of concern, then into one of tragedy and loss.

"It is Christophe," he said, his mind not yet fully comprehending my use of the past tense. I tried to keep my face neutral, but I must have shown some relief that it was a name I didn't recognise, and so selfishly relieved that I didn't have to grieve for a man I knew personally.

"I'm sorry, Roland," I said simply. Inadequately. He left me then, thankfully not asking questions about the specifics.

We were fed and given a place to sleep. Dan hated being away from Sanctuary, as did I, but I could feel the physical tension radiating from him like anxiety waves as he lay a few feet away from where I slept. I tried to sleep anyway, but my own nerves and stress kept me awake throughout portions of the night, and although I didn't know it at the time it was for good reason.

NIGHT OPERATIONS

Ahmad Gareer had taken a personal lead to dealing with the people inside that small fortified town on the edge of the coast nestled between the cliffs. He had sent crews out on small crafts in the dark of night moving slowly so that the people watching their mothership, their fuel tanker, had no idea how many men he had sent ashore.

It took only five days for them to return just after dark with news of the building at the fork in the road and the secrets the lone man there had yielded. Many of his crew were French speakers, and although the dialect there was very different they retained enough common vocabulary to speak.

The pirate leader, once a terrorist and internationally wanted criminal, moved his pieces around the chessboard. He had sent a crew ashore intentionally to spread fear and panic among the people inside the walled town that he wanted for himself, and he had to admit that the stories of what they had done, and the few women they had brought back to his ship alive, was a reward greater than any he had hoped for. He was certain that the men and women inside those walls would be enraged and terrified in equal measures. He wanted them angry, just as he wanted them scared, because that way he could manipulate their responses.

The only setback of his plan was the loss of the entire crew who had done such a fine job at spreading terror he had sent them back for another turn. A day later he looked through the massive set of binoculars that had hung from the arm of the ship's captain's chair, which he had taken as his throne, and saw their skiff anchored in the bay. He assumed them dead or captured but had no concerns of what they would tell anyone under interrogation, even if they told of everything they knew.

Gareer had a ship, they could say. They had come from East Africa. He had crews numbering close to fifty armed men. He had sent them ashore to have fun.

They could say nothing more of the plan because the only man among them to know it was him.

"*Boqor*?" a voice said from the open doorway of the tanker's bridge.

"What do you want?" he answered, not looking at the skinny youth who spoken to him as a mark of his superiority.

"It's the boat," he said, "they are signalling us." Gareer stood, snatching up the binoculars as he walked to the platform outside of the bridge. That bridge, like many large ships, was at the stern of the vessel and built high above to offer a commanding view ahead. He raised the powerful binoculars and scanned for half a minute, not wanting to ask where the crew was, until he located the boat in the distance towards the west, with the open expanse of the Atlantic behind them. They flashed a powerful ship's light towards the tanker giving the agreed signal.

"Signal them back," Gareer ordered, "and prepare everyone; we go ashore tonight."

The agreed signal, a simple one to inform the leader that the fighters had left the safety of their walls, meant that Gareer could launch his offensive on the town that he mistakenly thought would be unprotected. He wasn't to know that there were more than enough capable defenders left behind, but that he was banking on the best fighters being far from home was a sound strategy and one that no doubt worked.

"*Mamon?*" a little voice said from the doorway that Leah hadn't noticed creak open. Leah, startled but suppressing her reaction to swear loudly, turned and smiled at her daughter.

She's definitely yours, she thought, *she could sneak up on anything.*

"You know," she told Adalene after she had stopped her heart from thumping double time, "your grandfather would say we have to put a bell on you."

The girl frowned as she thought. "He says this all the time," she said in her accented English which she often mixed with fluent French as though she spoke a single mixed language. "What does this mean?"

Leah looked at the girl and smiled. She had been worried when her daughter hadn't spoken a single word until she turned three years old, but relieved and amazed when she did finally start speaking that she used whole sentences in both French and English, as though she had been waiting and listening to bide her time until she understood both tongues.

"It means," she told her as she reached out for a hug, "that Granddad is old and cranky and won't admit that he's going as deaf as he is blind so he accuses everyone of sneaking up on him."

"But why does he want me to wear a bell? Is it so he can hear me coming from far away?"

"That's right, clever pants," she said, unable to resist the urge to squeeze the girl's ribs and make her twist away in laughter.

"What are you writing now?" she asked her mother.

"The same thing I've been writing for a week," she told her kindly. "It's a very long story."

"Can you tell me some of it?" she asked hopefully as her face betrayed the need for attention more than knowledge of the actual story.

"Not yet, beautiful," Leah told her, "when you're older you can read it yourself, but… not yet." The girl's bottom lip extended automatically until her mother's next words lit up her face like a Christmas tree.

"I'm taking a break anyway," she told her, "because the next part of the story is very sad and I need to think about it a bit more. Let's do something together instead, shall we?"

"Papa wanted you," she told her mother.

"That's good," Leah said, "because I was just thinking about him."

~

Lucien took over from Neil on the sea wall in the early evening. He hadn't slept in the day as would have been sensible for someone taking a night shift, but with Leah away inland with what was to all intents and purposes a war party there was no way he could relax enough to sleep.

He always preferred to go to bed early, something which Leah couldn't understand as going to bed early was a thing adults made children do, but could just as easily stay up for a day and a night without suffering too much. Feeling as anxious as he did that day sleep was a thing that wouldn't happen in his near-future.

"All quiet," Neil said with a quivering salute, at least his midriff continued quivering when the remainder of his body had come to a halt.

"Thank you, Neil," Lucien answered, disappointing him by not returning the salute as he walked past and surveyed the darkening waters out towards the hulk blocking their idyllic sea view. As the shift commander of sorts he arrived before the members of the militia rostered for the chilly night duty, and saw the tired eyes of the men and women who had kept watch during the day. Some acknowledged him with smiles or greetings, whereas others just waited for their relief to show up after spending the afternoon trying to keep out of the hot sun. Lucien's arrival meant that the end of their shift was imminent, and that realisation made the last half an hour almost unbearable for some.

His people arrived in small groups and he replaced the guards from the furthest point in the defences for them to follow Neil back to the main keep where hot food would be waiting for them. When the sea wall was occupied by the ten fresh militia members Lucien settled in with a detached telescopic sight from a weapon to watch the horizon. He saw nothing, so called in to contact the three other areas connected by their makeshift communications technology.

He checked in with the gatehouse, giving in to the urge to ask if the party had returned yet and hiding his dismay when told that they had not. He called up the fort high above his position on the opposite end of their small, protected enclave and received the same information.

"Watchtower, this is Lucien," he said into the other handset, waiting a few seconds for an answer before preparing to call them again.

"Tower, here," came the answer in French even though he had automatically called in English as the last call had been in that language. "All clear, the bastards have not come back."

"Keep watch," Lucien warned, knowing that there must be some of them still ashore as Leah had gone to hunt them. He picked up his small scope again, leaving the rifle on his back until such time as he needed it, and scanned the darkening waters ahead with a sense of uncomfortable foreboding.

The crew who had ridden their small boat back out to the water under the high cliffs, blocking their sight of the watchtower, had sent their signal and returned to shore. They had left a handful of men to give the impression that the farm miles inland was the focus of their attention, and Gareer had told the leader of the boat crew that these men were expendable. Now, joined together, the two groups began a slow and treacherous climb up the uneven and untrodden rocks to gain the plateau high above the protected bay in the hope that they would be masters of the high ground by morning and force the town below to surrender.

That wasn't the entirety of their plan because, as brutal as Gareer was, their leader, their *Boqor*, was a thinker.

As soon as the night was fully dark, chosen for the lack of moonlight which had prompted their long wait at sea until the time was right, three boats would attack the bay under the cover of night.

The climb to the top of the cliffs didn't follow the plan, however, and after three of his men had slipped from the rocks to plummet noisily back down to their deaths, it became clear that they had little chance of successfully reaching the top without the light to pick their paths safely. Knowing this, but being more afraid of Gareer's displeasure than he was of falling to an agonising death, the leader of the crews forced the pirates upwards with threats of violence and shouts.

Those shouts, travelling much farther in the still, dark night than people unaccustomed to that time of day would expect, reached the ears of a sentry from the watchtower who had wandered outside to enjoy the cool night air. That enjoyment took the form of a lit pipe stuffed with the previous year's premium tobacco from their friends in Andorra, and a relaxing emptying of his bladder over the cliff edge which he had stepped carefully towards in the poor light.

The shouts from below stopped him mid-stream. He waited for a second in silence until his brain had convinced him that he had imagined it, that his mind played tricks on him in the night, and the stream resumed. He had done this many times and never before had the sound of it landing prompted noises of anger and disgust. The stream slowed and dried up as the dawning realisation hit him. He shouted to raise the alarm as he ran backwards zipping up his fly to snatch up his rifle.

The others from the tower ran towards the sound of his high-pitched yelling, bringing their own guns as they peered over the edge to see nothing but darkness below. The man swore that he had not imagined it, had not made it up for attention, and ran back inside to wrap a thin blanket around a log before setting it alight. He ignored the protests as he waited for it to catch alight properly and leaned over the side to drop the now burning log into the dark void.

Looking down as the sparks flew from each impact with the rocks, he was rewarded with the terrifying sight of two eyes, wide in shock and fear, looking back up at him from a dark-skinned face.

Bullets tore downwards, snatching the pirates from the rock face to add the sounds of bullets striking meat and bone to the panicked shouts and screams of falling men. One of the sentries, thinking more logically than the other three, ran back inside to pick up the large battery-powered lamp, and as an afterthought grabbed the thick rag to bring the pot of hot water from where it hung above the large fireplace.

Thrusting the big torch at one of his companions, the man prepared to tip the hot contents of the metal jug over the edge just as soon as he saw a target.

Startled from his semi-meditative state far below, Lucien launched himself up to the distant sound of gunfire. He barked an order in French for calls to be made but he knew from the direction of the noises that the source of the battle had to be the watchtower.

The attack, even though it failed, served a purpose in distracting the defenders beside the sea.

Neil's system of floating solar lamps, the kind of ones with the low output, showed the darkness of the two passing skiffs as the lights were obscured. By the time the defenders had noticed the silent boats sliding into the bay they were already hard under the edge of the sea wall and out of reach of the massive fifty calibre machine gun as the big barrel couldn't be depressed far enough to take aim. The rattle of gunfire erupted closer to the town, prompting screams and shouts as the darkness devolved their panic into chaos. Defenders were hit and fell from the wall, struck by the undisciplined barrage of bullets fired from inside the bay as the attackers splashed into the shallow water to forge their way through wet sand.

Lucien, cursing himself for being distracted by the far-off noises, swore loudly as he dropped low and tucked his body behind a stone pillar.

"Take cover! Take cover!" he yelled over and over in both French and English, hoping that at least some of the militia would heed his words. Struggling free of the sling to bring the assault rifle around to his front he peeked his head out of cover just long enough to see multiple muzzle flashes on the lower ground. His mind raced, telling him unhelpfully that had the tide been in there wouldn't have been the small stretch of sandy beach for them to land, but the savagely close ricochet of bullets forced his head back behind the protection of the ancient stone and his mind back to the immediate problem.

Flicking the safety catch forward with his thumb he rose and turned in one smooth movement towards the edge of the walkway to fire short bursts into the bodies of the pirates illuminated eerily by the muzzle flashes of their own loud weapons. He stalked along the wall, killing three who were exchanging fire with a few of his people huddle by the machine gun still uselessly pointing out to sea. When his magazine clicked dry he hit the release and shook the weapon to let it fall out as his left hand brought a fresh one up to seat it into the weapon. He clicked it home, wiggling it slightly to make sure it was there as he was operating by touch alone, before opening up again in bursts aimed at the remaining attackers, who were easy to pick out in the darkness thanks to the long, bright flames coming from the barrels of their guns.

But muzzle flashes in the dark worked both ways, and while his were less pronounced he was still a silhouetted target higher up on the wall as he stalked forwards killing them on the beach.

What he didn't see, what he couldn't have seen, was the one pirate who had a jammed gun and had yet to fire a single shot. Lucien passed directly by him, having killed the two men either side of him. The pirate fumbled desperately with the weapon, yanking out the magazine and pulling on the cocking handle to free up the mechanics before slotting the magazine back in and making the gun ready to fire. As he fumbled with it in the dark the sky above him burst into brightness forcing his eyes to half close at the harshness of the fire-work display.

It was a flare, or to be more precise a series of flares fired from the handheld guns taken from the many boats and ships salvaged over the years at Sanctuary. Not only were they being fired from somewhere at sea level, they arced out over the black expanse from the watchtower to descend slowly and light up the bay below. Now employed as a form of battlefield illumination the flares worked both ways, and the fire intensified at the shore.

Only one pirate crew pitched the staged battle there, as the second had slipped further into the bay where they loosely lashed their rusty skiff to a wooden post and clambered up onto the stone sides of the old port. They split into two groups; one headed into the narrow streets and the other up the long, sweeping stone ramp towards the main keep.

Unaware of this as he cycled his weapon for the second time, Lucien reached for the third magazine on his vest. The terrible whine of a ricocheting bullet combined with the sensation of having the reload snatched from his grip with a ferocity he wasn't expecting, made him turn instinctively in the direction the shot had come from. In the strange light of the moving flares he saw a young man staring back at him in wide-eyed shock as he fumbled with the malfunctioning weapon. Only a single bullet had left the barrel before the rifle jammed again, and his inexperience at trying to reload the same magazine cost him his life.

Dropping the carbine in his hand for it to be caught by the sling and bang his leg, Lucien drew the Glock from his right hip and gripped it tightly in two hands as he triggered off a half-dozen rounds into his attacker. As he dropped to slump soundlessly into the wet sand, Lucien's eyes darted around to search for another target until noises from further inside the town caught his attention.

Spinning back, his own eyes as wide as the boy who had almost killed him, he felt an impossibly hard thump to his back and pitched forward to crack his head against the stones.

NON-COMBATANTS

Leah stretched her back again, standing to hear the gathering array of cracks and clicks that accompanied periods of inactivity for her. Ares, thinking that it was time to go somewhere, pulled himself awkwardly to his feet only to sit heavily and bat at an oversized ear with an oversized back paw.

She thought about how to word the next part of the story, thinking that it needed a little explaining for anyone in the future reading it to understand how the next part happened as it did.

Her dog finished his scratching ritual, and as he hadn't been called on to leave the room he lay back down in the patch of sun shining through the narrow window and went back to sleep in order to be fully charged for the next time he was awoken.

Leah opened a battered canteen and took a long, pensive pull of water before sitting down and picking up the pen once more.

One of the things that Dan got wrong in my very humble, and also very private, opinion was that he didn't arm everyone he could from the beginning.

I know back then that we only had a few guns and no decent source of ammunition resupply, but we lived in the country back then and even rural England was stocked with enough shotguns to make a difference. It wasn't like people needed the laborious instruction of how to use an automatic weapon; how to reload fast on instinct through repetitive of hours of practice, but a shotgun was a very simple thing. You could point it in the general direction of someone you really didn't like, and if that wasn't enough to dissuade their offending behaviour then the wide spread of lead pellets often did the trick.

I'm not saying there's no skill at all involved in using one, but their simplicity made them effective and the training package lasted about five minutes.

All of us who had left the prison and the farms so long ago to chase the wild goose south and over the water had been armed, and that never really dropped off after we eventually found safety inside the ancient walls of Sanctuary. People didn't all walk around carrying their gun every day, but there was a kind of reassurance to know that those who possessed them had them hung over their fireplaces ready to use should that need ever arise again.

We kept the good stuff locked away, because a shotgun and a machine gun are very different animals, but at that point the town was full of weapons. Maybe they weren't expecting that.

One of the closest inhabited buildings to the docks was a thin, three-level house with the ground floor originally given over to the town's dive school. Alita had stayed there out of habit, living in one of the apartments above, so when she and Mitch had coupled they saw no reason to disrupt their current arrangements.

With her man away and her baby woken by the sounds of a

battle in the town to scream incessantly, Alita forced herself to prioritise and block out the sounds of the cries that tugged at her soul. She bypassed the room with the cot and her daughter, instead opening a cupboard at the head of the stairs and pulling out a shotgun which she knew Mitch kept loaded. She cradled it in her left arm and reached back inside to a higher shelf where her hand brought back a semi-automatic pistol and a magazine, which she slapped home and pulled back the slide.

She sat halfway up the first set of stairs, trying to ignore the sound of her baby's cries until her milk ran freely to soak two darkening circles on her grey top, and waited.

She didn't have to wait long. The door burst inwards in a spray of splintering wood which annoyed her as the door was unlocked. She saw a ragged man, black hair in tight curls and dirty beige clothing hanging loosely from his spare frame, and watched as he swept the barrel of a gun she recognised but couldn't name over her sitting room.

The shotgun was already aimed at the door, already pulled into her shoulder, so when the man appeared she just had to grip the weapon tighter and squeeze.

He was snatched off his feet, thrown in bloody ruin back onto the street where he had come from having been converted from dangerous invader to so much broken meat and bone in a heartbeat.

Alita racked a replacement cartridge into the chamber of the shotgun, muttering to herself that these bastards would never get near her baby. Sounds of crying forced their way down the narrow stairs and she called out in a soft voice to try and hush the baby torn from sleep by the loud boom of the gun, but she would not abandon her position in order to comfort her.

Few things in life can push most people to commit such acts without remorse, but the life of such a young child being put in danger had set Alita's resolve to previously unknown levels.

All over the town others were waking to the sounds of gunfire, more sporadic by then, and were arming themselves just as Alita had. One by one all of the pirates who had slunk into the dark alleys between the tall buildings fell to the weapons of the town's inhabitants.

The other half of that boat crew, six men led by one only slightly more ruthless and inhuman than the others, headed for the large wooden doors leading to the interior of the old castle. The only defenders in that part of the town were on the ramparts above the gate and on the other side of the big stone construction. They knew better than to abandon their post in case an attack came from their landward side, regardless of whatever noises they heard behind them.

The first two people inside the keep to confront the pirates died under a hail of gunfire to stain the old stones with fresh blood, which would take years to fade despite being scrubbed repeatedly. Nobody lived on that ground floor as it was where the cooking and congregating happened, but as people began to react to the attack they came down the multiple spiral staircases to find the confused invaders unsure of where to go as they were assaulted from the tight corridors and stairwells. Pinned down in the open with no cover, they split up on instinct to run for safety.

One of those men found himself reaching the first floor unscathed where his rapid, deep breathing was the only sound filling the echoing corridors. Noises behind him made him yelp in fear and point his rifle back down the stairs but relief that it was one of his own people washed over him.

They exchanged a few quick words, deciding to get out of there and back to the boats, when the sound of pursuit from below reached them. Running down the corridor to escape and find another exit they took refuge by tucking into a deep doorway. The door behind them opened and a moment of stunned silence reigned as the two pirates found themselves looking at a pair of women, one fair and one dark with tattoos visible all the way up both arms and on her chest under the collar bones. They moved quicker than the women, raising their guns to shout and intimidate just as the screams started. They were forced to their knees and both pleaded as they clung to one another in fear.

A sickening crack filled the room and one of the attackers clattered to the ground in a way that spoke of severe and unrecoverable injury. The surviving pirate spun to face the threat but was driven backwards to the ground as his rifle loudly discharged a pair of un-aimed bullets into the furniture in the room.

Dropping the wooden stool he had used to break the neck and crack open the skull of the first pirate, Joshua Bucknor fell upon the other one like a demon unleashed. As the rifle was dragged out of his fingers and forced up his chest where the cold metal crushed his windpipe and stopped any air from getting into his lungs, the pirate's eyes bulged unnaturally as he stared at his attacker and saw only bloodshot eyes above a beard and bared teeth that he half recognised.

Pouring out every ounce of hatred and fear and terrible, crushing guilt he could muster, the American leaned all of his body weight into the weapon as tears and mucus flowed down his face and into the beard he hadn't got around to shaving off fully. He heard screaming, only later realising that it came from his own mouth, as he forced the gun down again and again to the sounds of crunching until the limp body beneath him finally let him know that he had won.

He had dreamed of doing that for years, even planned it once as a way to end his life by forcing them to execute him for murder, but he had never seen the plan through. Rolling off the body to look at the deaths he had just caused, Joshua cried aloud as the rest of the pain left him. Saved from their uncertain fate, Kate and Sera knelt beside him and both wrapped their arms around the damaged sailor, just holding him as he sobbed and screamed almost silently as though the pressure was too great to come out.

Outside and below, rising above the other small sounds of the end of the fight, came the heavy clattering of the big machine gun pouring lead and murder out to sea.

WHILE YOU WERE AWAY

We woke with the dawn and set off fast for home, leaving a pair of the militia at the farms to bolster their defences until the situation had resolved itself. I initially argued against losing any more guns from Sanctuary, but the addition of just a single pair of fighters meant the world of difference for the farm and very little to us at the town.

Nobody spoke much; breath enough to talk meant that the pace could be increased and as I set the pace it was pretty brisk. Reaching the gates before the sun had climbed high enough in the sky to offer any real heat I was first inside the walls and asking where Lucien was. My stomach churned and my head pounded but thoughts of personal comfort were abandoned when I saw the looks they wore.

"We were attacked," said the olive-skinned Spaniard guarding the gates, "in the night." He looked drawn. Pale and tired as though he had been on duty since we had left the day before, which in truth he had been. I gave up asking them any more questions as I could tell by the smell that the fight hadn't happened there. I took the direct route to the bay, skipping over the sand towards the sea wall and finding my way blocked by the rising tide which forced me onto the lowest edge of the sloped castle walls. Nemesis followed, splashing in the low water without regard as though she shared my unspoken fear.

I saw bodies. Even from the distance I still had to cover I could tell that the bodies were both ours and theirs. Neil saw me coming and head me off before I got to the covered lines of corpses to throw off the blankets shrouding their faces. His left arm was in a crude sling and the sleeve of his shirt had been cut away to show a heavy dressing on the outer edge of his meaty arm, but my mind registered none of this; I showed no concern that one of my oldest friends had evidently been shot. Again.

"Easy, Leah," Neil said to soothe me. My eyes told him I wouldn't take anything easy, not until I knew.

"Where is he?" I demanded, my chin quivering and my voice starting to crack. "Where's Lucien?" He didn't answer me quickly enough so I sidestepped his girth and reached down for the first blanket which I tore back to expose the dull eyes of a dead pirate. Blood had dried as it ran from his mouth and my eyes ranged further down the body to see a series of neat holes through his chest beneath the dirty shirt. Next to him, in terrible juxtaposition, was the pale face of a French boy I had personally instructed in the use of the assault rifle that lay beside his body. His eyes were closed and his face seemed oddly untouched as though he just slept a very deep and still sleep, but further down I saw the bloody ruin of his legs where bullets had torn through his thighs to empty his body of blood in seconds. I stood, barely resisting the urge to kick the dead body of the pirate as though it would serve any logical purpose, and turned on Neil again.

"Tell me," I pleaded, tears running freely down my face as I begged him to break the news to me and not force me to pull back each blanket in turn until I found the broken body of the man I loved.

Of the man who would be the father of my child.

"He's not here," Neil said, his own voice thick with sorrow and anger, "I swear it."

"So where is he?" I demanded of Neil who shifted uncomfortably.

"We don't know. Nobody knows. We can't find his... we can't find him."

I swallowed, fighting down the rising bile in my stomach forced up by the emotions bouncing around my mind and body like a rocket. "Perhaps he fell into the water and..." Neil started, abandoning the train of thought as he watched me fall apart. I crumpled to the ground, kneeling beside the two bodies and sobbing out loud so that Nemesis, scared and unnerved by my display, whined and nudged me with her large muzzle where I hid my face in my hands.

Boots approached and I heard a quiet exchange between Dan and Neil as Mitch ran towards his home shouting Alita's name. Ash, similarly concerned by the sight and sound of me crying on my knees, came to push his wet nose under my hands as I continued to cry.

"Missing," I heard Neil say to Dan, "one of the militia saw him go down but his body isn't here..."

"Who saw what?" I snapped through my tears as I flew back to my feet in one single movement. "Did you say someone saw Lucien go down? Who? Where are they?" Both Neil and Dan lifted their hands to calm me down but I was having none of it. I turned on my heel and began demanding answers from the subdued militia members on the sea wall.

"*L'as-tu vu?Où est Lucien? Vite!*" None of them answered and I felt shame that they looked down to avoid my anger. I wasn't angry at them, not really, I was terrified that I had lost him. I continued shouting questions in English and French amidst the embarrassed gathering until Mitch jogged back to the position. He held no such regard for the dignity of the enemy dead and began pulling the remainder of the blankets aside until he found one with a gaping, ragged wound in place of his chest. To my horror, and to the surprise of everyone there, he dragged the body of the pirate out of the line and began kicking it like an out of control drunk in a street fight at three in the morning.

"You wee *bastard*!" he bawled, and he kicked and stamped, his eyes wild and devoid of all sense. "You fucking *bastard*!" he roared until Dan, having seen more than enough, stepped in to stop the brutality.

"That's enough mate," he said firmly but as kindly as he could manage, pacing a hand on his shoulder. My eyes went wide as Mitch shrugged him off angrily and launched another kick at the dead man's skull to bounce it around on the lifeless neck grotesquely. Dan, his own nerves frayed and his temper rising higher, tried again. This time he grabbed Mitch firmly by the thickly padded shoulder of his vest and yanked him off balance to bring his face closer.

"I said," he yelled, "*that's enough*." Mitch rounded on him, his face a rictus of uncontrolled rage as he drew back his head to throw it forward and connect the skulls of the two men. Stunned by the unexpected blow and the ringing sound of their heads banging together, Dan staggered back a pace and shook his head in shock that his friend had just cheap-shotted him so viciously. Friend or not, Dan stepped forwards and transformed into the person I had seen him become on more than a few occasions. He sidestepped Mitch's wild haymaker, stepping under the arm and throwing his own up with an open palm to connect with the soldier's chin. As this happened, Dan's right leg had hooked Mitch's and bent the knee to fold the Scotsman painfully back on himself onto the stone walkway. Dan held him there, chin pushed painfully upwards as the proximity of his upper body prevented the hands coming back to him, and the legs trapped underneath stopped any kicks.

"I said that's enough," Dan shouted again, removing his hand and stepping backwards and up quickly to avoid any wild lashing out. Mitch floundered, trying to untangle himself and failing to do so quickly. For the first time I saw Ash step in front of Dan ready to protect him against one of our own.

"Stop it, Mitch," yelled Alita's voice as she hurried towards us holding a bundle in her arms. "You silly bloody shite," she called her man as she switched to rapid-fire Spanish to berate him better in her native tongue. Chest heaving and eyes pouring with tears of fear and adrenaline, Mitch eyeballed Dan for a second longer until the moment passed, evaporating to bring him back to his senses. He answered Alita in accented Spanish. He mumbled apologies, explaining that the one he was trying to kill a second time over had broken into his home where Alita and their baby were sleeping. It was clear to me that she didn't need his help, given the state of the body even before Mitch had abused it, but I felt his pain; not being there to fight for other people was eating me up inside too, only my man was nowhere to be found.

That realisation hit me again, interrupted briefly by the display of the enraged Scot, and that ton of bricks drove me back down to the ground where I cried again.

~

"*Mamon?*" Adalene's voice startled Leah from the doorway. "Why do you cry?"

Leah wiped her tears away and sniffed with a small laugh. "Oh, I was just remembering something… *difficult*," she told her as she reached out for an embrace. Adalene went to her mother smiling, pouring out her need to comfort others as though her heart held more than enough love for everyone. Leah held onto her tightly, even after Adalene released her own squeeze on her, and thought of the day that she would have to show her how to shoot a gun.

The thought of her, of her little girl, going out into the dangerous outside world filled her with dread and she wanted to keep her shut up inside the walls forever. Leah knew that wouldn't happen, and if she took after either her mother or her father in any way then keeping her contained would crush her spirit. Leah released her, standing to close the heavy book which had filled with her scribbled words far quicker than she had anticipated. She knew where the story was going, knew where it ended and what they all went through to get there, but the next part wasn't her story to tell.

Just as she had when she transcribed Joshua's words, Leah called her dog and closed up the room she had adopted as her office, to go and find the man who could tell the next part of the story with the clarity it deserved.

A Different Perspective

I am no soldier, or at least I wasn't until I found myself far from home with no family and no idea what was happening in the world. It took many years and some strange events to put me where I am now, but that is not all for here.

I was a boy when it happened, but events forced me to become a man faster than the world before would have wanted. The time I first picked up a gun was only days before our little town, that we thought so invulnerable, was attacked. I never expected to go from school and boxing to explosions and gun battles in only a year, but that was where my life decided to go and I was just along for the ride.

I was just a boy, but the young girl who came with the English people was younger. She never strayed far from the big man with his dog and I don't remember ever speaking more than one or two words to her for many years.

I tried my hand at fishing but found it was not to my tastes. I spent a year at the farm learning how they worked their fields but grew bored. When word was spread that they wanted fighters to be trained I took that chance and found I had a good skill with a rifle. I could hit targets at very long range, and somehow the complexities of the physics involved came easily to me, even if the words of the soldier who taught me did not make as much sense.

I was given a new gun and sent up to the tower to keep watch over our small space and found that I enjoyed it. I thought I would miss other people, would feel isolated and alone, but in truth I liked being just slightly removed from everyone below. I spent some weeks back in the town when my time in the tower had to be changed, what they called 'rotating me out' which sounded strange to me, but I always looked forward to that long climb back up the rocky path to keep watch. When nobody watched me I tended to the graves of the people buried on the cliff top.

When the time came for me to be called up, for me to be taken on an adventure thanks to my skill with a rifle, I had no idea the direction of my life would be so changed again.

I say all of this not to waste the time of anyone who will read this story, but to hopefully let them better understand that I was not prepared for the world I found myself in that early summer night a decade ago.

~

I had the high ground, and while the distance was a lot closer than I was used to it was impossible for me to miss. I fired in bursts, cutting down the men who were just shadows to me, lit up by the bright flames pouring from the ends of their weapons. All around me I heard the terrible noises of gunfire and bullets bouncing from the stones and I remember thinking that I could be hit by one of those bullets flying so randomly at any time. That made me speed up, made me try to achieve the goal quicker than I should have, and I amazed myself at how fast and professional my magazine changed must have looked.

That vanity cost me, because the second time I changed magazines I was hit in my back and fell down to hit my head hard.

I woke up when it was still dark and tried to keep as still as I could. I knew I was on a boat from the sounds and movements, and I knew I had been shot in my vest because my entire back felt like I had been kicked by a mule. My head spun which, combining with the movement on the water, made me vomit. I tried to do it as quietly as possible, to try not to move, but in case anyone has ever tried to wake up with the egg of a goose on their forehead on a moving boat and be sick without moving, it is impossible.

I coughed and spat the acidic contents of my stomach down my front, forcing myself to sit up and gasp in a deep breath to cough again and try to get the rest of it out of my mouth and nose. They started shouting at me, very angry and one of them hit me in the head again with his gun. The blow was not hard, at least not hard enough to make me lose consciousness, but it hurt and gave me an excuse to lie back down and pretend to be stunned as a loop of rough rope was tied around my wrists.

I kept my eyes closed and tried to think.

I slowly felt down to my right hip and found the holster for my gun. It was empty, and I cursed myself for thinking that it would have been missed by these people. I still had spare magazines for the pistol I no longer owned, and I also had two spare magazines for my other weapon which was nowhere to be seen, but what I didn't have was my knife.

Forcing myself to stay calm and failing, my breathing stayed fast and deep as I bounced painfully around in the small boat. I couldn't understand their words, but their tone made me think they had messed up very badly. There were only three voices in the boat that

I could make out, and from what I could guess they were arguing amongst themselves. I stayed quiet and as still as possible, not having to wait long before the screaming engine stopped revving and just emitted a coughing chugging sound as the boat rocked back and forth in the water without the forward momentum it had previously. My stomach threatened to empty itself again and my head pounded like Satan himself was a blacksmith and my skull his anvil.

More shouting and a noise I couldn't place made me open my eyes to curse the lightness of the dawn sky as it brought a fresh stab of pain to my head. I closed my eyes again but in my mind I looked at the images of what I had seen. A wooden platform was being lowered to the water like the kind of contraption that would be used to paint the sides of tall buildings. Or the sides of big ships. A man was on it, skinny and dressed in dirty clothes like all of them I had seen and he carried the same kind of weapon as the majority of them did.

He shouted at the men and they shouted back, none of them seeming to speak for them as a whole.

Ils sont si mal disciplinés qu'il me fait peur, I thought to myself. They were so badly disciplined it frightened me.

I kept my eyes shut and tried to listen, as Leah would say, between the lines.

She said this when she did not know the language people spoke well enough and tried instead to read the tone of the conversation. She made me do it when she spoke in English with Mitch and he used the words that do not show in any translation dictionary I have ever found, and I realised in that moment what she meant.

Now, listening between the lines of their shouted conversation, I got the impression that they had failed and the man on the rickety lift was unhappy about it. They argued that it wasn't their fault. They blamed other people, perhaps, maybe even each other as their shouts grew angrier until two of the men in the boat stood to point their weapons at one another only a few feet above my face. I held my breath, willing my chest not to heave as my lungs tried to force as much air into my body as possible.

Orders were shouted down from higher up, from the deck of the big ship, and thankfully whatever was said made them put their guns down. I was dragged to my feet and rolled onto the rough wooden boards of the lift which squeaked upwards with jerking movements. That made it difficult to pretend I was still unconscious as I would have fallen off the side and back down to the water level if I didn't reach out and grab hold of the side of a plank of wood, unable to let go even though I now had a handful of splinters. More shouts and I was prodded with a gun barrel until I lifted my head.

I saw over the metal side of the deck, taking in a disorganised rabble of more pirates all pointing and shouting at me. I was dragged aboard and my weapons were laid out in front of me like I was some deconstructed delicacy offered up to appease an angry and malevolent god.

That flippant description so easily given in my head turned out to be worryingly accurate, as the man who advanced towards me seemed so different to the others in his bearing and obvious authority that he could have been from a different species.

They told him things I did not understand as I tried to keep my eyes off the man, but I was drawn to the richly embroidered scarf he wore wound loosely around his neck and the better quality clothing he wore. What marked him out as really different, despite being clean and so obviously in charge, was the coldness of his piercing eyes. They promised, without him saying a word, to kill me without remorse if it served any purpose for him.

He stepped forwards to pick up my Glock and checked the action with practiced hands. Nodding his approval he gave more orders and I stood still as the holster and vest were pulled from my body. The gun evidently belonged to him now, as would the vest have done if he hadn't turned it over and tutted his annoyance at the hole in the material. I saw where the hole was and tried not to think what would have happened had the bullet gone through; it was dead centre and would have cut through my spine to paralyse me had I lived. He walked away with the Glock and spare magazines giving a final order over his shoulder without giving me even a second look.

Hands grabbed me and shoved me along as the others jeered at me, leaning in to fill my vision with filthy teeth as they laughed at their newest prisoner.

Hostage, my mind told me, *not prisoner. You are their hostage now.*

Hopelessly outnumbered, I decided I would show at least some defiance rather than die slowly; when I reached the metal door one of them unlocked by spinning a wheel in the centre and I was pushed inside, I turned and held up my bound hands, asking in French for them to release my bonds. One hesitated, glancing at the others for permission or support, I could not tell which, until he summoned the bravery to step forwards and raise a rusted blade the size of his forearm to cut the ropes. I smiled when my hands were free, rubbing the wrists to check everything still worked and feeling the slight numbness in both hands which I knew would be a blessing for what I wanted to do next.

"Before you go?" I asked them as they turned for the door and made them turn back to face me. I guessed they wouldn't kill me for no reason, but that the chances of getting off the boat alive were non-existent, so I decided to do things my way and to hell with it.

As the first one turned my right fist hit him with a hook that dislocated his jaw and sent him towards the metal deck in slow motion. The next nearest was the man who had cut free the ropes and still had the machete in his hand which he started to raise. I jabbed him hard in the throat with my left fist, following up with a second to the end of his nose which was rewarded by a crunch and a pop as blood instantly covered his mouth and chin. The third man in the doorway was out of my reach and reacting fast. Before I could step over the unconscious form of the first man I had punched he had raised his gun barrel at my chest and started shouting for me to get back.

I knew this because he screamed it in English, but at first my mind didn't seem able to translate what he had said until he shouted it a fourth or fifth time. I held up both hands, happy that I had hurt two of them badly enough to soothe the wound of being captured, and stepped backwards.

Come on, I thought, *shoot me if you're going to shoot me.*

They didn't. Instead they backed off dragging the unconscious one with them, shutting the door to leave me in the darkened gloom. Feeling faint from the exertion and my throbbing head I staggered, shooting out a hand to lean against the cold metal wall to stop my head from hitting something again. As I steadied myself with deep breaths, I noticed for the first time that I wasn't alone in the dark room.

THE PLAN

"They must have taken him," I insisted to Dan, my eyes still puffy and red but my face a tense mask of anger. "It's the only explanation that makes sense."

"Leah," he began in a tone of voice that I recognised but I wasn't in the mood to be coddled and treated with sympathy.

"No!" I interrupted. "Don't tell me to forget about it. Don't tell me it's pointless and *don't* tell me he's dead." I breathed hard as I kept my mouth tightly shut to keep in the tears that threatened to come again.

"I was going to ask," Dan said softly, "how you planned to *get* there?"

I looked at him, surprised and yet not at the same time. We shared a kindred spirit of wanting to do things that no sane person would, and I knew he would be itching to get onboard that ship even without the chance that our own people were imprisoned there.

"I... I..." I said, my face twisting with angry frustration as I knew I didn't have the first clue how to get onboard the massive ship. I couldn't even think of a way to get close enough to it without being detected.

"Mitch is dead against it now," Dan said. I wasn't surprised. He had scared just about everyone who had seen his display with the body and his subsequent clash with my father. The two men had taken themselves away after the uncomfortable altercation and returned as though nothing had happened, like the two friends who had been close for years hadn't just fought in front of half the town. It was all very… *male* of them to just pretend it hadn't happened.

"He'd rather stay defensive," Dan went on, "rather kill them off as they try to come ashore until they've lost enough people to make staying here a thing for the 'too difficult' box." I made a huffing noise to show what I thought of the plan to wait them out, but I didn't judge Mitch for it; he had come too close to losing his family and that would have long-lasting effects.

"You know as well as I do that won't work," I told him, "you also know that doesn't help us get our people back." Dan's mouth tightened, probably forcing down the urge to remind me there was no guarantee that Lucien was captured and not dead. I had argued all day with everyone who tried to comfort and console me, even having it laid out that he must have been taken out with the tide or else he would return to the water's surface in the next day or so, as though the harsh truth would snap me out of my denial. We were saved another disagreement by a tentative rapping on the doorframe of the room we were in.

"Knock, knock," Adam said pointlessly, giving verbal subtitles to what he'd actually just done. Both Dan and I bit back telling him this, as he had been in tears of guilt when we had spoken with him, having been in command of the day watch and in an exhausted slumber when the attack happened. He had managed to throw on some trousers and grab his vest and gun in time to see the last of the group who had infiltrated the main castle go down to a hail of small arms fire. Marie, we later found out as she hadn't told us, had been leading that group of terrified people and formed them together as she lead them up the spiral staircases and over the first floor to descend behind their attackers to kill them. She had conveniently left that part out of her story, glossing over it with the most innocent detail, but the fact that she had pulled a trigger was a big deal. Luckily, enough of them had pulled their triggers so that the death of the man with the noisy rifle couldn't be attributed to any single one person's guilt, because taking a life would have affected Marie, I thought.

"What do you need?" Dan said kindly, leaning away from me as our heads had been bent closer together as we spoke.

"Thought you'd both want to know straight away," Adam said as he walked in, unslinging his rifle which had become as much a part of him as our own weapons and resting it on a wooden sideboard. "Danielle here saw something I thought you should know." He turned to the bewildered Frenchman and nudged him with his elbow, saying, "Tell 'em, then."

French Dan looked between us and Adam, mouth hanging slightly open with the unspoken threat of his remaining senses escaping via that opening, and closed it to swallow before speaking in gruff French.

"I saw them take a man on their boat. He looked like he was hurt, so I guessed it was one of their own. I didn't realise until today, after I had slept, that I didn't see any of them with blonde hair…"

"Sooo…" Dan said slowly with raised eyebrows almost meeting in the middle of his confused face, "you thought the blonde-haired person was one of the African pirates?"

The question hung in the air for a moment before French Dan shrugged. "They could have been from South Africa," he explained lamely. I realised my own mouth was open then, and as stupid as the assumption obviously was I couldn't help but accept the logic of his words, even if they were unsupported by any level of common sense. The facts of what he saw also raised my heart through the roof because it made me absolutely certain that they had taken Lucien when the few who had reportedly survived their failed attack fled in one of their boats.

I turned to Dan, seeing in his expression that he could no longer deny my beliefs, and nodded before thanking Adam and French Dan.

"Ad?" Dan said as the two men walked out of the room, making him poke his expectant face back around the corner in silent question. "You know it's just the French way of pronouncing Daniel, right?" Dan said in a low, conspiratorial voice. "You know he's not *actually* called Danielle, don't you?" Adam's face fell in mild shock that was quickly recovered.

"Yeah," he chuckled in a way that I was sure he thought sounded natural, "'course I do!" His face disappeared again and ours met.

"Told you," I said seriously. In any other scenario Dan would probably have taken the opportunity to get a dig in about Lucien, who he still called pretty boy as his looks hadn't faded one bit in the last couple of years, but the severity of what we faced took all the remaining humour out of him.

"You did," he said seriously, reaching into his vest pouch for a stale French cigarette which, under normal circumstances, wouldn't be smoked inside. I watched in silence as he lit it, shaking the pack to double check there wasn't another hiding inside somewhere before he crumpled it in his fist and patted a leg pocket for his secondary packet. If he'd gone through a full pack already by that time of day then he must have been stressed.

"So how do we get on that ship?" I asked.

"I don't know," Dan said before he inhaled, screwing his eyes up as the harsh smoke didn't seem to agree with him like the menthols he preferred. Exhaling, he looked me in the eye as his lips turned to blow the smoke away to one side and said, "So we had better figure it out pretty sharpish."

The resonating finality of his words, combined with the smoke falling from his mouth as he spoke, was a memory that stayed with me in great detail for a very long time.

The ship was in the water. Very deep water to be precise, so I started asking innocuous questions of the people I knew who had experience of such things. Neil was my first stop, not because he was any kind of marine expert but more because he had an answer or an ingenious solution to any problem. I didn't start straight in with, 'hey, how would *you* get onboard… let's say that big ship out there? Asking for a friend…' but instead started slowly by asking him how his arm felt.

"Just creased me a little bit," he said in very untypical Neil fashion by using his own voice and not quoting a film. I'm sure if I'd have asked him at the time when the adrenaline was high he'd have said that he didn't have time to bleed or one of his other favourite quotes, but I could tell it had shaken him up and was hurting. I smiled and reached into a leg pocket before theatrically looking from side to side to check for anyone watching before I slid my hand palm down across the table towards him.

He played along, doing his own surreptitious checks for any

surveillance as he took them without looking.

"Little something for later," I muttered with a wink. "Now, I was wondering—" I said, though I didn't the chance to finish my thought as he cut me off.

"How to get onboard a boat that's too far away from shore to reach without being seen and too high to hop over the railings?" His eyebrows were up and his words soft and inquisitive. I deflated, knowing I had already let the cat out of the bag by not denying it quickly enough.

"Yes," I told him simply. Neil smiled, leaning closer and lowering his voice.

"Now," he said, "I don't know if this is one hundred per cent true, but it was one of Rich's stories and he didn't strike me as a bullshitter."

"Nor me," I said, remembering one of my mentors of almost a decade ago in a bubble of fondness that was quickly burst by the recollection of his assumed death. "If anything he was quite the opposite."

"Exactly," Neil said, "so I have no reason to think this one isn't real. He told me about an old boy he served with, who was posted up in Scotland which is where they hide all the nuclear subs – all deep-water inlets and the like – and not just our subs but the American's as well."

"Go on," I said, unsure if I was going to be leaving with a recommendation of requisitioning a submarine from somewhere.

"Well, this old boy told him that some American SEAL told them over drinks about the time they were given a training exercise to infiltrate one of their own boats. One of those exercises people hand out when they're bored or want to make a name for themselves. Well, this team of SEALs, you know what SEALs are, right?" I nodded. "Well this team split off into pairs and tried three different approaches; one pair tried to get aboard with hooky IDs and got pinched at the docks, another tried to nab one of the smaller boats by force but failed somehow, and the last pair decided to swim out and climb the anchor chains in the dead of night..." He waggled his eyebrows at me as though he had just imparted the secret of a magic trick.

"And they succeeded?" I asked, hopeful.

"Oh god no, one of them didn't make it up the chain because the cold water had sapped him and the other one got battered by two cooks who clocked him slipping over the railing."

"Neil," I said, "you're filling me with confidence..." He shrugged.

"Well they were only elite special forces," he explained, "they weren't Nikitas." Despite myself I laughed, unable to see any sensible reason why trained men at the peak of their abilities and experience couldn't get onboard, but some mongrel of a girl, who could shoot and won most of her fights because nobody expected to get coldclocked by a girl or because a dog messed someone up for her, could.

"Well," I said as I stood up, "thanks anyway." I reached out to pat him on the shoulder, only stopping myself in time to not make contact with the body part that had had a brush with high-speed lead but not quickly enough to stop him hurting himself with the flinch of reaction. I backed away amidst his hisses of pain until they subsided and he turned to the secret offering I had given him.

It's probably worth mentioning to people who used to remember how the medical world worked that France had a strange way of administering painkillers. Back at home, when everything still worked normally, you'd just buy paracetamol in almost any shop but would need a prescription for anything stronger. In France they preferred to administer their pain meds a different way, which took a lot of getting used to.

Neil looked at the packet, his eyes widening slowly as he realised firstly what the medicine was, and secondly how he had to take it.

"Really?" he yelled at my retreating back. "A suppository?" I laughed at his tone and the last words of his I heard echoing to me as I turned towards the docks. "For all the good this will do, I may as well shove it up my…"

THE RECRUITER

Neil's story, while full of encouragement and rousing tales of success, had got me thinking. I knew I could climb up an anchor chain, especially one with links as big as that ship would have because it would be like climbing a ladder more than a rope, but the problem of how to get there was bugging me. There was no way I'd be able to swim that far out, even without my fear of deep water, not if I expected to be able to do anything but drown before I got there. That left a boat, and for the plan I had in mind to work I'd need to bring someone else in on the gig before I recruited a driver.

I walked the familiar route to the familiar house, finding the only unfamiliar part to be the wide, dark bloodstain on the cobblestones outside the open front door. I paused in the doorway, calling out "Knock, knock," and wincing as I'd just realised I'd done one of the most annoying things in the world. Alita was there, eyes tired but the rest of her quiet face a mask of resolve that showed no adverse effects of having created the bloodstain outside.

"Got a minute?" I asked her.

"Mitch is not at home," she said, misunderstanding who I was looking for.

"That's alright," I said trying to sound light-hearted, "I've had enough of him after the last few days anyway." She didn't seem amused, perhaps because my acting skills weren't my strongest point. She kissed the forehead of the loosely wrapped bundle she carried and laid it down gently in the small wooden crib. She rocked it with expert care, shushing the baby without seeming to have to concentrate on which actions occupied different parts of her body and mind.

"You have a look on you," Alita said with narrowed eyes, as though my body language had already given away the fact that I was after some off-the-books information.

"Do I?" I asked innocently, trying and failing to recover my poise.

"You do," she replied, "and I know why." I said nothing, doing what Dan had taught me to do and let others fill the silence. "You are worried about Lucien, are you not?"

I deflated. Of course I was worried about Lucien. My chest burned with pain as though my heart was going to implode whenever I thought about him and what they would do to him. I shook away that pain, that hopelessness, in case it consumed me like it threatened to and instead steeled myself for action.

"I need to know if you have any scuba gear left," I said, my words obviously coming from way out of the blue as she seemed physically taken aback by the subject change. Her mind whirred as her mouth flapped in shock to emit only strangled sounds as they didn't seem to be able to form any coherent sentence. "And I need you to show me how to use it," I added. "Today."

Alita sat, mouth still open and the rocking of the crib forgotten.

"Have you ever done it before?" she asked, surprising me by ignoring the fifty or more questions I was expecting before I convinced her to reach the training part.

"No," I said, "but I used a snorkel once in a swimming pool…" Alita's mouth closed a little more tightly than was natural, pressing her lips together to make a slight whitening of the olive skin surrounding her mouth. I knew that meant that my claims of snorkelling expertise were so far removed from what I was asking her to teach me, but I appreciated her not telling me.

"Scuba is…" she began, "scuba is very different. You don't breathe the air, but have to suck it in and blow it out instead. It is not a natural thing for the body to do and you have to concentrate to not fall into the panic. Tell me what you want to do and I will tell you if I can help."

"You promise not to tell anyone else?" I asked hopefully.

"It depends on whether you will be putting anyone else at risk with your plan. I have a conscience."

As she said that, her momentarily forgotten infant woke with a sudden, ear-piercing shriek that stabbed through my senses and feelings, and made certain parts of my chest throb with sudden discomfort. Stifling the urge to reach inside my vest with both hands to try and sooth them, I fought internally to stop Alita from finding out the secret I, quite literally, carried with me.

~

"This," Alita told me as she showed me a thumbs up sign, "does not mean that everything is okays." She switched the hand gesture smoothly to an 'o' with her forefinger and thumb and spread the other digits out in a fan. "*This* means that you are okay. The other one means that you are needing to going up to the surface."

"Roger," I said, trying to take in a whole new world of skills in an hour. We were in a quiet part of the bay, but I soon realised there was no way of keeping what I was doing a secret from anyone. Sanctuary was effectively a very small, and very close-knit town where everyone knew everyone else and anything that didn't happen behind closed doors was everyone's business. Even a lot of the stuff that happened behind closed doors became everyone's business but that was just human nature.

Suddenly deciding to use up a couple of bottles of compressed air in the midst of a full-blown crisis under the weak guise of learning something new to try and take my mind off things, was about as believable as a wolf wearing a white coat and saying 'baaa'. A small crowd of the town's children gathered on the sand to watch as we practised going down about a metre where I was shown via scuba sign language how to change my regulator or swap for the backup one in case there was a problem. I felt like I was doing underwater Tai-Chi as I swept my right arm around in an exaggerated loop to find the breathing thingy and put it in my mouth to blow out the salty water before I could breathe.

Alita was right; it was the most alien thing I think I'd ever done, and it took every ounce of concentration not to panic when we graduated to the deeper water further out in the bay. She taught me how to use the compressed air to fill the vest and remain at a certain depth, and the biggest problem I had then was learning how to move with the big flippers on my feet as my body seemed to just want to rotate sideways and tip me upside down which had the added bonus of terrifying me by showing the darker, deeper water that I couldn't see the bottom of.

Three hours later, emerging from the water exhausted, I helped Alita put the equipment back on the old cart designed for just that purpose and looked up to see the bored eyes of my dog who some-how knew that she wouldn't be allowed to play on this one. I smiled at her, my bottom lip protruding in sympathy, when I saw the scowl on the face of the woman behind Nemesis. My own face dropped as I saw Kate shooting me the dirtiest look of disapproval I had ever seen.

"A word?" she said brusquely, making it a demand and not a request.

"Just need to help Alita get th—"

"A. Word. Please," she said, barely able to keep her words above a growl. "Unless you'd rather discuss it out here?"

I smiled, defeated by her powerful knowledge of something I didn't want the world to know. I looked around, seeing the open door of a shed used to house various buoys and fishing net floatation things. "Please, my office…"

"Are you insane?" Kate demanded in a hiss. "You really think I believe this is just recreational? In your condition you can't possibly think you can go swimming out there and—"

"Relax," I said, smoothly transitioning into the lie I had decided on in the last few seconds, "it's a defensive capability Dan and I came up with and he's about as natural in the water as a cow is at driving."

"What kind of *defensive capability*?" she asked, evidently un-swayed.

"We're looking at rigging some steel lines across the bay which will mess up their little boats if they come back." She stopped, her mind ticking over the explanation and finding no overt dishonesty on my face. It pained me to lie to her, especially as she was the kind-est, most thoughtful person I had met, who put herself in harm's way without question just to try and save the lives of people she didn't know and often didn't like. Her previous occupation wasn't just a job, but truly was her calling. Just like Dan and I were born with that internal switch that made us run *towards* danger, Kate was cut from that same cloth.

"You think I'm going out into deep water a mile off shore with a scuba tank on my back?" I asked, attempting to solidify my cover. "How would I even get onboard? What would I do on my own? Relax, Kate, I'm not going to do anything stupid." She looked hard at me, deciding whether or not to play her final card.

"Do I have to tell Dan about your… *situation*?" she asked pointedly. My face dropped in a mask of neutrality which hid the anger and frustration I felt. Like I didn't know? Like it wasn't on my mind every minute of every day? She wasn't to know that the thought of losing a baby was as terrifying to me as the thought of raising said baby without the father and only able to tell a few stories about him, eventually having to admit that I had let him get carried away by a bunch of pirates who probably chopped his head off with a rusty machete.

That was even if Sanctuary survived their presence for much longer.

"No," I said firmly, "you do not." She hesitated a moment longer, searching my face for any signs of disobedience, before turning and walking away.

I watched her walk away, my nose suddenly picking up the smell of tobacco and turning my head towards the source. Dan leaned against a wall, a dog at each heel as he smoked and smiled at me. The smell of his cigarette turned my stomach and I hoped he would finish it before we spoke. He did, luckily, tossing the soggy end of the hand-rolled smoke into the water and strolling towards me with the dogs silently flanking him without orders.

"Figured it out?" he asked.

"Yes," I told him, "one part of it at least."

"I think I've got you covered on the other part," he said in a tone of voice that I feared was a little resigned. "Come on, let's talk."

BEST KEPT BETWEEN OURSELVES

Other than Alita, Mitch was brought into the inner circle along with Neil. The list of co-conspirators was unsurprising, but the pain of leaving Marie out of it was a sting that both Dan and I would have to work hard to heal.

If we made it back.

Dan and I had both pulled the night shift, in theory, but with Neil and Mitch lurking to take over when we went on our way. The moon still offered next to no light but we could see well enough for Dan to pilot the small boat, towing the other, larger one that had been recovered from the outer bay and stuffed with yet more bodies of dead pirates. Given our respective numbers, we were definitely ahead in score terms. Not that it mattered, because we would be forced to leave or else starve if we didn't get them away from our home.

I was dressed in a jet black wetsuit, the reflective strips picked off by Alita that afternoon, and I had to admit it felt quite good to be in something so form fitting for this kind of work. It also meant that my footfalls on the ship would be grippy and silent if my plan worked. I wrapped my equipment in plastic bags, sealing them in turn before adding more and more layers to keep the water out of their working parts.

I took a second bundle, a larger one containing a bag in which was stuffed Dan's vest, shotgun, carbine and ammunition. Again something that involved the plan working as we hoped it would.

The journey out over the black water was filled with the foul smells of decaying bodies and wind whipping past us which thankfully took the stench away with it for the most part. It didn't take long, actually it was quicker than I had hoped it would be as I had timed my psyching-up process wrong and had to condense the last few minutes as Dan backed off the throttle and made the boat full of rotting cargo bump into our stern. I fought back the urge to vomit and splashed my mask in the cold water like I had been shown before strapping it tightly over my face. I turned on the air, tied my airtight bundles to the weight belt Alita had given me, and looked at Dan for a long second before he broke and reached out to me.

The small boat rocked unnervingly as he embraced me, whispering into my ear to come back for him and make the bastards pay. I hugged him back, put the regulator in my mouth, and slipped silently into the dark water to descend before the boats moved off again.

This was the most frightening part. In fact, it was the most frightening thing I had ever done and as I worked my legs to make the flippers propel me towards the front of the ship, I was overwhelmed by the sensation of floating in space and not being ten feet below the water just off the coast of southern France. It didn't take me long to find the ship, being like an enormous building descending far below the level I swam at, but it took me another thirty minutes to feel my way around in search of the forward anchor chain we had studied with the most powerful optic we could find that afternoon.

I was on the verge of panic when I found it, ready to kick for the surface and breathe normal air as I back-stroked for shore in shameful defeat, but the thought of Lucien and now Dan on board that big bastard boat kept me focused. Finding the anchor chain by way of banging my head into it, I struggled out of my scuba gear and attached it to the chain using the big clip on it for just that purpose. With my two sealed burdens floating silently on the surface, I peeled open my own and wrapped my legs around the huge chain to steady myself as I slipped on the vest and unwrapped the suppressed gun. Pointing it upwards and holding my breath I expected to see heads appear in the slightly lighter dark above, followed by shouts of alarm and long muzzle flashes to signify my death.

None came, and I lowered the gun to poke my toes in between the gaps of the big metal chain links as I started to climb. Halfway up I slipped, yelping involuntarily as flailed to regain my grip on a slimy piece of steel. Clinging to the chain, grateful that I couldn't see how far from the surface of the water I was, I muttered to myself reassuringly.

"Let's just keep that bit to ourselves, shall we?"

When I had slowed my heartrate enough, I reached up and placed a careful gloved hand over the railing to lift my head and check if the coast was clear.

⁓

Dan shone a torch as he approached, not wanting to startle any ill-disciplined sentry into emptying the magazine of whatever he carried in his general direction. Lights shone back from the far side of the ship: he had intentionally gone to that side to give Leah as much cover as possible, and shouts rang down to him.

"I've brought your people back," he yelled up as he smiled. He pretended not to understand the accented English yelled back at him, preferring to have his discussions face to face and stalling for as much time as possible. He waited as the squeaking noise from above him manifested into a lowered wooden platform which seemed to serve as their lift to sea level. Two men rode the rudimentary elevator, both pointing weapons at him which back in the world would have bothered him but nowadays seemed par for the course of meeting new people.

"Greeting, shitheads," Dan intoned formally, "take me to your leader!" They looked at one another, confused. "Nothing? Seriously?" Dan complained with clear disappointment. "Come on, fuckwits, take me up." He pointed upwards, stepping up to climb on the wooden platform and being pushed back hard so that he landed hard on his back. Without the vest he usually wore to cushion the fall he felt the breath driven from his chest and pain lance up and down his spine which had already taken more than enough abuse in the years he had been on the planet.

"Ooh," he groaned, "that's going to cost you…" The one who hadn't knocked him back reached down to half drag and half help him up, keeping the barrel of his rifle pressed painfully into Dan's chest.

"I like you," he said in an attempt at an Austrian accent, "I'm going to kill you last."

The pirate said nothing in response as the other one had pulled back the rough canvas covering on the second boat to reel backwards yelling in obvious anger and disgust. The platform was raised and Dan took deep breaths ready to take the pain he knew was coming, hoping against all odds that Leah was winning her own battles.

I slipped over the railing, my body dropping silently but the bundles of Dan's and my own equipment clanging onto the metal deck with a noise that sounded to me like the ringing of a dinner gong.

I stayed still and silent, waiting for any response to my noisy arrival but finding none. Feeling my way through my equipment with only my hands as my eyes stayed glued to the darkness ahead, I found my vest and slipped it over my head, my left hand touching all the things I would need to locate quickly. I unwrapped Dan's bundle, fixing it to my back and pulling the straps tight. I rose, feeling the fat suppressor of Dan's gun hit me in the hip as I moved, and stepped heel-toe, heel-toe on crouched legs towards the middle of the ship. I was exhausted in seconds, my legs already burned out from the stress of the swim and the climb. My shoulders ached from the exertion and I was forced to rest because my breath was louder than the surrounding sounds.

Inactivity was agony, but I knew stumbling into contact when I was this exhausted was a guarantee of ensuring failure. Rested, I stood and headed towards the distant lights near the middle of the big ship only to drop to one knee in silence after thirty careful paces. Voices ahead, no sound of urgency and more importantly not seeming to be searching for anything. I made out the silhouettes of two of them, their guns as recognisable as their human forms, and moved slowly to my right into deeper shadow for them to pass by my position. They moved carelessly, talking as they went and I tried to fathom how they would find any enemy unless their plan was to get one of them killed as a signal. I looked behind them, seeing no follow up patrol in case that was their actual plan, and stalked them back the way I had come.

They were heading towards the very front of the ship, so logic dictated they would turn around at some point and head back. I wanted them stopped at the furthest point, so my stalking distance was narrowed as they reached the front of the vessel where the two railings met in a rounded point. They paused, turning slowly to begin their boring return trip, when I rose up from the shadows and drilled a three-round burst into both of them in turn. The rapid coughing noises from my weapon sounded unbelievably loud in the darkness that seemed to amplify sounds I didn't want to make.

One crumpled where he stood, but the second one staggered backwards under the weight of the lead hitting his chest. His lower back hit the railing and slowly his upper body began the tip as physics took hold of him. I didn't want the noise of a dead body slamming into the sea below to raise any alarms, so I rushed forwards to grab a handful of his thin T-shirt and hauled him back over the metal rail before he tipped too far and dragged me with him.

With both bodies seeping dark blood onto the deck I froze, taking a knee and keeping my gun raised in case anyone else came from the shadows ahead to investigate the sounds I had caused. I waited a full minute, counting down from sixty silently in my head until I forced myself to believe that no planned assault was heading my way.

Grabbing a bare ankle I dragged them one by one to the darkest shadow of some kind of big vent on the deck and hid their bodies against it before retracing my steps back towards the busier part of the ship.

~

Dan was jostled and pushed into what he guessed was the bridge of the ship after climbing a series of metal staircases. Rough hands patted him down and he resisted the gloating urge to laugh when their untrained hands missed three places he could have hidden a weapon. He didn't take the risk of hiding anything on his person, trusting instead in the drive and ability of the young woman he hoped by now would be stalking the ship looking for friendly faces.

He had toyed with the idea of bringing one of the few grenades they possessed, envisioning himself holding the pin aloft in one hand and the small bomb in the other, but decided against it as he didn't much fancy holding onto it for any length of time and risk blowing his arm off at best.

"Sit down," he was told in English so heavily accented that it took him back years to the time he had visited Africa as a young man. The words had come from the man who had pulled him up from the skiff he had piloted and he seemed to shake with nervous apprehension.

Dan, in contrast, kept his terror firmly shut up inside and radiated the calm demeanour of a man holding bargaining chips.

Another man, striding purposefully and clearly in charge, walked in and made a direct line for Dan. He slapped him hard across the face, marking a long string of what he guessed were curses in a language Dan didn't understand. The backhand blow stung, but the pain wasn't as high as the spike of anger he felt at being mistreated.

"Why are you here?" the man snapped at Dan. "What do you want?"

"You in charge?" Dan enquired, working his jaw to soothe the ache caused by the humiliating blow.

"I am Ahmad Gareer," he said proudly in decent English, "and you have attacked and killed my men."

"Your men attacked and killed innocent civilians," Dan countered, "I was just returning them to you." Gareer's face flashed in anger again and he struck another savage backhand blow with the other hand to Dan's opposite cheek. His head was flung to the other side, his mouth opening and closing as his eyebrows went up and down to deal with the blow before he turned to fix the man with a cold stare of promise.

"That one will cost you," he said softly, hoping that the man would lean in closer to better hear his words so he could employ the trick he had used once before and crack his nose across his face with his forehead. Gareer stayed annoyingly out of reach and smiled at Dan. His mind worked, trying to figure out the man's play by coming unarmed to his domain bearing the insult of the bodies of his men.

His smile dropped as he saw no way that the move wasn't a ploy as part of a larger attack.

"Get everyone up," he demanded as he spun away, "put everyone on guard now."

Dan leaned back and tested the weakness of his bound hands.

It's on you now, kid, he thought.

INCENTIVE

I heard the commotion ahead of me, and automatically angled away from it as I didn't want to link up with Dan when he had the full attention of everyone onboard. I watched from the shadows as I saw what I hoped was Dan being brought up and escorted out of sight up the switchback metal steps to the high windows towards the back of the boat.

My job, as far as I saw it, was to find and free Lucien and any other prisoners, which was why I was lugging two heavy and ungainly AK-47s looped over my shoulder and threatening to hit every metal surface in reach to make noise, as though the stolen weapons themselves still tried to raise the alarm.

I moved slowly, mature and experienced enough to not rush into a fight and instead bide my time. The forward section of the boat was an unruly mess of crates and other items I couldn't make out, but it was a minefield of potential cover spots which both acted in my favour and to shred my already taught nerves.

I didn't have to wait long before activity seemed to blossom far ahead and more tired pirates were sent out to patrol in ones and twos. I picked off four more over the next twenty minutes as they wandered aimlessly in the dark. It was a simple thing for me, which made me feel a little arrogant and almost as though the fight was unfair, until I reminded myself that unfair was perfectly acceptable so long as it was in your favour.

I had a stash of five rifles and a few spare magazines, electing to leave the huge PKM like the one Mitch had so lovingly restored as I couldn't carry what I had already. I wrapped the bundle of rifles in a rough blanket left on the deck, using a piece of brightly coloured twine to bind it. Lights were switched on all over the ship now, removing my advantage among large parts of the deck where I could no longer rely on my invisibility. Patches of shadow still existed that allowed me to advance, but they felt like bottlenecks where ambushes could be set so I increased my levels of caution accordingly.

I watched and waited, seeing increased activity ahead of me where men seemed to be congregating like they were guarding something. I kept checking my watch, not wanting to leave it too long but anxious to be doing something as my nerves began to fray even more.

One more man walked towards me lazily, his gun resting over his shoulder and his finger on the trigger in a disgraceful display of weapon indiscipline. Using a trick I had developed as a child, I took a spent bullet casing from a pouch on my vest and spun it in my fingers as the man approached ready to fling it ahead and distract him.

I tossed it, hearing the answering ring of brass on steel as he turned instinctively to look over his left shoulder. I rose, weapon up and tucked in tight, but my suppressor caught the very edge of the metal drum I hid behind and made a second, louder noise than my distraction. He spun back to face my direction as I pulled the trigger to snap his head back. A bright flash lit up the dark night as his dead finger curled around the trigger of his gun to fire a single shot that echoed loudly over the silence.

"Shit!" I hissed, dropping my gun on its sling and advancing as the dead pirate slumped in a kneeling position against a wooden crate. "Fuck, fuck, *fuck*," I said as my mind tried to decide what to do next. The body being discovered would tell them someone was onboard, and where I was, which would lead to my capture or death. Bad option. Dumping the body overboard would make a splash and have the same results as option one. I looked at the body, the position he fell in giving me and idea which I ran with as shouts already began far ahead and started to move in my direction. I picked up his dropped rifle and switched it around, curling his dead hand against the grip and the tip of the barrel against the hole in his skull I had created. His hand fell away and the head lolled back but the gun stayed in position and gave what I hoped was the indication that he had chosen to take his own life.

I knew it wouldn't stand up to close scrutiny, mostly because the size of the bullet hole through his head didn't match with the kind of ammunition he was carrying, but I hoped it would give me enough time to get ahead of the response that was coming fast. Slipping away to the opposite side of the ship I moved slowly around the men who came to investigate. Looking ahead, I saw that the ones who had responded to the shot had left the room they were guarding unattended.

~

Dan heard the gunshot. Heard the shouts in response and smiled that they were running around in the dark and probably dying at the hands of a young woman he suspected was rather better at what he did than he was. Or at least would be one day.

His smile faded when he thought of the girl, *his* girl, out there on her own and decided it was time to call a change to the plan and began working his hands loose at a faster and more painful rate than before.

"Quiet," Lucien said in the dark, "did you hear that?"

The others in the dark storeroom said nothing, straining their ears to listen but hearing nothing.

"There!" he said. "Again." One of the others murmured a hesitant agreement, but before any further discussion came the sound of ringing metal was loud outside their prison cell like hail stones on a car roof. The door creaked as the locking wheel was spun open and a slight figure stepped inside with a familiar weapon tucked into her shoulder.

"Leah," Lucien said, barely able to keep the tears from his voice as he stumbled forwards. She dropped her gun, wrapping her arms around his neck and crushing her lips into his face to prompt sounds of pain as most of his body hurt.

"I am okay," he assured her, kissing her back, "I am okay. What are you doing here? How did you—"

"No time," she said, interrupting him, "here." She dropped a bundle at his feet and he fumbled at the bindings to expose the handful of stolen weapons. Lucien asked the others still hiding back in the shadows if any of them knew how to use a gun and Leah's mouth opened in shock as only two of the dozen prisoners stepped forward. She wasn't shocked at the lack of rifle use, but more of the number of people held captive who had obviously been snatched recently from the area she thought she knew well and claimed to be a protector of.

"Tell them to stay here," she told him, "just us until this rat's nest is cleared." Lucien passed on her orders, taking the spare ammunition for all but two rifles which were left in the hands of two men instructed to guard the door. Leah slipped out of the metal hatch after glancing in both directions and he followed.

The door of the bridge burst open again and the man calling himself Gareer stomped towards Dan with an angry purpose written all over his face. Dan tried to look scared, tried to show an anticipation of fear and violence, but he couldn't help himself and his smile betrayed him just before Gareer reached him. He stood quickly, his hands coming from behind his back to show that they were no longer tied together as his right fist swung savagely down at the pirate captain's head.

Unaccustomed to losing many fights, Dan let out a cry of surprise and a little fear when the blow didn't connect to fell his enemy like a dead animal.

Gareer saw the blow coming a mile away and stepped out of reach to deliver his own attack and hit Dan in the throat to send him stumbling and choking to the deck. He scrambled to his feet, eyes wide with rage and shock, to step forwards and have his next three blows deflected with ease until he left himself flat-footed and open to attack. Gareer punished his mistake and planted a heavy boot into his chest to send him backwards in a heap of flailing limbs.

"You fight like a child, Englishman," Gareer goaded him as he bounced on his feet and warmed up to the enjoyment of fighting an inferior opponent. Dan stood, one eye closed in pain and his neck cricked over to one side.

"Yeah," he groaned, "and you hit like a bitch." Gareer's smile dropped as he advanced to prove the man wrong.

~

"Watch left," I told Lucien as I rose and moved to the right, "they'll be coming, just don't shoot this way." I knew he had heard me, and my concentration was running at maximum as I flicked the safety catch all the way up to automatic. I stitched the gaggle of confused pirates with an entire magazine before dropping and moving backwards as I reloaded, already ducking the incoming volley of badly aimed bullets from the survivors. As I had expected, or hoped really, they ran straight towards where the bullets had come from and didn't think to move with any kind of coherence like I had been trained to do. Instead they just ran in a pack, putting me in mind of young children playing football in a gaggle surrounding the ball with no concept of tactical spacing.

Lucien cut them down with bursts from his liberated AK, leaving only one for me to pop up and engage.

"Come on," I shouted, pointing upwards to the highest windows above us in my desperation to reach Dan and give him the heavy burden on my back.

~

Dan's head bounced off a radar console, one of the old switches cutting his eyebrow to add another scar to his already-battered face. He didn't have time to take a second and recover from the blow as a boot stamped down on the back of his thigh to try and cripple him through blunt trauma. He rolled, lashing out with his own boots and scoring only a glancing blow which made the man he had underestimated chuckle with cruel laughter.

"Where are you going, Englishman?" he asked as he stalked behind the crawling prisoner. Dan spun onto his back ready to defend himself with his feet, seeing for the first time that Gareer had a gun holstered on his left hip in a cross-draw position. He could have taken the weapon out at any point and killed him, but he seemed to prefer the option of beating him to death for sport.

Dan always said that when you know what a person wants, you know how to control them.

"That all you got?" he moaned through swollen lips as he struggled to his feet slower than he knew he could manage. He stood up and swayed, feigning exhaustion only slightly ahead of the inevitable reality, and raised his hands to invite more pain. Gareer advanced, wanting to beat the smug man into submission before locking him up to keep him and prolong the enjoyment he got from causing pain. He drew back a punch, only half delivering it as Dan fell onto him in a half collapse like a tired boxer clenching his opponent in the ring. He lowered his legs and put both hands on Dan's chest to throw him off, to shove him away like a piece of dead meat, but never completed the move. The air left his lungs in the same instant his knees stopped holding his body upright, and a weak sound of unfathomable pain leaked from his open mouth.

Dan, in a move that he defended for years afterwards, delivered an uppercut with every ounce of strength his failing body could muster. The clenched fist connected with Gareer's body in a very personal manner with the instant effect of stunning, winding and crippling him in one punch.

As the pirate leader dropped to the deck on his knees with both hands clutching at his groin, Dan stood with the gun from his attacker's holster in his right hand. He looked at it, recognising a Glock so well maintained that he guessed it was one of their own, and checked for a round in the chamber. The glint of brass told him there was and without ceremony he placed the short barrel under Gareer's chin and lifted his face.

"I'm not going anywhere, you fucker," he whispered in his face, pulling the trigger once to splash hot blood on his own skin.

AFTERMATH

Leah stood and stretched her back again, annoyed at herself for stay-ing still too long and feeling as though writing the story had made her an inch shorter. She thought about what had happened after that. How she and Lucien had burst into the bridge to find Dan slumped in the captain's chair with fresh blood all over him. He had waved them away, assuring them that he was fine, when it was obvious that he had taken a beating in payment for his victory.

Seeing that her awkwardly long-legged puppy still snoozed in the shaft of sunlight, she bent her head back to the pages in the hope of finishing the task and returning to normality, vowing to let others write down the next tale for her.

When dawn broke over the ship the remaining pirates had been rounded up and those who didn't feel rebellious enough to get them-selves shot had begged to be allowed to take the boat. They were mostly the type not to be carrying weapons, at least they weren't when they had surrendered, and more than a few had been ousted by the collection of cooks and engineers who refused to be bracketed with one of the raiders. Against all ruthless good sense, an old man had asked for and been granted Dan's permission to take the ship away and never return. Having satisfied himself that the cruel element of the crew had been dispatched, especially seeing as how they had treated the body of Gareer which, even though he was an evil bastard, was not to our liking.

We took a large skiff and the collection of prisoners back to Sanctuary, suffering the shouting and berating from a few key people as we returned. It turned out that the gunfire had been heard on shore and word soon spread fearing another attack. When our absence was noticed, the truth of what was happening came out.

The prisoners, some of them from settlements we hadn't even found yet, were treated for their injuries and fed before being given fresh clothing and the promise of an escort home. A few, the surviving women from the homestead, elected to stay in Sanctuary as returning to their burned home was an impossibility.

By the time the arguing had abated and people hugged us in gratitude and relief that we came back, the horizon was clear but for the shrinking silhouette of a large ship heading west for the Atlantic.

Kate was the angriest of everyone, and that anger was directed at me. She forced the confrontation in front of everyone, which I guess I deserved a little, but she would never understand my reason for putting my life and the life of my unborn baby at risk; raising my child without its father would be something I could never get over, and as far as I saw it the risk was my own to take.

"Kate's upset with me because she advised me not to do anything strenuous… in my condition."

Dan choked on the water he drank, dropping his cigarette as he took a strangled breath in to cough again and burp before turning his streaming, wide eyes on me. Marie gasped out loud and Mitch and Alita just smiled. I knew she'd tell Mitch and I wasn't cross in the slightest.

The one person who hadn't responded was Lucien. I turned to face him, seeing such a youthful innocence on his face mixed with a look of guilty shock.

"You…" he said in a weak croak as his eyes began to leak. "You are…?"

"Yes," I told him, my own tears now flowing to match his. "I am."

EPILOGUE

"Have you finished your story, *Mamon*?" Adalene asked from the doorway. Leah rested her pen down, wiggling her fingers to loosen up the cramp as she realised she had been staring at the page for a long time just thinking.

"*Oui chérie*," Leah said kindly, reaching out to hug her girl as her mind conjured up the memory of what had happened after that point in the story. It didn't need writing down that she had gone out of her mind with the inactivity and discomfort of being pregnant through a hot summer and giving birth during a cruelly cold winter. How much she hated not being able to go anywhere or do anything, and how all of that faded into absolute nothingness when the time came.

To this day Leah had never experienced pain like it, and she'd probably be the first person to level a targeting gaze on any man who likens any pain he feels to childbirth.

All of that pain, along with the frustration and the discomfort that came before it, vanished the moment they put her little girl in her arms and she felt her tiny, shaky movements as her fingers spread wide and her eyes screwed tightly shut. She sucked in a long breath, deafening her mother in an instant with a lip-wobbling cry which to this day was one of the greatest sounds Leah has ever heard.

She had grown to be a boisterous toddler and an inquisitive young girl, to become the sensitive and intuitive little lady who always wanted to learn something new.

"Come on," Leah told her as she stood, seeing Ares spin on his back again to follow them with a sneeze that shook his whole head and made him stagger. "Let's take a walk."

Adalene bounded ahead of her mother, going up the spiral stone staircases like a mountain goat. Like Leah used to, before the physical stress of carrying her had left her pelvis feeling like she'd barely survived a helicopter crash. When they reached the ramparts and Adalene ran ahead, Leah looked down to see Ares looking up expectantly.

"Go on then," she told him, laughing out loud as his bandy legs seemed to belong to a bigger dog and threatened to trip him up as he chased after the girl. She stopped in a patch of sun, looking out over the sea as she was still able to recall the menacing shape of that ship out there a decade ago. Then she glanced up to the watchtower, thinking of those under the earth there and hoping that she still made them proud of her.

Leah was proud of them. Proud of the people of the town and everywhere else. Those people were survivors, all of them. Not everyone could shoot a gun or climb an anchor chain, that much was obvious, but in their own way every single person under her influence and protection was a survivor. They deserved to be there. They deserved to be flourishing and forging new futures, and Leah hoped that one day they would do so under the protection of her own family.

There was a time, there were many times in fact, when Leah felt overwhelmed; when the pressures of life and the demands on her were too much for one person to satisfy. She persevered, just as those before her had shown her how and she hoped how those in the future would take their inspiration from her and how she acted.

Adalene raced back to her, the awkward dog having grown accustomed to his legs and running at a steady speed beside her, and Leah took them back down the steps to get some food.

The evening meal was as basic as it was tasty and full of fresh goodness. Leah sat at the central table among familiar faces, many of them much older than when they had first arrived, which included her own. They spoke, they laughed, they enjoyed life, until the door burst open and a red-faced member of the militia stood there, eyes wildly searching for someone.

Leah stood, knowing that someone would be her, and walked over to him with her hands up in a calming gesture.

"Not here," she said softly in French, "not in front of everyone." She turned him by the shoulder and walked him out of the room until they were alone in a corridor.

"The fort," he said, "they say there are people coming."

"Calm down," she said, "what people?"

"They say it is a war party."

Leah stopped, knowing that the defence of their way of life was something that would never end.

ABOUT THE AUTHOR

Devon C Ford is from the UK and lives in the Midlands. His career in public services started in his teens and has provided a wealth of experiences, both good and some very bad, which form the basis of the books ideas that cause regular insomnia.

Facebook: @devoncfordofficial

Twitter: @DevonFordAuthor

Website: www.devoncford.com

Also by Devon C Ford:

Burning Skies: The Fall is book one of the innovative multi-author series following Cal as he finds himself in the middle of a domestic terror attack in New York.

ARC, book one of the brilliant *New Earth* series sees Earth on the brink of destruction, with one man charged with saving us all from extinction!